Wandering Star

———★———

a novel by
J. M. G. Le Clézio

translated by C. Dickson

CURBSTONE PRESS

A LANNAN TRANSLATION SELECTION
WITH SPECIAL THANKS TO PATRICK LANNAN AND
THE LANNAN FOUNDATION BOARD OF DIRECTORS

FIRST EDITION, 2004
Translation copyright © 2004 C. Dickson
ALL RIGHTS RESERVED.

Printed in Canada on acid-free paper by Transcontinental Book Group
Cover design: Susan Shapiro
Cover artwork: Ben Shahn (1898-1969); "Father and Child," 1946;
tempura on cardboard, 39 7/8 x 30"; gift of James Thrall Soby, The
Museum of Modern Art, New York, NY; © Estate of Ben Shahn /
lic. by VAGA, New York, NY.
Digital image © MOMA / lic. by SCALA/Art Resource, NY.

This book was published with the support of the
Connecticut Commission on Culture & Tourism,
Lannan Foundation, National Endowment for
the Arts, and donations from many individuals.
We are very grateful for all of their support.

Library of Congress Cataloging-in-Publication Data

Le Clézio, J.-M. G. (Jean-Marie Gustave), 1940-
    [Etoile errante. English]
    Wandering star : a novel / by J.M.G. Le Clézio ; translated by
C. Dickson.— 1st ed.
    p. cm.
    ISBN 1-931896-11-9 (pbk. : alk. paper)
    I. Dickson, C. II. Title.
PQ2672.E25E7613 2004
843'.914—dc22   2004013695

published by
CURBSTONE PRESS   321 Jackson Street   Willimantic CT 06226
        phone: 860-423-5110   e-mail: info@curbstone.org
                    www.curbstone.org

To the captured children

Estrella errante
Amor pasajero
Sigue tu camino
Por mares y tierras
Quebra tus cadenas
    (Peruvian song)

Wandering star
Transitory love
Follows your path
Through seas and lands
It breaks your chains
    (translated by
    Jack Hirschman)

Hélène

Saint-Martin-Vésubie, summer 1943

She knew that winter was over when she heard the sound of water. In winter, snow covered the village, the roofs of the houses and the fields were white. Icicles formed on the edges of the roofs. Then the sun started burning down, the snow melted, and water started trickling drop by drop from all the roofs, the joists, the tree branches, and all of the drops ran together forming rivulets, the rivulets ran into streams, and the water leapt joyously down all the streets in the village.

That sound of water might be her very first memory. She recalled the first winter in the mountains and the music of water in spring. When was that? She was walking between her mother and father down the village street, holding their hands. One arm was pulled higher because her father was so tall. And the water was running down on all sides, making that music, those whooshing, swishing, drumming sounds. Every time she remembered that she felt like laughing because it was a strange and gentle sound, like a caress. She was laughing then, walking between her mother and father, and the water in the gutters and the stream answered her, rippling, rushing.

Now, with the burning summer heat, the deep blue sky, her entire body was filled with a feeling of happiness that was almost frightening. More than anything, she loved the vast grassy slope that rose up toward the sky above the village. She didn't go all the way up to the top because everyone said there were vipers up there. She'd stroll a little way along the edge of the field, just far enough to feel the cool earth, the sharp blades against her lips. In places, the grass was so high she completely disappeared. She was thirteen years old and her name was Hélène Grève, but her father called her Esther.

School had closed in the beginning of June because the teacher, Mr. Seligman, had fallen ill. There was also old Heinrich Ferne who gave lessons in the morning, but he didn't want to come alone. For the children, the holidays that had begun were going to be quite long. They didn't know that for many of them the summer would end in death.

Every morning at dawn, they went out and didn't come back until lunchtime—in a rush—then left again to run in the fields or play in the narrow streets of the village with an old ball that had gone flat several times and been repaired with rubber bicycle patches.

In the beginning of summer most of the children were like little savages—sunbrowned faces, arms and legs, bits of grass tangled in their hair, torn, dirt-smudged clothes. Esther loved going out with the children every morning, in that mixed group of boys and girls, Jewish children and children from the village, all rowdy, tousled—Mr. Seligman's class. With them, she ran through the still-cool, narrow village streets, then across the large square making dogs bark and old people sitting in the sun grumble. They followed the street with the stream down toward the river, cut through the fields to reach the cemetery. When the sun burned down hot, they bathed in the icy waters of the torrent. The boys stayed down below and the girls climbed up the torrent to hide behind the huge boulders. But they knew the boys came into the bushes to spy on them, they could hear their muffled snickering and they splashed water around haphazardly and let out shrill shrieks.

Esther was the wildest of them all with her black curly hair cropped short, her brown face, and when her mother saw her come home for lunch she said, "Hélène, you look like a gypsy!" That pleased her father and so he said her name in Spanish, "Estrellita, little star."

He was the one who'd first shown her the vast grassy fields high above the village, above the torrent. Still farther up began the road leading to the mountains, the dark forest of larches—but that was another world. Gasparini said that in winter there were wolves in the forest and if you listened at night, you could hear them howl far off in the distance. But as hard as she listened at night in her bed, Esther had never heard their howling, maybe because of the sound of the water that was constantly streaming down the middle of the street.

One day before summer her father took her to the mouth of the valley, the place where the river becomes a thin stream of water bounding from rock to rock. On each side of the valley the mountains rose, like the walls of a fortress, covered with forests. Her father pointed to the floor of the valley, to the chaotic crowd of mountains, and he said, "Italy is over that way." Esther tried to imagine what was on the other side of the mountains beyond. "Is it a long way to Italy?" Her father answered, "If you could fly like a bird, you'd be there this very evening. But for you, it's a long walk, maybe two days." She would like to have been a bird, to get there that very evening. After that, her father had never spoken of Italy again, or of anything that was on the other side of the mountains.

The Italians were never seen outside of the village. They lived at the Hotel Terminus, a big white building with green shutters right on the square. Most of the time they stayed in the hotel, in the large dining room on the ground floor, talking and playing cards. When the weather was fine, they went out into the square and walked up and down in groups of two or three, policemen and soldiers. Under their breaths, the children poked fun at their hats decorated with a cock feather. When Esther walked past the hotel with other girls, the carabinieri would joke around a little, mixing French words in with Italian. Once a day, the Jews had to line up in front of the hotel to be signed into the register and have their ration cards checked. Each time, Esther went with her mother and father. They walked into the large dim room. The carabinieri put one of the restaurant tables by the door and each person who went in gave his name so the officer could tick it off the list.

Even so, Esther's father didn't resent the Italians. He said they weren't mean like the Germans. One day, during a meeting in the kitchen at Esther's house, someone said something against the Italians, and her father got angry. "Keep quiet, they're the ones who saved us when Prefect Ribière gave the order to turn us over to the Germans." But he hardly ever spoke about the war, about any of that, he hardly ever said, "the Jews", because he didn't believe in religion and because he was a communist. When Mr. Seligman wanted to enroll Esther in religious studies where the Jewish children went every evening—the chalet high up in the village—her father refused. So then the other children made fun of her and they even said, *goy*, which means "heathen." They also said, "communist!" Esther fought with them. But her father didn't give in. He just said, "Let them be. They'll tire of it before you do." He was right, the children in Mr. Seligman's class forgot about it, they didn't say "heathen" or "communist" anymore. Anyway, there were other children that didn't go to religious studies, like Gasparini, or like Tristan, who was half English and whose mother was Italian, a pretty brunette who wore wide-brimmed hats.

Esther liked Mr. Heinrich Ferne very much because of the piano. He lived on the ground floor of an old, somewhat run-down villa just below the square, on the street that led down to the cemetery. It wasn't a pretty house, you might even say it was rather sinister, with its neglected garden overrun with acanthuses and the upstairs shutters always closed. When Mr. Ferne wasn't teaching at the school, he stayed shut up in his kitchen and played the piano. It was the only piano in the village and there might not have been another one in all the mountain villages as far as Nice and Monte Carlo. People said that when the Italians moved into the hotel, the captain of the carabinieri, whose name was Mondoloni and who loved music, wanted to put the piano in the dining room. But Mr. Ferne said, "You can take the piano, of course, because you are the victors. But know that I will never play for you there."

He played for no one. He lived alone in that dilapidated villa, and sometimes in the afternoon when she walked past, Esther heard the music spilling out the kitchen door. It was like the sound of streams in spring, a soft, light, fleeting sound that seemed to be coming from everywhere at once. Esther stopped in the street near the gate and listened. When it was over, she walked quickly away so he wouldn't see her. One day she'd mentioned the piano to her mother and her mother said that Mr. Ferne used to be a famous pianist, long ago in Vienna, before the war. He gave evening concerts attended by women in long gowns and men in black coats. When the Germans invaded Austria, they put all the Jews in prison and they took Mr. Ferne's wife away and he was able to escape. But ever since that day, he never wanted to play the piano for anyone. When he came to the village, he didn't have a piano. He found one for sale on the coast, he had it brought up in a truck, hidden under tarpaulins, and moved into his kitchen.

Now that she knew the story, Esther hardly dared go near the gate. She listened to the notes of music, the gentle streaming notes, and it seemed to her that there was something sad about it, something that made tears well up in her eyes.

On that particular afternoon it was hot and everything in the village seemed to be asleep. Esther walked over to Mr. Ferne's house. In the garden there was a tall mulberry tree. Using the gate, Esther pulled herself up onto the wall in the shade of the mulberry tree. Through the kitchen window, she saw Mr. Ferne's silhouette leaning over the piano. The ivory keys gleamed in the half-light. The notes slid smoothly out, hesitated, started up again, as if it were a language, as if Mr. Ferne wasn't really sure where to begin anymore. Esther peered into the kitchen as hard as she could until her eyes began to smart. Then the music truly began, it sprang from the piano all of a sudden and filled the entire house, the garden, and the street, it filled everything with its power, its order, and then it grew soft, mysterious. Now it was surging up, pouring out like the water in the streams, it went straight up to the sky, to the clouds, mixed with the light. It spilled over the mountains, went all the way to the source of the two torrents, it was as powerful as the river.

With her hands gripping the rusty gate, Esther listened

to Mr. Ferne's language. He didn't sound like the schoolteacher now. He was telling strange stories, stories she couldn't remember, like the stories in dreams. In them, people were free, there was no war, no Italians or Germans, nothing that could be frightening or stop life. And yet it was sad as well, and the music slowed down, questioning. At times everything tore apart, shattered. Then silence.

The music started up again, she listened to every phrase that came. Never had anything been so important, except maybe when her mother sang a song or her father read passages from her favorite books, like when Mr. Pickwick is sent to the London prison or when Nicolas Nickleby meets his uncle.

Esther pushed open the gate, crossed the garden. Without a sound, she went into the kitchen and walked over to the piano. She watched each ivory key sinking down with precision under the old man's nervous fingers; she listened closely to each phrase.

Suddenly Mr. Ferne stopped, and the silence grew heavy, threatening. Esther started to back away, but Mr. Ferne turned toward her. The light shone upon his white face with its strange little goat's beard.

He said, "What's your name?"

"Hélène," said Esther.

"Well, come in then."

As if it were as natural as could be, as if he knew the young girl.

Then he started playing again, without paying any attention to her. She listened to him, standing by the piano, not daring to breathe. Never had music seemed so beautiful to her. In the semi-darkness, the black piano blotted everything out. The long hands of the old man ran over the keys, stopped, started out again. Sometimes Mr. Ferne looked through a pile of notebooks with mysterious names written on them.

Sonaten fûr Pianoforte
Von W. A Mozart

Czerny
Preliminary Studies in Finger Dexterity, op. 636

Beethoven
Sonaten, vol. II, par Moszkowski

Liszt
Klavierwerke, Band IV

Bach
Englische suiten, 4-6

He turned toward Esther, "Would you like to play?"
Esther looked at him, astonished.
"It's that I don't know how."
He shrugged his shoulders. "It doesn't matter. Try, watch what my fingers do."
He had her sit down on the bench next to him. He had a strange way of making his fingers run over the keys, like a thin, nervous animal.
Esther tried to imitate him, and to her great surprise she succeeded in imitating him.
"You see? It's simple. Now the other hand."
He watched her hand, he seemed impatient.
"All right, you'll need to have lessons, you might be able to play. But it's a lot of work. Try the chords."
He put Esther's hands on the keyboard, spread out her

fingers. His own hands were long and slender, not the hands of an old man, but young, strong hands, with bulging veins. The sounds of chords sprang up, magically. Vibrated under the young girl's fingers, echoed deep within her.

"You'll have to learn how to read the notes. When you know how to do that, come back to see me."

Ever since then, Esther went back whenever she could get away in the afternoons. She pushed open the gate of the villa, went noiselessly into the kitchen while Mr. Ferne was playing. At some point, without turning his head, he would know she was there. He'd say, "Come in, sit down."

Esther sat down beside him on the bench and she watched the long hands running over the keyboard as if they themselves were creating the notes. It lasted such a long time that she forgot everything else, even where she was. Mr. Ferne showed her how to let her fingers run over the keys. On a sheet of white paper he had written some notes; he wanted her to sing them and play them at the same time. His eyes shone, his little goat's beard twitched. "You have a lovely voice, but I'm not sure if you'll really be able to play the piano." When she made a mistake, he got angry. "That's all for today, go away, leave me alone!" But he held her back by the arm, and for her he played one of Mozart's sonatas, the one he preferred. When Esther went out into the street, she was dazed by the sunlight and the silence; it took her a few minutes to get oriented again.

Late in the afternoon, Esther saw Mr. Ferne in the village square. People came up to greet him, and he talked about anything but music. They were rich people that lived in the chalets on the other side of the torrent, amidst gardens where tall chestnut trees grew. Esther's father didn't like them much, but he wouldn't stand for anyone to speak ill of them because they helped the poor people that came from Russia or from Poland. Mr. Ferne greeted everyone ceremoniously, sharing a few words with each, then he went back to his run-down house.

Near evening the square livened up, people came from all the streets in Saint-Martin, wealthy people from the villas and the poor who lived in hotel rooms, farmers back from the war, village women in aprons, young girls walking in groups of three under the watchful eyes of the carabinieri and the Italian soldiers, diamond-dealers, tailors, furriers from northern Europe. Children ran across the square, laughing and bumping into the girls, or playing hide and seek behind the trees. Esther just sat on the low wall on the edge of the square, watching all the people. She listened to the sounds of voices, the calls, the shouts of children erupting suddenly like the squawking of birds.

Then the sun slipped behind the mountain and a sort of milky haze blurred the village. Shadows crept into the square. Everything seemed strange, far away. Esther thought of her father who was walking through the tall grass somewhere in the mountains, on the way back from his meeting. Elizabeth never came to the square, she waited at home, knitting with bits of yarn, trying not to worry. Esther just couldn't understand what it all meant, the men and the women, all so different, speaking all kinds of languages, coming from all over the world to this square. She watched the old Jews wearing their long black coats, the peasant women with their clothing worn thin from working in the fields, and the young girls circling the fountain in their pale-colored dresses.

When the light disappeared, the square slowly emptied. Everyone went back to their homes, the voices faded away one after the other. You could hear the gurgling of the fountain and the cries of children running after each other through the streets. Elizabeth walked into the square. She took Esther by the hand and they went down to the dark little apartment together. They walked in step, their shoes echoing in unison down the street. Esther liked that. She held her mother's hand very tightly; it was as if they were both thirteen years old, and had their whole lives in front of them.

Tristan could still remember his mother's hands playing the black piano in the afternoon when everything around seemed to be drowsing. In the living room there were sometimes guests, he heard voices, the laughter of his mother's friends. Tristan couldn't remember their names anymore. He only saw the movement of hands over the piano keys, and the music burst forth. That was very long ago. He didn't know when she'd told him the name of that music, *La Cathédrale engloutie*, with the sound of bells ringing under the sea. It was in Cannes, in another time, in another world. Then he wanted to go back to that life, like in a dream. The piano music swelled, filled the small hotel room, slipped out into the hallways, reaching every floor. It rang out loudly in the night silence. Tristan could hear his heart beating in rhythm to the music and suddenly he awoke from his dream, terrified, his back soaked with sweat; he sat up in his bed to listen, to make sure that no one else had heard the music. He listened to the peaceful breathing of his sleeping mother and, on the other side of the shutters, the sound of the water in the fountain.

They lived on the second floor of the Hotel Victoria, a small room with a balcony looking out over the square. All the floors were filled with poor families that the Italians had put under house arrest and there were so many people that in the daytime the hotel buzzed like a beehive. When Mrs. O'Rourke had arrived in Saint-Martin on the bus, Tristan was a lonely, shy boy of twelve. His straight blond hair was trimmed around his head in a "bowl cut", he wore strange English clothes—gray flannel shorts that were too long, woolen stockings and odd-looking vests. Everything about him was foreign. In Cannes, they'd lived with a small circle of English expatriates in summer residences that the war had pared down even more. War had broken out and Tristan's father, who was a businessman in equatorial Africa, had enrolled in the colonial armed forces. Since then, they had no news of him. Tristan stopped going to school and his mother gave him lessons at home. And so, when they'd reached the mountains, Mrs. O'Rourke didn't want to enroll Tristan in Mr. Seligman's school. The first memory Esther had of him was his silhouette in strange clothing as he stood in the doorway of the hotel watching the children on their way to school.

Mrs. O'Rourke was beautiful. Her long dresses and wide-brimmed hats contrasted with her sober face, the slightly melancholy cast to her eyes. She spoke very pure French, with no accent, and people said she was a spy working for the carabinieri, or that she was a criminal in hiding. It was mostly the girls that whispered stories to each other. It was the same when they talked about Rachel who was seeing the captain of the carabinieri in secret.

So at first Tristan didn't want to mix with the other children. He walked around the village alone, or sometimes he went out into the fields, walked down the slope till he reached the river. When he found other children there, he climbed back up without turning around. Maybe he was afraid of them. He wanted to show he didn't need anyone.

Evenings, Esther saw him walking around in the square, offering his arm ceremoniously to his mother. They strolled under the plane trees to the other end of the square where the carabinieri were. Then they turned and started back the other way. People didn't talk much with Mrs. O'Rourke. But she exchanged a few words with old Heinrich Ferne because he was a musician. She never went with the others to have her name checked on the list at the Hotel Terminus. She wasn't Jewish.

Time had passed, it was almost summer. Now everyone knew that Mrs. O'Rourke wasn't rich. They even said that she had no money at all, because she went to see the diamond dealers to borrow money in exchange for her jewelry. They said she hardly had anything left to pawn, just a few lockets, some ivory necklaces, some trinkets.

Tristan looked at his mother as if he'd never seen her before. He wanted to remember the days in the house in Cannes, the mimosas in the afternoon light, the birds singing outside, his mother's voice, and always the hands playing *La Cathédrale engloutie*, the music—so very brutal one minute, so very sad the next. The scene was getting blurry, drifting away.

Tristan couldn't bear it in the hotel room anymore. The sun had burned his face and hands, had bleached his hair that had grown too long. His clothes were ragged and dirty from running through the bushes. One day on the road leading out of the village, he'd gotten into a fight with Gasparini because the boy was flirting with Esther. Gasparini was older, stronger, and he'd put a neck-lock on Tristan; his face was contorted with hatred, he said, "Go ahead, say you're a jerk! Say it!" Tristan had held out till he fainted. In the end, Gasparini let go of him; he let the others think that Tristan had given in.

Ever since that day, everything had changed. Now it was summer, the days had grown long. Tristan left the hotel every morning while his mother still slept in the narrow room. He didn't come back till noon, starving, his legs scratched by brambles. His mother didn't say anything, but she had a pretty good idea. One day as he was going out, she said in an odd voice, "You know, Tristan, that young girl isn't for you." He stopped short. "What on earth are you talking about? What young girl?" She simply repeated, "She's not for you, Tristan." But she never brought it up again.

In the morning, Tristan was in the village square just when the Jews were lining up in front of the door to the Hotel Terminus. The men and women waited their turn to go in, to have their names checked off in the register, and receive their ration cards.

Half-hidden behind the trees, Tristan watched Esther and her parents as they waited. He was a little ashamed because he and his mother didn't have to stand in line; they weren't like the others. It was right there in that square that Esther had looked at him for the first time. It was raining off and on. The women wrapped themselves tightly in their shawls, opened their big black umbrellas. The children stayed close by, not running, not shouting. In the shade of the plane trees, Tristan watched Esther standing in the middle of the line. Her head was bare, drops of rain sparkled in her black hair. She was holding her mother's arm, and her father looked very tall next to her. She wasn't talking; no one was talking, not even the carabinieri standing in front of the door to the restaurant. Every time the door opened, Tristan caught a quick glimpse of the large room lit by the French doors thrown open onto the garden. The carabinieri were standing near the windows smoking. One of them was sitting at a table with an open register in front of him, he was checking off the names. For Tristan, there was something awful, something mysterious about it all, as if the people that went into the room wouldn't come out again. On the side of the hotel facing the square, the windows were closed, curtains drawn. When night fell, the Italians closed the shutters and barricaded themselves inside the hotel. The square was pitch-dark, as if uninhabited. No one was allowed to go out.

It was the silence that drew Tristan to the hotel. He'd left the tepid room where his mother was breathing softly, the dream of music and gardens, to come and watch Esther amidst all the dark shapes waiting in the square. The carabinieri wrote down her name. She went in with her mother and father, and the man with the register marked her name in the notebook at the bottom of the list with all the other names. Tristan would have liked to be with her in the line, move up with her till they reached the table; he couldn't sleep in the room at the Hotel Victoria while that was happening. The silence in the square was too heavy. The only sound was that of the water in the basin of the fountain, a dog barked somewhere.

Afterward, Esther came back out. She walked in the square a little off to one side of her mother and father. When she went past the trees, she saw Tristan and there was a blaze in her black eyes, something like anger, or disdain, a violent flame that had made the boy's heart beat too fast. He stepped back. He wanted to say, you're beautiful, I can't think of anything but you, I love you. But the silhouettes were already hurrying off toward the narrow streets.

The sun rose in the sky, the light burned down between the clouds. In the fields, the grass was razor sharp, the bushes whipped at your legs. Tristan was running to get away, he went all the way down to the icy stream. The air was full of smells, of pollen, of flies.

It was as if there had never been a summer before that one. The sun scorched the grasses in the fields, the stones in the torrent, and the mountains seemed so distant against the dark blue sky. Esther often walked down to the river, deep in the valley, to the place where the two torrents met and the valley grew very wide. The circle of mountains seemed even more distant there. In the morning, the air was smooth and cold, the sky utterly blue. Then, after noon, clouds appeared above the peaks to the north and east, roiling up into bright billows. The light vibrated over the river water. The vibration was everywhere; when you turned your head, it merged with the sound of the water and the song of crickets.

One day, Gasparini came down to the river with Esther. When the sun was in mid-sky, Esther started to walk back up the slope toward home, and Gasparini took her hand.

"Come on, let's go down to see my cousin cutting the wheat in Roquebillière." Esther hesitated. "It's not far, just a little farther down, we'll go in my grandfather's cart," said Gasparini.

Esther had seen the harvest once, long ago, with her father, but she wasn't sure she remembered what the wheat looked like. In the end she climbed up into the cart. There were women with scarves on their heads, children. Old Grandfather Gasparini was leading the horse. The cart followed the curves of the track down into the valley. There were no more houses, only the river shimmering in the sunlight, the green fields. The track was rutted out, the cart lurched to and fro and it made the women laugh. Shortly before reaching Roquebillière, the valley widened out. Before seeing anything, Esther heard sounds: shouts, women's voices, shrill laughter that floated over on the hot wind, and a rustling sound, soft and even, like the sound of rain.

"We're almost there, the wheatfields are over that way," Gasparini said.

Then the track joined the road and suddenly Esther saw all the people at work. There was quite a crowd, carts waiting as their horses grazed on the banks of the road, children playing. Near the carts, older men were busy loading the wheat using wooden pitchforks. Most of the fields had already been harvested; women wearing headscarves were leaning over sheaves that they bound together and then pushed out toward the road near the carts. Near them, babies, little tots, were playing with the ears of wheat fallen on the ground. Other children, older ones, were gleaning in the field, stuffing ears into gunnysacks.

The young men were working at the end of the field. Standing a few steps apart from one another, forming a line like infantry soldiers, they moved slowly forward through the wheat, swinging their scythes. That was what Esther had heard from afar when she arrived. With mechanical regularity, the scythes lifted up behind the men, their long blades glinting in the sun, they remained immobile for a moment then suddenly fell back down with a crunching sound into the wheat, and the men made a deep sound with their throats and chests. A hmph! that echoed through the valley.

Esther hid behind the carts because she didn't want anyone to see her, but Gasparini pulled her by the hand and forced her to walk right down the middle of the field. The stubble was sharp and stiff, it pierced through their rope-soled espadrilles, scratched their ankles. The most striking thing was the smell, a smell Esther wasn't familiar with, and maybe it was because of the smell that she'd been frightened when she first arrived. A bitter smell of dust and sweat, a smell that was a mixture of humans and plants. The sun was blinding, it burned your eyelids, your face, your hands. All around them in the field there were women and children in worn clothing that Esther had never seen before. With a sort of fervent haste, they were gathering up the ears that had fallen from the sheaves and putting them into their gunnysacks. "They're Italians," Gasparini said with a hint of condescension in his voice. "There's no wheat in their country, so they come and glean here." Esther watched the young women in rags intently, their faces half-hidden with faded headscarves. "Where do they come from?" Gasparini pointed to the mountains at the far end of the valley. "They come from Valdieri, from Santa Anna (he said Santanna), they come on foot through the mountains because they're hungry in their country." Esther was surprised, she'd never dreamt that Italians could look like these women and children. But Gasparini was pulling her over toward the line of harvesters. "Look, he's my cousin." A young man in an undershirt, face and arms reddened from the sun, had stopped swinging his scythe. "So, are you going to introduce me to your fiancée?" He burst out laughing, and the other men also stopped to stare at them. Gasparini shrugged his shoulders. With Esther, he walked over to the far end of the field to sit down on an embankment. From there all they could hear was the whooshing of the scythes in the wheat and the deep grunting of the men: hmph! hmph! Gasparini said, "My father says that the Italians are going to lose the war because they have nothing to eat in their country." Esther replied, "Then maybe they'll come to live here?" Gasparini answered unhesitatingly, "We wouldn't let them. We'd throw them out. Besides, the English and the Americans are going to win the war. My father says that the Germans and the Italians will soon be defeated." Then, he lowered his voice a little, "My father is in the Maquis, what about yours?" Esther thought it over. She wasn't really sure she should answer. Then she said the same thing, "Mine too, he's in the Maquis." Gasparini asked, "What does he do?" Esther said, "He helps Jews get across the mountains, he helps them hide." Gasparini seemed a little irritated, "That's not the same. That's not what helping the Maquis is about." Esther already regretted having talked about all of that. Her mother and father had told her that she should never talk about the war, or about the people that came to their house, to anyone. They had told her that the Italian soldiers gave people money to turn others in. Maybe Gasparini was going to repeat everything to Captain Mondoloni? They both remained silent for a long time, nibbling on the grains of wheat that they picked one by one from their transparent hulls. Finally, he said, "What does your father do? I mean what did he do before the war?" Esther answered, "He was a teacher." Gasparini seemed interested, "What did he teach?" Esther said, "He taught History in high school. History and Geography." Gasparini didn't say anything else. He stared straight out in front of himself, his face was closed. Esther thought about the way, a little while ago, he had said, "They don't have anything to eat in their country." A little later, Gasparini said, "My father has a rifle, he still has it, it's hidden at our place, in the barn. If you like, I can show it to you one day." He and Esther again sat there for a while without saying anything, listening to the sound of the scythes and the grunting men. The sun hung very still in the center of the sky, there were no shadows on the ground. Between the spikes of stubble, huge black ants scurried forward, stopped, struck out again. They too were searching for grains of wheat fallen from the sheaves.

"Is it true you're a Jew?" Gasparini asked. Esther looked at him as if she didn't understand. "Tell me, is it true?" the boy repeated. Suddenly there was such an anxious look on his face that Esther answered very rapidly, angrily, "Me? No, no!" Gasparini's face hadn't relaxed. Now he said, "My father says that if the Germans come here, they'll kill all the Jews." Suddenly Esther felt her heart beating faster, painfully, the blood swelled in the veins in her neck, beat in her temples and in her ears. She didn't understand why, but her eyes were full of tears. It was because she'd lied, that was it. She heard the slow, insistent voice of the boy, and her own voice echoing, repeating, "Me? No, no!" Fear, or pain was spilling from her eyes. Up above the fields the sky was almost blackish blue, the light shone on the scythes, on the rocks in the mountains. The sun was scorching her back and shoulders through her dress. Out in the middle of the field, like tireless ants, the women and children in rags continued searching hungrily through the stubble, and their fingers were cut and bloody.

All of a sudden, without saying a word, Esther stood up and left, walking at first, with the spikes of the stubble poking through her espadrilles. Behind her, the slightly hoarse voice of the boy was shouting, "Hélène! Hélène, wait for me! Where are you going?" When she got to the road, where the carts were awaiting their loads of sheaves, she started running as fast as she could toward the village. She was running without looking back, without losing a second, imagining there was a mad dog at her heels so that she could run even faster. The cool air of the valley slipped over her;

after the heat of the wheat fields it felt like water.

She ran till she got a pain in her side and couldn't breathe anymore. Then she sat on the edge of the road, and the silence was terrifying. A truck came along surrounded by a cloud of blue smoke, driven by two carabinieri. The Italians had her climb up in the back and a few minutes later, Esther got off in the town square. She didn't tell her mother what had happened down there where the people were harvesting. The bitter taste of the grains of wheat stayed in her mouth for a long time.

The Italians ended up carting off Mr. Ferne's piano early one morning, in the rain. The news spread quickly, no one knew how. All the children in the town were there, and some old women in aprons too, and Jews wearing their winter caftans, because of the rain. Then the massive, magical piano, all shiny-black with copper candlesticks in the shape of devils, started moving up the street, carried by four Italian soldiers in uniform. Esther watched the strange troop file past, the piano teetering and tottering like a huge coffin, and the black plumes on the soldiers hats bouncing with each step. Several times the soldiers had to stop to catch their breath, and every time they set the piano down on the pavement the cords hummed with a long vibration that sounded like a lament.

That was the day that Esther talked to Rachel for the first time. She followed the cortege from a distance, and then she picked out the shape of Mr. Ferne who was also walking up the street in the rain. Esther hid in the recess of a doorway, to wait, and Rachel stopped right next to her. Drops of water wet Rachel's beautiful red hair, ran down onto her face like tears. Maybe that was why Esther had wanted to become her friend. But the piano had already disappeared at the top of the street, near the Terminus Hotel. Mr. Ferne walked past the girls without seeing them, there was a peculiar grimace on his white face, because of worry, or maybe because of the rain. His thin little gray beard was quivering, as if he were talking to himself, maybe he was cursing the Italian soldiers in his own language. It was comical and sad at the same time, and Esther felt a lump in her throat, because she suddenly understood what war was all about. When there was a war, men, police, and soldiers with strange plumed hats could just come and brazenly take Mr. Ferne's piano from his house and carry it into the dining room of the Terminus Hotel. They could do that even though Mr. Ferne loved his piano more than anything in the world and it was the only thing that mattered to him in life.

Then Rachel walked up the street toward the town square and Esther walked beside her. When they reached the square, they took shelter under a plane tree and watched the rain coming down. When Rachel spoke, a little cloud of steam formed around her lips. Esther was happy to be there, in spite of Mr. Ferne's piano, because she'd wanted to talk to Rachel for a long time but had never dared to. Esther loved her long red hair that fell loosely down onto her shoulders. It shocked a lot of the townspeople, the peasant women and also the religious Jews, that Rachel didn't go to the ceremonies anymore, and that she often talked with the Italian carabinieri in front of the hotel. But she was so beautiful that Esther thought it didn't matter that she wasn't like the others. Esther had often followed Rachel without her knowing—through the streets of the village when she went shopping or when she went for an afternoon stroll in the square with her mother and father. People said a lot of things about her, the boys said she went out at night, in spite of the curfew, and that she went swimming nude in the river. The girls told less extraordinary, but more spiteful stories.

They said that Rachel was dating Captain Mondoloni, that she went to see him at the Terminus Hotel and that they went out on the road together in the armored car. When the war was over and when the Italians were defeated, they would cut off her beautiful hair and put her in front of a firing squad, like all the members of the Gestapo and the Italian army. Esther knew perfectly well they said all of that because they were jealous.

On that day Esther and Rachel stayed together for a long time talking and watching the rain riddling the surface of the puddles. When it stopped raining, people came out into the square as they did every morning, peasant women in aprons and headscarves, and old men wearing hats and long black caftans. Children started running around too, most of them barefoot and in rags.

Then Rachel pointed to Mr. Ferne. He too was in the square, hiding on the other side of the fountain. He was looking over in the direction of the hotel, as if he would be able to get a glimpse of his piano. There was something both ridiculous and pitiful about his thin shape slipping from tree to tree, craning his neck to try and see inside the hotel while the carabinieri stood smoking by the door, something that made Esther feel ashamed. All of a sudden, she had stood it long enough. She took Rachel's hand and dragged her over to the street with the stream, and they went all the way down to the road above the river. They walked together along the road, still shiny with rain, without saying anything until they reached the bridge. Underneath, the two torrents met, forming whirlpools. A path led to a narrow shingle beach by the converging waters. The sound of the torrents was deafening but Esther thought it was really fine. In that place, nothing else existed in the world, and you couldn't talk to one another. The clouds had parted, the sun shone down on the stones, made the whitewater sparkle.

Esther and Rachel sat on the wet stones for a long time, watching the eddying waters. Rachel pulled out some cigarettes, a strange packet, marked in English. She started smoking and the sweet acrid smoke of the cigarette twirled around her and attracted wasps. At one point, she passed the cigarette to Esther for her to try it, but the smoke made her cough, and Rachel started laughing.

Afterward, they climbed back up the bank because they were cold and they sat on a low wall in the sunshine. Rachel started talking about her parents in a funny voice—hard, almost cruel. She didn't love them because they were always afraid, and because they'd fled their home in Poland and gone into hiding in France. She didn't talk about the Italians, or about Mondoloni, but all of a sudden she started digging in the pocket of her dress and held out a ring in her open palm.

"Look, someone gave this to me."

It was a very beautiful antique ring, with a dark blue stone that shone out amid other smaller, very white stones.

"It's a sapphire," Rachel said. "And the little ones around it are diamonds."

Esther had never seen anything like it.

"Is it pretty?"

"Yes," said Esther. But she didn't like that dark stone. It had a strange glint that was a little frightening. Esther thought that it was like the war, like the piano that the carabinieri had taken from Mr. Ferne's house. She didn't say anything, but Rachel understood and she immediately put the ring back in her pocket.

"What will you do when the war is over?" Rachel asked. And before Esther had time to think about it, she continued,

"I know what I would like to do. I would like to make music like Mr. Ferne, play the piano, sing. Go to the big cities, to Vienna, Paris, Berlin, to America, everywhere."

She lit up another cigarette, and while she talked about all of that, Esther watched her profile, haloed in her luminous red hair, she watched her arms, her fingers with their long nails. Maybe because of the smoke from the cigarette, because of the sunlight, Esther felt herself getting a bit dizzy. Rachel spoke of the nightlife in Paris, in Warsaw, in Rome, as if she'd really experienced all of that. When Esther talked about Mr. Ferne's music, Rachel suddenly got angry. She said he was an old fool, a bum, with his piano in his kitchen. Esther didn't argue, trying not to destroy the image of Rachel, her delicate profile with its halo of red hair, wanting simply to remain by her side as long as possible and smell the fragrance of her cigarette. But it was sad to hear her talk like that, and think about Mr. Ferne's piano all alone in the vast smoke-filled room at the Terminus Hotel where the carabinieri were drinking and playing cards. It made her think of war, of death, of the image that was forever popping into her mind: that of her father walking through the vast grassy fields, far from the village, disappearing, as if he would never come back.

When Rachel had finished her English cigarette, she threw the stub down into the valley and stood up, brushing off the back of her dress with her hands. Together, not saying a word, they went back toward the village where the chimneys were smoking for the noon meal.

It was already August. Every evening of late, the sky filled with huge white or gray clouds that piled up in fantastic shapes. For several days Esther's father had been leaving early in the morning, wearing his gray flannel suit, carrying a child's school-satchel, the same one that he used to carry when he went to teach History and Geography at the high school in Nice. Esther watched his tense dark face anxiously. He opened the door to the apartment, down below the level of the still-dark narrow street, and he turned around to kiss his daughter. One day Esther asked him, "Where are you going?" He answered almost harshly, "I'm going to see some people." Then he added, "Don't ask me questions, Estrellita. You mustn't speak about any of this, ever, do you understand?" Esther knew that he was going to help the Jews cross the mountains, but she didn't ask anything more. That's why the summer seemed terrifying, despite the beauty of the blue sky, despite the fields with grasses grown so high, despite the song of crickets and the sound of the water rushing over the stones in the torrents. Esther couldn't sit still for a minute in the apartment. On her mother's face she saw her own worry, the silence, the burden of waiting. So, as soon as she drank the morning bowl of hot milk, she opened the door of the apartment and climbed the stairs to the street. She was outside when she heard her mother's voice saying, "Hélène? Are you going out already?" Her mother never called her Esther when someone outside might hear. One evening, as she lay in her bed in the dark room, Esther heard her mother complaining that she spent all her time roaming around, and her father simply responded, "Let her be, these might be her last days..." Ever since then, those words had stuck in her mind: her last days...That was what lured her so irresistibly out of doors. That was what made the sky so blue, the sun so bright, the mountains and the grassy field so fascinating, so all-consuming. At the crack of dawn, Esther started watching the light through the chinks in the cardboard that blocked off the small ventilator window, she waited for the brief cries of birds to call to her, the twittering of sparrows, the shrill whistle of swifts inviting her to come outside. When she could finally open the door and go out into the fresh air in the street, with the icy stream running down the middle of the cobblestones, she had an extraordinary sensation of freedom, a feeling of limitless bliss. She could walk down to the last houses in the village, look out over the whole stretch of the valley—still immense in the morning mist—and her father's words would fade away. Then she'd start running through the big grassy field above the river, without even thinking of vipers, and she reached the place where the path led up toward the high mountains. That's where her father went every morning, up into the unknown. Eyes blinded with the morning light, she tried to glimpse the highest peaks, the forest of larches, the gorges, the treacherous ravines. Below, on the floor of the valley, she could hear the voices of children in the river. They were busy catching crayfish, wading into the water up to their thighs, feet sunk deep in the sandy bottoms of the torrent's pools. Esther could distinctly hear the girls laughing, their sharp calls, "Maryse! Maryse!..." She kept walking through the field until the voices and laughter grew faint, disappeared. On the other side of the valley rose the dark slope of the mountain, the screes of red-colored rocks scattered with small thorn bushes. In the grassy field, the sun was already burning hot and Esther felt sweat running down her face, under her arms. Farther up, in the shelter of a few boulders, there was no wind, not a breath, not a sound. That was what Esther came here for, that silence. When there was not a human sound to be heard, only the shrill whirring of insects, and the brief cry of a skylark from time to time, and the rustling grasses, Esther felt so fine. She listened to her heart beating with slow heavy thumps, she even listened to the sound of the air coming out of her nostrils. She didn't understand why she desired that silence. It was just simply right, it was necessary. And so, little by little, the fear dissipated. The sunlight, the sky in which all the clouds were just beginning to swell, and the vast grassy fields where the flies and the bees hung suspended in the light, the somber walls of the mountains and the forests, all of that would go on and on. It wasn't the last day yet, she knew that then, all of it could still remain there, keep going, no one would stop it.

One day Esther wanted to show that place, that secret, to someone. She led Gasparini through the tall grasses all the way up to the boulders. Luckily, Gasparini hadn't mentioned vipers, maybe just to show that he wasn't afraid. But as they neared the screes, Gasparini had said very quickly, "This isn't a good place, I'm going back down." And he turned and ran away. Esther wasn't angry. She was merely surprised that she understood why the boy had run off so rapidly. He didn't need to know that everything would last, that everything had to keep going day after day, for years and centuries, and that no one could stop it.

It wasn't the fields full of viper grass that Esther was afraid of. What frightened her was the harvest. The fields of wheat were like trees shedding their leaves. Esther went back to see the harvest once again, back to the place she'd gone with Gasparini, way down in the valley, near Roquebillière.

This time the wheat was almost entirely cut. The line of men armed with their long glittering blades had broken up, there were only a few isolated groups. They were cutting the wheat higher up in the fields, in narrow terraces on the flanks of the mountain. The children were binding the last sheaves. The poor women and children were wandering through the stubble but their sacks remained empty.

Esther sat on the embankment looking out on the bare fields. She didn't understand why she felt so sad, so angry, with such a blue sky and the sun beating down on the stubbled fields. Gasparini came and sat down beside her. They didn't say anything. They watched the harvesters moving along the terraces. Gasparini was holding a fistful of ears and they crunched on the grains of wheat, slowly savoring the bittersweet taste. Now Gasparini never spoke of the war anymore, or of Jews. He seemed tense and worried. He was a boy of fifteen or sixteen, but already broad and strong as a man, with cheeks that flushed easily like a girl's. Esther felt very different from him, but she quite liked him anyway. When his friends walked by on the road they jibed him and he looked at them angrily, got half way up as if he were going to fight them.

One day Gasparini came to get Esther at her house, early in the morning. He came down the little stairway from the road and knocked at the door. Esther's mother opened the door. She looked at him for a moment, not understanding, then she recognized him and asked him to come into the kitchen. It was the first time he'd been to Esther's house. He looked around—the dark narrow room, the wooden table with benches, the cast-iron stove, the pots sitting balanced on a board. When Esther came in she almost burst out laughing seeing him looking so sheepish standing in front of the table, his eyes trained on the waxed tablecloth. From time to time, he shooed a fly away with the back of his hand.

Elizabeth brought out a bottle of cherry juice that she'd made in the spring. Gasparini drank the glass of juice, then he took a handkerchief from his pocket to wipe his mouth. The silence in the kitchen made everything seem to last much longer. Finally he decided to talk, in a slightly gruff voice. "I wanted to ask permission to take Hélène to church on Friday, for the celebration." He looked at Esther standing there in front of him as if she could help him. "What celebration?" asked Elizabeth. "Friday is the celebration of the Madonna," explained Gasparini. "The Madonna should return to the mountains, she'll be leaving the church." Elizabeth turned to her daughter, "Well? I suppose it's up to you to decide?" Esther said soberly, "If my parents consent, I'll go." Elizabeth said, "You have my permission, but you'll have to ask your father too."

The ceremony took place on Friday, as planned. The carabinieri issued an authorization and first thing in the morning people started gathering in the little village square in front of the church. Inside the church, children had lit candles and hung bouquets of flowers. There were mostly old men and women because many of the younger men were prisoners and hadn't come back from the war. But the teenage girls came wearing their low-necked summer dresses, barelegged, with espadrilles on their feet and only a shawl over their hair. Gasparini came to pick up Esther. He was wearing a light gray suit with knickers that belonged to his older brother who had worn them only once, on the day of his Solemn Communion. For the first time in his life, he had put on a tie, it was burgundy colored. Esther's mother smiled a little mockingly at the young peasant dressed in his Sunday best, but Esther shot a reproachful glance at her. Esther's father shook Gasparini's hand and said a few friendly words. Gasparini was very impressed with the tall figure Esther's father cut and also because he was a teacher. When Esther had asked her father's permission, he'd said without hesitating, "Yes, it's important for you to go to this celebration." He'd said that so seriously that it intrigued Esther.

Now, seeing the church filled with people, she understood why it was so important. The crowd had come from all over, even from isolated farms up in the mountains, from the sheepfolds of the Boréon, or Mollières. In the open square in front of the Terminus Hotel with the Italian flag flying from its roof, the carabinieri and soldiers watched the throngs go by.

Around ten o'clock the ceremony began. The priest entered the chapel followed by part of the crowd. In its midst were three men dressed in dark blue suits. Gasparini whispered in Esther's ear, "Look, that's my cousin." Esther recognized the young man that had been harvesting the wheat near Roquebillière. "When the war is over, he'll be the one who will carry the Madonna into the mountains." The church was packed and there was not enough room for the children. They waited on the porch in front of the church in the sun. When the bell started ringing, a ripple went through the crowd and the three men appeared carrying the statue. It was the first time that Esther had seen the statue of the Madonna. It represented a small woman with a waxen face, holding in her arms a baby with a strangely adult look in his eyes. The statue was draped in a large cloak of blue satin that shone in the sunlight. Its hair also shone, it was black and thick as a horse's mane. People moved aside to make way for the statue that rocked back and forth over the heads of the crowd, and the three men went back inside the church. From the hubbub, rose the first notes of Ave Maria. "When the war is over, my cousin will go with the others, they'll take the statue up to the sanctuary in the mountains," repeated Gasparini rather impatiently. When the ceremony was finished, everyone flooded out into the square. Esther stood on her tiptoes to try and get a glimpse of the Italian soldiers. Their gray uniforms stood out starkly in the shade of the lime trees. But it was really Rachel that Esther wanted to see.

A little off to one side, the old Jews were watching too. You could pick them out in the distance because of their black clothing, their hats, the scarves on the women's heads, their pallid faces. Despite the hot sporadic bursts of sun, they kept their caftans on. They stood there looking on without speaking to one another, stroking their beards. The Jewish children didn't mingle with the well-dressed crowd. They stood very still next to their parents.

All of a sudden, Esther saw Tristan. He was standing on the edge of the square with the Jewish children. He wasn't moving, just standing there staring. He had a funny expression on his face, a grimace against the bright sunlight.

Esther felt the blood rushing under her skin. She pulled away from Gasparini's hand and marched straight over to Tristan. Her heart was pounding heavily, she thought it was anger. "Why are you always watching me? Why do you spy on me?" He stepped back a little. His deep blue eyes shone, but he didn't respond. "Go away! Find something else to do, leave me alone, you're not my brother!" Esther heard Gasparini's voice calling her, "Hélène! Come back, where are you going?" There was such an anxious look in Tristan's eyes that she stopped for a moment and her voice grew softer, she said to him, "I'll be back, I'm sorry, I don't know why I said that to you." She pushed through the crowd with her head down, without answering Gasparini. The girls stepped aside to let her by. She started walking down the street with the stream; it was deserted. But she didn't want to go back home, she didn't want to have to answer her mother's questions. Once far from the square, she heard the sound of human voices swelling, laughter, calls, and over it all, a sort of humming, the voice of the priest chanting in the church, *Ave, Ave, Ave Maria...*

As the afternoon drew to a close, Esther went back to the square. Most of the people were gone, but there was a group of boys and girls over by the lime trees. When she walked up to them, Esther heard the sound of accordion music. In the center of the square, by the fountain, women were dancing with each other, or else with very young boys that only came up to their shoulders. The Italian soldiers were standing in front of the hotel, smoking and listening to the music.

Now Esther was looking for Rachel. Slowly, she walked over toward the hotel, her heart racing. She glanced over in the direction of the main room, and through the open door she saw the soldiers and the carabinieri. On Mr. Ferne's piano a gramophone was playing a slow, nasal-sounding mazurka. Outside, the women spun around, their red faces shining in the sunlight. Esther walked past them, past the boys, past the carabinieri, she walked up to the door of the hotel. The sun was very low in the sky, it barely lit the inside of the main room through the windows overlooking the garden. The light was painful for Esther, it made her dizzy. Maybe it was because of what her father had said, that everything had to stop. When Esther went into the room, she felt relieved. But her heart still beat heavily in her chest. She saw Rachel. She was with the plumed soldiers, in the middle of the room in which the tables and chairs had been pushed back against the walls, and she was dancing with Mondoloni. There were other women in the room, but Rachel was the only one dancing. The others were watching her, how she turned and whirled around, with her pale-colored dress flying up and showing her slender legs, how her bare arm lay lightly on the soldier's shoulder. At times, the carabinieri and the soldiers stopped in front of her, and

Esther had to stand on her tiptoes to see. Because of the loud music, Esther couldn't hear Rachel's voice, but she thought she heard an exclamation, a burst of laughter from time to time. Never had Rachel seemed so beautiful to her. She must have already had quite a lot to drink, but she was the sort who could hold her liquor well. She simply held herself very straight as she turned and turned to the sound of the mazurka, and her long dark red hair swept lightly across her back. In vain, Esther tried to attract her attention. Her brown face was thrown backward, she was gone, far from that place, in another world, being swept along with the dancing and the sounds of the music. The soldiers and the carabinieri were all turned facing her, watching her as they smoked and drank, and Esther thought she heard them laughing. The children had come up and were standing in front of the door, trying to see in, the women were leaning forward in an attempt to make out the lithe silhouette dancing in the main room. Then the carabinieri turned around, they motioned with their hands, and everyone drew back. Outside in the square, the young people kept their distance, on the other side of the fountain. None of them seemed to be paying any attention. That's what made Esther's heart beat so fast. She felt like something wasn't right, it was as if there was a lie somewhere. The young people were pretending that they didn't see, but it was Rachel they were thinking of—deep down, they hated her even more than the Italian soldiers.

The music continued, with the nasal voice, the polkas beat out on Mr. Ferne's piano, the strangled voice of the clarinet knotted in the air.

When Esther left the hotel, Gasparini came up and stood in front of her. His eyes glinted with anger. "Come on, we're going for a walk." Esther shook her head. She walked down the narrow street till she came to the place where you can see out over the valley. She wanted to be alone, not hear the music or the voices anymore. At one point, Gasparini grabbed hold of her wrist and pulled her over to him clumsily, holding her by the waist, as if he wanted to dance. His face was red from the heat, the tie was strangling him. He leaned toward Esther, tried to kiss her. His smell filled Esther's nostrils, a heavy smell that frightened and attracted her at the same time, a man-smell. She started pushing him away, saying at first, "leave me alone, go away!" Then she started struggling fiercely, she scratched him and he just stood in the middle of the street, puzzled. The boys were forming a circle around them, laughing. Then Tristan jumped on Gasparini, grabbing him around the neck, he was trying to get a good hold on him, but he was too light, he was left hanging there, his feet dangling in the air. With a mere jab of the elbow, Gasparini threw him off and sent him rolling on the ground. He shouted, "You little snot, try that again and I'll beat your head in!" Esther started running through the streets as fast as she could, then she headed down through the fields to the torrent. She stopped running, listened to her heart thudding in her chest, in her throat. Even there near the river she could still hear the sad, whining music of the party, the clarinet endlessly repeating the same phrase on the record while Rachel swung around the room with Mondoloni, her pale face impervious and distant like that of a blind woman.

Nights were very dark, because of the curfew. You had to draw the curtains at the windows, plug up all the cracks with rags and cardboard. Sometimes the men from the Maquis came in the afternoon. They sat down on the benches around the table covered with a wax cloth in the narrow kitchen. Esther knew them well, but she didn't know most of their names. Some came from the village or nearby, they left before nightfall. Some came from far away, from Nice or Cannes, sent by Ignace Finck, Gutman, Wister, Appel. Some even came from the Italian Maquis. Amongst them, there was one whom Esther liked very much. He was a lad with hair as red as Rachel's, and his name was Mario. He came from beyond the mountains, where the Italian peasants and shepherds were fighting against the fascists. Whenever he came, he was always so tired that he stayed overnight, sleeping on some cushions on the kitchen floor. He didn't talk much with the other maquisards. He spent his time with Esther instead. He told her funny stories, half in French, half in Italian, punctuated with great bursts of laughter. He had small eyes that were surprisingly green, snake eyes, thought Esther. Sometimes when he'd spent the night in the kitchen, he took Esther for a walk around the village at dawn, without even worrying about the soldiers in the Terminus Hotel.

She went with him out into the fields, up above the river. Together they walked through the tall grass, him in front, her following in the path he made in the grass. He was the one who mentioned vipers first. But he wasn't afraid of them. He said that he could tame them, and even catch them, by whistling at them like dogs.

One morning he took Esther out even farther into the fields, beyond the place where the two streams met. Esther was walking behind him, her heart racing wildly, listening to Mario who was making odd whistling sounds—soft and shrill—a sort of music she'd never heard before. The heat of the sun was already swirling thickly in the grasses and the mountains around the valley looked like giant walls from which the clouds sprang into being. They walked for a long time through the tall grass with Mario's soft whistling sounds that seemed to come from all sides at once, it gave you a slightly dizzy feeling. Suddenly Mario stopped, holding his hand up in the air. Esther slipped noiselessly up against his back. Mario turned toward her. His green eyes shone. In a whisper he said, "Look!" Through the grass, Esther saw something she wasn't quite sure of laying on the shingle beach by the riverbank. It looked like a thick rope made of two short twisted fibers—the color of dead leaves— that shone in the light as if someone had just taken it out of the water. Suddenly Esther shuddered—the rope was moving! Horrified, Esther watched through the grass as the two intertwined vipers slithered and twisted over the beach. At one point their heads parted, two short snouts, eyes with vertical pupils, mouths open. The vipers remained stuck together, staring fixedly at each other, as if in ecstasy. Then their bodies started twisting on the rocks again, slithering between the pebbles, coiling to one side. Clinging to one another in knots that slipped up and down, came undone, lashing their tails like whips. They continued to slide, roll, and, despite the crashing of the river, Esther thought she heard the scraping sound of scales running over one another.

"Are they fighting?" Esther asked trying her best to speak softly. Mario was watching the snakes. The whole of his thick face was concentrated in his gaze, his two narrowly slit eyes, like those of snakes. He turned toward Esther and said, "No, they're making love." Then Esther watched even more intently as the two entangled vipers slithered over the beach, through the pebbles, without noticing their presence. It lasted a very long time, the snakes remaining motionless and cold at times like bits of branch, then suddenly quivering and whipping the ground, so closely joined that you couldn't see their heads anymore. In the end, their bodies relaxed and their heads dropped to the ground, each to one side. Esther could see the frozen pupil, like a treacherous loophole, and their bodies puffed up with their breathing and the light shining on their scales. Very slowly, one of the vipers loosened the knot, it slipped away and disappeared in the grass by the river. When the other began moving away, Mario started whistling in his strange way, between his teeth, almost without opening his lips, a tenuous whistling—soft, almost inaudible. The snake lifted its head and stared straight at Mario and Esther standing there in the grass. Under that gaze, Esther felt her heart dip and waver. The viper hesitated a moment, its wide head making a right angle to its upright body. Then, in the wink of an eye, it too disappeared across the grassy field.

Mario and Esther went back toward the village. They didn't say anything the whole way, walking through the tall grass, simply being careful about where they put their feet. When they got to the road, Esther asked, "You never kill them?" Mario started laughing. "Yes, yes, I know how to kill them too." He picked up a small stick on the edge of the road and showed her how to do it, giving a sharp rap on the snake's neck, near the head. Esther asked again, "And could

41

you have killed them today?" A strange look came over Mario's face. He shook his head. "No, today I couldn't have. It would have been wrong to kill them."

That was why Esther liked Mario so much. One day, instead of telling her stories, he had told her a little about his life, just a few snatches. Before the war he was a shepherd, over by Valdieri. He hadn't wanted to go to war, he had hidden in the mountains. But the fascists killed all his sheep and his dog, and Mario had joined the Maquis.

Now Esther had phony papers. One afternoon, some men came with Mario into the kitchen and they put ID cards down on the table for everyone, for Esther, for her mother and father, for Mario too. Esther looked at the bit of yellow cardboard with her father's photo on it for a long time. Written there she saw:

Name: JAUFFERT. First name: Pierre. Middle name: Michel

Date of birth: April 10, 1910. Place of birth: Marseille (Bouches-du-Rhône).

Profession: Salesman

Features:

    Nose:

        Bridge: straight

        Base: medium

        Size: medium

    General shape of face: long

    Complexion: fair

    Eyes: green

    Hair: light brown

Then her mother's card, Name: JAUFFERT, Maiden name: Leroy, First name: Madeleine, born February 3, 1912 in

Pontivy (Morbihan), No profession. And her own, JAUFFERT Hélène, born February 22, 1931, in Nice (Alpes-Maritimes), no profession. Features: Nose: Bridge: straight, Base: medium, Size: medium, General shape of face: oval, Complexion: fair, Eyes: green, Hair: black.

The men talked for a long time sitting around the table, their faces lit fantastically by the oil lamp. Esther tried to listen to what they were saying, without understanding, as if they were train robbers planning a job. She watched Mario's broad face, his red hair, his narrow, slanting eyes, and she thought that maybe he was dreaming about the vipers in the grassy fields, or about the hares that he caught in his traps on full-moon nights.

When the men spoke with her father, there was always a name that she couldn't forget because it sounded so fine, like the name of a hero in one of her father's history books: Angelo Donati. Angelo Donati said this, did that, and the men all nodded in agreement. Angelo Donati had a boat ready in Livorno, a big motorized sailboat that would take all the fugitives aboard and save them. The boat would cross the sea and take the Jews to Jerusalem, far from the Germans. Esther listened to that, lying on the floor on the cushions that Mario used for a bed and she fell half way asleep, dreaming of Angelo Donati's boat, of the long journey across the sea to Jerusalem. Then Elizabeth got up, she wrapped her arms around Esther and together they walked to the little alcove room where Esther's bed was. Before going to sleep, Esther asked: "Tell me, when will we go away on Angelo Donati's boat? When will we go to Jerusalem?" Esther's mother kissed her, told her jokingly, but in a low voice, her throat tightening with worry: "Go to sleep now, never speak of Angelo Donati to anyone, do you understand? It's a secret." Esther said, "But is it true that the boat will take everyone to Jerusalem?" Elizabeth answered, "It's true, and we'll go too, maybe, we'll go to Jerusalem." Esther kept her eyes opened wide in the darkness, she listened to the sound of the voices echoing softly in the little kitchen, Mario's laughter. Then there were footsteps outside dying away, the door closed. When her mother and father lay down in the big bed next to hers and she could hear them breathing, she went to sleep.

It was already the end of summer, with rain every afternoon and the sound of water streaming down over the roof and through all the gutters. In the morning the sun shone brightly over the mountains and Esther would hardly take time to swallow her bowl of milk to get outdoors more quickly. She waited for Tristan in the square by the fountain and then they and the other children ran down the street with the stream all the way to the river. The rains had barely troubled the crashing, cold waters of the Boréon. The boys waited down at the bottom and Esther went up with the other girls to the place where the torrent cascaded down between two blocks of rock. They undressed in the bushes. Like most of the girls, Esther bathed in her panties, but there were some, like Judith, who were too shy to take off their slips. The greatest part was getting into the water, hanging on to the rocks, right where the current was strongest, and letting the water run over your body. The smooth water poured down, pushing against your shoulders and chest, sliding over your hips and along your legs making its unbroken sound. Then you could forget everything, the cold water cleansed you to the very core, washed away everything that was bothering you, burning within you. Judith, Esther's friend (she wasn't really her friend, not like Rachel was, but they sat together in Mr. Seligman's class), had talked about baptism absolving sins. Esther thought that this is what it must feel like, a smooth, cold river flowing over you and cleansing you. When Esther came out of the torrent into the sunlight and stood unsteadily on the flat rock, she felt as if she were brand new and as if all the bad feelings and all the anger had disappeared. Afterward, the girls went back down to where the boys were waiting. They'd been scavenging around in vain in the holes of the torrent looking for crayfish, and to get even for not having caught anything, they splashed water at the girls.

So then everyone sat down on a large flat rock above the torrent and waited, watching the water. The sun climbed in the still-cloudless sky. Light filtered into the forest of birch and chestnut trees. Irritated wasps flew about, drawn by the drops of water caught in their hair, on their bare skin. Esther was very attentive to every detail, every shadow, she watched with an almost pained scrutiny everything near and far: the line of Caïres' ridge against the sky, the pines bristling on the hilltops, the prickly grasses, the stones, the gnats hanging suspended in the light. The shouts of children, the laughter of girls, each word echoed strangely in her ears, two or three times, like the barking of dogs. They were unrecognizable, incomprehensible, Gasparini, with his red face, his short-cropped hair, his broad man-shoulders, and the others, Maryse, Anne, Bernard, Judith, all so thin in their wet clothing, their eyes hidden in the shadows of their brows, their silhouettes, both frail and distant at the same time. But Tristan wasn't like the others. He was so awkward, he had such gentle eyes. Of late, whenever they went for a walk around the village, Esther would hold his hand. They were playing at being in love. They went down to the torrent and she would lure him into the gorge, jumping from rock to rock. She thought that was the thing she was best at in life: running through the rocks, leaping lightly, calculating her stride, choosing which route to take in a quarter of a second. Tristan tried to follow, but Esther was too fast for him. She bounded along so quickly that no one could have followed her. She jumped without thinking, barefoot, holding her espadrilles, then she would stop, listening for the panting breath of the boy who wasn't able to keep up with her. When she'd gone quite a ways up the torrent, she stopped by the water's edge, hidden by a mass of rock, listening acutely to all the sounds—cracking things, insects whirring—mingling with the crashing flow of water. She could hear dogs barking far off in the distance and then, Tristan's voice calling her name "Hélène! Hé-lè-ne!" She enjoyed not answering, staying there huddled up in the shelter of the rock, because it was as if she were in charge of her life, as if she could decide everything that would ever happen to her. It was a game, but she didn't tell anyone about it. Who would have understood? When Tristan had grown hoarse from calling, he followed the torrent back down and Esther came out of her hiding place. She climbed the steep slope up to the path, went over to the cemetery. From there, she would wave her arms and shout so that Tristan would see her. But sometimes she went back down to the village alone, walked home, threw herself on her bed with her face buried in the pillow, and cried. She didn't know what about.

It was the end, the most scorching part of the summer, when the grass fields turned yellow and straw stalks fermented at the edge of the fields with pungent warmth. Esther had never been out that far alone, past the place where the shepherds kept their flocks in winter—windowless drystone huts, vaulted cellars like caves. Suddenly the clouds appeared, cutting off the light as if a giant hand had opened up in the sky. Esther had gone so far she thought she was lost, just like in her dreams, when her father would disappear in the field of tall grass. It wasn't really all that terrifying, feeling like you were lost at the mouth of the gorges, deep in the dark mountains. It made you shudder a bit on account of the wolf stories. Mario had told her about the wolves in Italy, they walked through the winter snow in single file, went down into the valleys to carry off lambs and young goats. But maybe Esther had shuddered because of the sharp wind that was bearing the rain along in its path. Standing up on a rock above the bushes, she could see the gray clouds covering the flanks of the mountains, making their way up the narrow valley. The sweeping curtain was engulfing rocky cliffs, forests, great boulders. The wind began to blow harder, bitterly cold after the warmth of the fermenting straw. Esther started running, trying to make it back to the shepherds' huts before the rain. But the icy drops were already spattering heavily on the ground. Life was taking its revenge, catching up on the time Esther had stolen in her hiding places. She was running, her heart leaping wildly in her chest.

The sheepfold was immense, like a cave. It formed a long tunnel penetrating far back into the mountain. There were bats up in the shadows of the ceiling. Esther huddled in the doorway, half obstructed with a tangle of roots. Now that the rain was falling, Esther felt a little calmer. Flashes of lightning lit up the clouds. Water was beginning to flood down the side of the hill, forming large red streams. Soon Mr. Seligman would reopen school, the days would be getting shorter and shorter and snow would fall in the mountains. Esther thought about that as she watched the rain coming down and the streams rushing past her. She thought something was going to happen, something no one knew about.

Lately, these last few days, people just weren't the same as they used to be. There was something hurried about them, in the way they spoke, in the way they moved. The children had changed most of all. They were impatient, irritable, when they were playing, when they went fishing or swimming in the torrent, even when they were running about in the square. Gasparini had said again, "The Germans will be coming soon, they'll take all the Jews away." He said that as if it were an absolute certainty, and Esther had felt her throat tighten because that was what time was bringing and what she wanted to prevent. She said: "Then they'll take me away too." Gasparini looked at her sharply, "If you have false papers, they won't take you away." He said: "Hélène, that's not a Jewish name." Esther answered immediately, in a calm, cold voice: "My name's not Hélène, my name's Esther. It's a Jewish name." Gasparini said, "If the Germans come, you'll have to hide." He seemed unsure of himself for the first time. He added, "If the German's come, I'll hide you in the barn."

In the square, the boys were talking about Rachel. When Esther came up to them, they jabbed her away with their elbows, "Get lost! You're too little!" But Anne knew what they were talking about because her older brother was in the group. She heard them say that they'd found out where Captain Mondoloni went with Rachel—an old barn on the other side of the bridge down by the river. It was midday, but instead of going to eat lunch, Esther ran down the road all the way to the bridge, then she set out across the fields toward the barn. When she reached it, she heard the cawing of crows in the silent afternoon, and she thought that the boys had made the whole story up. But when she drew nearer to the old barn, she saw them hiding behind the bushes. There were several boys, older ones, and some girls too. The barn was built straddling two terraced embankments, down below the road level. Esther went down the slope without making a sound, over to the barn. Three boys were lying in the grass, and they were peeking into the barn through an opening above the wall, just under the roof. When Esther reached them, they stood up and started beating her, without saying a word. They kicked and punched her while one of them held her arms. Esther was thrashing around, her eyes were filled with tears, but she wasn't crying out loud. She tried to get a neck-lock on the boy who was holding her and he stumbled backwards. The boy backed away with Esther hanging on to his neck with all her might while the others pummeled her on the back to make her let go. Finally she fell to the ground, her eyes blurred with a cloud of blood. The boys climbed back up the embankment and ran off down the road. Then the barn door opened and through the red haze Esther saw Rachel looking at her. She was wearing her pretty pale-colored dress, the sun made her hair shine like copper. Then the captain came out after her, straightening his clothes. He had his revolver in his hand. When he saw Esther on the bank of the road and the boys running off, he burst out laughing and said something in Italian. At the same time, Rachel started screaming, in a strangely shrill and vulgar voice that Esther didn't recognize. She was climbing up the slope of the embankment with her gleaming hair, and she was picking up stones and throwing them awkwardly at the fleeing boys without succeeding in hitting them. Esther was in such pain that she couldn't get to her feet. She started crawling up the bank, desperately seeking some hole to hide in, to block out the shame and the fear. But Rachel came over, sat down in the grass beside her and stroked her hair and face. In a strange voice, hoarse from having screamed, she was saying: "It's nothing, sweetheart, it's all over..." and so they sat there alone in the sunshine on the grassy slope. Esther was trembling with cold and with exhaustion, she was watching the light in Rachel's red hair, smelling the odor of her body. Afterward, they went down to the torrent and

Rachel carefully helped her wash her face where the blood had dried. Esther was so tired that she needed to lean on Rachel to walk back up the slope to the village. She wished it would start raining right then and not stop until winter.

That was the evening Esther learned of Mario's death. There had been a faint tapping at the door in the night and Esther's father let some men in, a Jew named Gutman, and two men from Lantosque. Esther got out of bed and cracked open the bedroom door, squinting her eyes in the light from the kitchen. She stood in the doorway watching the men whispering around the table as if they were talking to the oil lamp. Elizabeth was sitting with them, she too was watching the lamp flame, saying nothing. Esther understood right away that something serious had happened. When the three men went out into the night again, Esther's father noticed her standing there at the door in her nightgown, and at first he said to her, almost harshly, "What are you doing there? Go back to bed!" Then he came over and held her closely in his arms, as if he were sorry to have scolded her. Elizabeth came over with tears running from her eyes. She said: "It's Mario, he's dead." Her father explained what had happened. It was only words, and yet for Esther, they were interminable, it was a story that repeated itself over and over again, incessantly, like in your dreams. That afternoon, while Esther was going down the road to the abandoned barn, the place where Rachel went to meet Captain Mondoloni, Mario was walking through the mountains, his knapsack filled with plastic explosives and delayed-action detonators, and dynamite sticks too, on his way to join the group that was going to blow up the power lines to Berthemont, where the Germans had recently set up their headquarters. The sun was

J. M. G. Le Clézio

shining down on the grass as Esther walked toward the deserted barn, and at that very same instant, Mario was walking alone through the fields at the foot of the mountains, and while he walked, he must certainly have been whistling gently to the vipers, just as he always did, and he was looking up at the very same sky that she was, hearing the very same crows cawing. Mario had hair as red as Rachel's, Rachel standing in the sunlight with her pale dress unhooked in the back, her white shoulders glowing in the sun, so alive, so attractive. Mario liked Rachel a lot, he told Esther so himself one day and when he'd confided that to her, he blushed—or more precisely, he turned bright red—and Esther had burst out laughing because of the color of his cheeks. He told Esther that when the war was over, he would take Rachel dancing on Saturdays, and Esther didn't have the heart to tell him that he wasn't Rachel's type, that she liked Italian officers, that she went dancing with Captain Mondoloni, and that people said she was a whore, and that they'd crop off her hair when the war was over. Mario was taking the sack of explosives to the men in the Maquis, over Berthemont way, he was walking quickly through the fields in order to get there before nightfall because he wanted to get back to spend the night in Saint-Martin. That was why Esther got up when the three men knocked at the door, because she thought it was Mario. Esther was slipping through the dry grass, toward the ruined barn. In the warm, damp barn Rachel was lying close against the captain, and he...he was kissing her on the mouth, down her neck, all over. It was the girls that said all of that, but they hadn't seen a thing, because it was much too dark in the barn. Only they'd listened to the sounds, the sighing, and the rustling of clothing. So when they finished beating Esther up, the boys fled, ran up to the road, disappeared, and she was dragging herself through the grass

53

on the bank with that red cloud before her eyes. And that was when she had heard the sound of the explosion, far away in the distance, down in the valley. That was why the captain came out of the barn holding his revolver, because he too, had heard the explosion. But Esther hadn't paid much attention to it because just then, at that very same instant, Rachel was standing there in front of the barn with all that red hair shining like a mane, and she was screaming insults at the boys and sitting down next to Esther. And the captain had started laughing and walked off down the road just as Rachel was sitting down in the grass to stroke Esther's hair. There had only been one explosion, such a terrific one that Esther had felt the pressure of the blast in her eardrums. When the men from the Maquis arrived, all they found was a huge crater in the grass, a gaping hole with burnt edges, smelling of powder. Searching through the grass around the hole, they'd also found a clump of red hair, and that's how they knew that Mario was dead. That was all that was left of him. Nothing but a clump of red hair. Now Esther was crying in her father's arms. She could feel the tears come brimming up out of her eyes, go running down her cheeks, along her nose and chin, dribbling off onto her father's shirt. And he was saying things about Mario, about everything he'd done, about his courage, but Esther wasn't really crying about that. She didn't know what she was crying about. Maybe it was on account of all these days that she'd spent running through the grass, in the sunshine, on account of the exhaustion, and also on account of Mr. Ferne's music. Maybe it was because the summer was burning itself out, the harvest, and the straw stalks moldering, the black clouds that gathered every evening, and the rain falling in cold drops, giving birth to red streams that rutted the mountain. She was so very tired, she wanted to go to sleep, forget everything, be somewhere else, be someone else, with another name, a real one, not some phony name on an identification card. Her mother came and picked her up, carried her gently over to the alcove where the bed was. Her forehead was burning hot, she was shivering as if she had a fever. In a cracked, ridiculous voice she asked, "When is Angelo Donati's boat going to leave? When will it take us to Jerusalem?" Elizabeth murmured, like in a song, "I don't know, my little love, my little life, go to sleep now." She sat down on the bed next to Esther, she was stroking her hair just like when she was a little girl. "Tell me about Jerusalem, please." In the silent night Elizabeth's voice murmured on, repeating the same old story, the one Esther had been hearing ever since she had learned to talk, the magical name that she knew without understanding, the city of light, of fountains, the place where all of the world's paths meet, Eretzraël, Eretzraël.

At the bottom of the gorge, everything was mysterious, new, disquieting. Never had Tristan felt like that before. As he made his way up the torrent, the boulders steadily increased in size, grew darker, in a tumble of chaos, as if a giant had thrown them down from the top of the mountains. The forest was also dark, it grew almost all the way down to the water and in the spaces between the rocks, ferns and brambles lived, all tangled together, barring the way like animals. That morning Tristan followed Esther even farther. The group of boys and girls had stayed down at the mouth of the gorges. For a while Tristan could hear their shouts, their calls, then their voices were drowned out by the sound of the water cascading down between the boulders. The sky over the valley was utterly blue, a hard, taut color that hurt your eyes. Tristan followed Esther through the gorge without calling to her, without saying a word. It was a game, and yet he could feel his heart beating faster, as if it were real, as if it were an adventure. He could feel the blood pulsing in the arteries of his neck, in his ears. It made an odd kind of tremor that echoed in the earth too, that blended in with the pounding of the water in the torrent. The shade in the gorge was cold but when Tristan breathed in, the air ripped through his body, whistling as if through an open window, through a cleft in the mountain. That was why everything was so new here, mysterious and disquieting. It was the kind of place he'd never dreamt of, even when he listened to his mother reading books, The Fifth Voyage of Sinbad the Sailor, when he comes upon the desert island where the Rocs live.

It was deep down inside of him, a painful, a giddy feeling—he wasn't sure. Maybe it came from the overly blue sky, from the crashing of the torrent that drowned out all the other sounds, or else from the dark trees hanging over the valley. At the bottom of the ravine, the shade was cold, Tristan could smell the peculiar odor of the earth. Dead leaves rotted between the rocks. Underfoot, his tracks filled with bubbling black water.

Up ahead of him, the light, fleeting figure of the girl appeared briefly now and again. She bounded from rock to rock, disappeared in the hollows, reappeared farther up. Tristan would have liked to call out her name, "Hélène!" like the other boys did, but he couldn't. It was a game, you had to jump through the rocks, heart pounding, eyes sharp, searching every dark recess, reading the trail.

As they went up the torrent, the gorge narrowed. The blocks of rock were enormous, dark, waterworn. It was as if the sunlight were trapped inside of them. They looked like gigantic petrified animals around which the water of the torrent swirled. Above them, the sides of the gorge were covered with thick black forest. Everything was wild. Everything disappeared, was swept away, cleansed by the water in the torrent. All that remained were the rocks, the sound of water, the cruel sky.

He caught up with Esther in the middle of a circle of dark-colored rocks where the water of the torrent formed a pool. She was squatting down by the water, rinsing off her arms. Then, with quick gestures, she took off her dress and jumped into the pool—not feet first like girls usually do, but head first, holding her nose. The flash of light on her very white body made Tristan shudder. He stayed up on the rocks, motionless, watching Esther swim. She had a very peculiar way of swimming, throwing one arm over her head and disappearing underwater. When she reached the other side of the pool, she lifted her head and motioned Tristan to join her.

After a slight hesitation, Tristan undressed awkwardly between the rocks and he too went into the icy water. The torrent crashed down into the pool and flowed slowly out over it. Tristan swam as fast as he could to the other side, swallowing lots of water. On the other side of the pool a huge rock looked out over the gorge. Esther got out of the water and Tristan again saw the light gleam on her white skin, on her back, on her slender legs. She shook out her black hair scattering the droplets behind her. She scaled agilely up the rock and sat down at its top in the sun. Tristan was ashamed of his naked body, of his white skin. He made his way slowly to the top of the rock to sit down next to Esther. After swimming across the pool, he felt his skin burning.

Esther was sitting up on the rock, her legs dangling over the edge. She looked at him as if it were all perfectly natural. Her body was long and muscular, like that of a boy, but there was already the tenderness of breasts, a faint shadow, a flutter.

The rushing sound of the water filled the narrow valley all the way up to the sky. There was no one but them in that gorge; it was as if they were alone in the world. For the first time in his life, Tristan felt free. It made his whole body buzz, as if suddenly the rest of the world had disappeared and all that was left was that dark rock, a sort of island hanging over the wilderness of the torrent. Tristan no longer thought of the square where the black figures waited in the rain before entering the Hotel Terminus. He no longer thought of his mother, of her sad, drawn face when she went to try and sell her cheap necklaces to the diamond dealers in order to buy milk, meat, potatoes.

On the smooth rock, Esther was leaning backward, eyes closed. Tristan watched her, without daring to draw closer, without daring to put his lips on her glistening shoulders, to taste the drops of water that still clung to her skin. He could forget about the bitter looks of the boys, the scornful words of the girls in the square when they spoke of Rachel. Tristan felt his heart beating very heavily in his chest, he could feel the warmth of his blood rippling outwards, all of the sunlight that had penetrated the black rocks and that was now radiating through their bodies. Tristan took Esther's hand and suddenly, without knowing how he dared, he put his lips on those of the young girl. At first Esther turned her face toward him, then abruptly kissed him on the mouth extremely violently. It was the first time she'd ever done that, she closed her eyes and she kissed him, as if she were drawing in his breath and smothering his words, as if the fear she felt should disappear in that embrace, and there would be nothing left before or after, only the sensation that was both sweet and burning at the same time, the taste of their saliva mixing together, and their tongues touching, the sound of their teeth knocking together, their shallow breaths, the beating of their hearts. There was a whirlwind of light. The cold water and the sunlight were inebriating, almost nauseating. Esther pushed Tristan's face away with her hands; she lay down on the rock with her eyes closed. She said, "You'll never leave me?" Her voice was gruff and filled with pain. "Now I'm like a sister to you, you won't tell anyone?" Tristan didn't understand. "I'll never leave you." He said that so solemnly it made Esther laugh. She ran her hand through his hair, pulled his head down onto her chest. "Listen to my heart." She lay there very still, her back against the smooth rock, her eyes closing out the sun. Against Tristan's ear, Esther's skin was soft and burning hot, as if with fever, and he listened to the dull thudding of her heart, he gazed at the intensely blue sky, heard the crashing of the water as it cascaded around their island.

The Germans were very near now. Gasparini said he'd seen tracer bullets one evening over near Berthemont. He said the Italians had lost the war; that they were going to surrender. So the Germans were coming to occupy all the villages, all the mountains. His father had told him so.

That evening in the square, everyone gathered in front of the hotel, they were talking amongst themselves, the men and the women from the village, but also the Jews, the old men dressed in their caftans and their large hats, and the rich Jews from the villas, and Mr. Heinrich Ferne, and even Tristan's mother was there with her long dress and her extraordinary hat.

While the people were discussing the dramatic turn of events, the children ran through the square as usual, maybe they ran even harder and let out shriller cries on purpose, to allay their fears. Esther had come to the square with her mother and they were standing still by a wall waiting, listening to the people talk. But it wasn't what the people were saying that interested Esther. She was looking hard at the Terminus Hotel, trying to catch a glimpse of Rachel. The boys and girls said that Rachel had quarreled with her parents and that now she was living at the hotel with Captain Mondoloni. But no one had seen her go in or come out. That evening the green shutters of the hotel were all closed, except the ones that opened onto the garden on the other side. The soldiers were staying inside, in the large room, smoking and talking. Esther walked a little closer; she could hear the sounds of their voices. That morning other military men had come up from down in the valley in a truck. Gasparini said the Italians were afraid after what happened to Mario and that's why they didn't dare come out into the village anymore.

Esther sat perfectly still on the wall, watching the front of the hotel because she wanted to see Rachel. When her mother went back down, she remained, sitting in the shadows. For days now, she'd been looking for Rachel. She'd even gone all the way out to the abandoned barn, and she'd gone into the old ruin, heart pounding, legs shaking, as if she were doing something forbidden. She'd waited until her eyes grew accustomed to the dark. But there was nothing there, just the pile of grass that had served as bedding for the livestock, and the acrid smell of urine and mildew.

She wanted to see Rachel, just for a minute. She'd gone over in her mind what she would say to her—that she was wrong, she hadn't gone to the barn to spy on her, that none of it mattered, that she'd gotten into the fight to defend her. She'd say, "It's not true! It's not true!" with all her might, so Rachel would know that she believed her, that she was still her friend and she believed her, that she didn't believe what the others said, she didn't laugh with them. She would show her the marks of the beating she'd taken, the bruises on her ribs, on her back, and that's why she couldn't talk or walk the other day, because she was in so much pain she couldn't stand up straight.

Where was Rachel? Maybe they'd already put her in a car at night when no one was watching and they'd taken her away to Italy, somewhere on the other side of the mountains, or even worse, northward where the Germans put the Jews in prison.

In the square that evening people came and went

nervously, they talked in all their languages and no one was thinking about Rachel. They acted liked they hadn't noticed anything. Esther went up to them one after the other to ask them, "You haven't seen Rachel, have you?" "You wouldn't know where Rachel is, would you?" But they simply turned their heads away, looking embarrassed, they acted as if they didn't know, as if they didn't understand. Even Mr. Ferne said nothing, he shook his head without saying anything. There was so much cruelty and jealousy—that's what frightened Esther, what hurt her. The shutters of the hotel remained closed and Esther couldn't imagine what was in those sad, dark, cave-like rooms. Maybe Rachel was locked up in one of them and she was peering through the cracks watching the people coming and going in the square, talking. Maybe she could see her too and she thought she was like all the others, that she hid in the tall grass to spy on her and laugh with the others. Thinking that made her head reel. In the twilight, Esther went down to the bottom of the village from where you could see a kind of mist illuminating the valley and the tall shapes of the mountains.

The next morning, there was a sound of music down below the square, over by the villa with its mulberry tree. Esther ran as fast as she could. In the steep street, in front of the gate, some women had stopped, some children too. Esther climbed up on the wall, gripping the gate, to her spot in the shade of the tree and she saw Mr. Ferne sitting in the kitchen in front of his black piano. "They brought it back! They gave the piano back to Mr. Ferne!" Esther felt like turning around and shouting that out to the people. But it wasn't necessary. All of them had the same expression on their faces. Gradually people gathered in the street to listen to Mr. Ferne play. And it's true he'd never played like that before. From the dark kitchen door, the notes took flight, rose in the light air, filled the entire street, the entire village. The piano that had been silent too long seemed to be playing all by itself. The music flowed out, soared, sparkled. Hanging onto the gate in the shade of the mulberry tree, Esther listened, barely breathing because the piano notes were going so fast, filling up her body, her chest. She was thinking that now everything would be as it was before. She could once again sit next to Mr. Ferne and learn to make her hands slide over the keys, read the music on the sheets of paper he prepared. She was thinking that nothing was coming to an end because Mr. Ferne's piano had come back. Everything would be simple, people wouldn't be afraid anymore, wouldn't seek revenge anymore. Rachel would start walking in the streets again, go shopping for her parents, she'd go to the square, and her hair would shine like red copper in the sun. In the morning, she'd wait for Esther near the fountain and they would go and sit in the shade of the plane trees to talk. She'd talk about what she was going to do later on, when the war was over, and about how she'd be a singer in Vienna, in Rome, in Berlin. Mr. Ferne's music was like that: it stopped time, and it even made it go backwards. Then, when he'd finished playing, Mr. Ferne appeared in the kitchen door. He looked at everyone with his eyes blinking in the bright sunlight and his little beard twitching. There was an odd expression on his face, as if he were crying. He took a few steps into the garden toward the people standing in the street and he spread out his arms, bowing his head slightly as if to say, Thank you, thank you my friends. And the people started clapping, first a few men and women that were out in the street, then everyone, even the children, and they were shouting too, cheering him. Esther clapped too, she thought it was like in the old days in

Vienna when Mr. Ferne played in front of gentlemen in tailcoats and ladies in evening dresses, back in the days of his youth.

It was on a Friday that, for the very first time, Esther entered the synagogue high up in the village where the Shabbat ceremony was held. It was the same every Friday: Mr. Yacov, who was old Reb Eïzik Salanter's assistant, went from house to house knocking on the doors where he knew Jews were living. He knocked at the door of Esther's house each time, but no one went to the Shabbat because neither her mother nor her father believed in religion. When Esther asked one day why they didn't go to the chalet for the Shabbat, her father simply said, "If you want to go, you're free to do so." He always thought that religion was a matter of freedom.

Several times she'd gone up in front of the chalet just when the women and girls were going in to prepare for the Shabbat. Through the open door, she'd seen the lights shining, heard the droning of prayers. Today, facing the open door she felt the same apprehension. Women dressed in black walked past without looking at her, went into the room. She recognized Judith, the girl who sat next to her in school. She had a black scarf on her head and when she went into the chalet with her mother, she turned toward Esther and made a little sign.

Esther stood across the street for a long time looking at the open door. Then suddenly, without knowing why, she walked up to the door and went into the chalet. Inside, because night was falling, it was as dark as a cave. Esther walked over to the closest wall, as if she wanted to hide. Before her, the women stood draped in their black shawls and paid no attention to her, except for one or two little girls who turned around. The black eyes of the children shone insistently in the semi-darkness. Then one of the little girls, whose name was Cécile, and who was also in Mr. Seligman's school, came over to Esther and handed her a scarf, murmuring, "Cover your hair with this." She went back to the center of the room. Esther put the scarf on her head and stepped forward to join the group of young girls. She felt better now that the scarf was hiding her hair and face.

Around Mr. Yacov, women were busily preparing the lectern, bringing water, arranging the gilt candleholders. All of a sudden, a light began to shine somewhere in the room and all eyes turned toward it. Starbursts of light appeared, one after another—wavering at first—then the flames took root and cast out long rays of light. Some women were going from candelabra to candelabra carrying a lit candle, and the light grew brighter. At the same time, there was a murmur of voices like an underground chanting and Esther saw people filing into the chalet, men and women, and in their midst walked old Reb Eïzik Salanter. They went to the center of the room, facing the lights, speaking their strange language. Esther looked in astonishment at their long white shawls draping down on either side of their faces. As they entered, the light grew brighter, the voices louder. Now they were chanting and the women in black were answering with softer voices. Inside the room, the alternating voices made a sound like the wind, or the rain, that slowly died away, then rose again, echoing loudly off the too narrow walls, made the flames of the candles flicker.

All around her, the teenage and younger girls, faces turned toward the light, repeated the mysterious words rocking their bodies back and forth. The smell of the soot from the candles mingled with the smell of sweat, the rhythmic chant, and it was like being drunk. She didn't dare move and yet, without even realizing it, she started swaying her bust forward, backward, following the movements of the women around her. She tried to read the strange words on people's lips, in the language that was so beautiful, that was speaking deep within her, as if the syllables were awakening memories. As she watched the star-shaped flames of the candles in the half-light of that mysterious cave, she was overcome with a feeling of giddiness. Never had she seen such a light, never had she heard such a chant. The voices rose, rang out, faded, then surged up elsewhere. At times, a voice spoke alone, the clear voice of a woman, chanting a long phrase, and Esther watched her veiled body rocking back and forth even harder, her arms slightly spread, her face stretching toward the flames. When she ceased speaking, a low murmur rose in the crowd saying amen, amen. Then a man's voice responded elsewhere, bellowed out strange words, words like music. For the first time, Esther knew what prayer was. She didn't know how it had come to her, but she was absolutely certain: it was the muffled sound of voices, suddenly bursting forth with the incantation of language, the rhythmic rocking of bodies, the star-flamed candles, the warm darkness filled with smells. It was the vortex of words.

Here in this room, nothing else could be of any importance. Nothing could be threatening anymore, not Mario's death, or the Germans who were coming up the valley with their armored vehicles, or even the tall figure of her father walking toward the mountains at dawn, disappearing into the tall grass, like someone sinking into death.

Esther rocked her body slowly forward, backward, her eyes trained on the lights, and deep down inside of her the voices of the men and women called out and responded, high toned, resonant, saying all those words in the mysterious language, and Esther could soar over time and over the mountains like the black bird her father had pointed out to her, all the way to the other side of the seas, to the place where light was born, all the way to Eretzraël.

Saturday September 8, Esther was awakened by a sound. A sound, a rumbling that was coming from all sides at once, filling the valley, echoing through the streets of the village, penetrating the very heart of the houses. Esther got up and in the gray light of the alcove she saw that her parents' bed was empty. In the kitchen her mother was already dressed, standing near the open door. It was the look in her eyes that made Esther shudder: a look dark with concern, and the look was a response to the rumbling that came from outside. Before Esther had time to ask a question, Elizabeth said, "Your father left during the night, he didn't want to wake you." The rumbling sound grew fainter, came back, seemed unreal. Elizabeth said, "It's American planes flying to Genoa...The Italians lost the war, they signed the armistice." Esther threw her arms around her mother. "So the Italians will be leaving?" Now she too was paralyzed with fear, it coursed through her hands, her legs like an icy tide creeping over her. It slowed her breathing, her thoughts. The rumbling of the airplanes faded out, rolling off into the distance like the sound of a thunderstorm. But now Esther heard a different, clearer rumbling. It was the sound of Italian trucks driving along the floor of the valley, making their way toward the village, fleeing the German army. "The war isn't over," Elizabeth said slowly. "Now the Germans will come. We have to leave. Everyone has to leave." She corrected herself, "All the Jews have to leave very quickly, before the Germans get here." The sound of the trucks was very loud now, they were taking the last curve before entering the village. Elizabeth grabbed a packed suitcase by the door, the old leather suitcase in which she kept all of her precious objects. "Go and get dressed. Put on warm clothes, your good shoes. We'll be going through the mountains. Your father will join us over there." She moved in feverish haste, bumping into chairs, looking for something useful she might have forgotten. Esther dressed quickly. Over her sweater, she put the sheepskin that Mario had left on the back of a chair the day he died. She knotted the black scarf that Cécile had given her on the Shabbat night around her head.

Outside in the large square the sun was shining, tracing the shadows of the leaves on the ground. The dome of the church gleamed. There were lovely, very white clouds in the sky. Esther looked sharply, painfully, at everything around her. On all sides, people were coming into the square. The poor Jews came out of the narrow streets, out of the basement apartments where they'd been living for so many years; they came with their bags, their old cardboard suitcases, their bundles of clothing, their provisions in gunnysacks. The older ones, like Reb Eïzik Salanter, Yacov, and the Polish people, had put on their heavy winter caftans, astrakhan caps. The women sometimes wore two coats, one on top of the other, and all of them were carrying their black shawls. The rich Jews were arriving too, with nicer suitcases and new clothes, but many of them had not even brought any bags because they hadn't had time to prepare themselves. Some came in taxis from the coast, their faces were drawn and pale and Esther thought maybe none of them would ever see any of this again, this square, these houses, the fountain, the blue mountains off in the distance.

The sound of the truck motors boomed through the square and would have prevented any talking anyway. The trucks were stopped in the square, one behind the other along the roadside all the way down to the big park with chestnut trees. The motors rumbled, a blue cloud hovered over the road. The people were crowded around the fountain, and the children were there too, but they weren't running around. They were dressed in rags, and stayed close to their mothers, sitting on the bundles of clothing, looking stunned. The soldiers in the Fourth Italian Army were in front of the hotel, waiting for the signal to depart. Esther approached them and was struck by the expression on their faces—disoriented, blank looks. Many must not have slept the night before, waiting for the news that would confirm their defeat and the signing of the armistice. The soldiers weren't looking at anyone. They stood there waiting in front of the hotel while the motors of the trucks chugged away on the other side of the square. The Jews came and went around the fountain, carting their bags from one place to another as if they were looking for the best place in which to wait. The people from the village and the farmers were there too, but a little off to one side; they stood under the arcades of the town hall watching the Jews gather around the fountain.

In the shadows of the arcades, Tristan stood motionless, half hidden. His handsome face was pale, with large circles under his eyes. He seemed to be shivering and remote in his English outfit, now threadbare from summer ramblings. He too had been awakened by the rumbling sound that filled the valley and he'd dressed hurriedly. Just as he was leaving the hotel room his mother had called to him, "Where are you going?" And since he didn't answer, she'd said in an anxious voice that cracked oddly, "No stay! You shouldn't go to the square, it's dangerous." But he was already outside.

He looked for Esther in the square, amidst the people who were waiting. When he saw her, he got ready to run over to her, then stopped. There were too many people. The women all looked tense. Then Mrs. O'Rourke came. She'd thrown on whatever she found, she who was usually so elegant had simply put a raincoat on over her dress, she wasn't wearing a hat. Her long blond hair fell in waves over her shoulders. Her face was also distraught, her eyes tired.

It was Esther who crossed the square, she went up to Tristan, she couldn't say a thing, she didn't know what to say, there was a knot in her throat. She gave Tristan a light kiss, then she shook Mrs. O'Rourke's hand. Tristan's mother smiled at her, she took her in her arms and hugged her, she kissed her on the cheek and said a few words, maybe "good luck", she had a deep voice, it was the first time she'd spoken to Esther. Esther went back to her mother's side. A moment later, when she looked back toward the arcades, Tristan and Mrs. O'Rourke had disappeared.

Now the sun beat heavily down. The lovely white clouds rose in the east, slipping slowly across the sky. From time to time, a cold shadow fell over the square, blotted out the patterns of leaves on the ground. Esther thought it was a beautiful day to go on a journey. She pictured her father walking in the mountains, right along the crest line, with the immensity of the valleys still in darkness. Maybe up where he was he could see the village with its tiny square and the black crowd that must look like a bunch of ants.

Maybe he was making his way down into the bottom of the still-dark valley, through the fields of yellowing grasses, over by Nantelle or Châtaigniers, where he'd arranged to meet up with the Jews coming from Nice, from Cannes, or even farther away, fleeing the advancing Germans?

All of a sudden there was a roaring of motors in the square and the Italians began to leave. They had undoubtedly received the signal they had been waiting for since dawn, or else they'd grown impatient and couldn't stand waiting any longer. They left one after the other, in groups, most of them on foot. They left amidst the rumbling of motors, without talking, or calling out to one another. The trucks pulled away and began moving up the road toward the high mountains along the Boréon valley. The rumbling of the motors swelled, bounced off the valley bottom, returned like echoing thunder. As the soldiers hurried along, Esther moved closer to the hotel. Maybe she would catch a glimpse of Rachel at some point, when she'd come out of the hotel with Captain Mondoloni. There were some men in civilian clothing, wearing raincoats and felt hats, some women too, but Rachel wasn't with them. Everything was happening so quickly, with such crowding and pushing, that Rachel might have gone by without Esther noticing, maybe she'd climbed into one of the trucks with those people. Esther's heart was beating very fast, she felt her throat tightening as she watched the last Italian soldiers clustering around the vehicles, jumping onto the tarpaulined truck beds as they drove away. Everything was so gray and sad, Esther would have liked so much to see Rachel's copper hair one last time. The people in the square said that the officers had left very early, before ten o'clock. So Rachel was already walking in the mountains, she was crossing the border at Ciriega Pass.

Now the people started leaving. In the middle of the square, near the fountain, a group of men had gathered around Mr. Seligman, the schoolteacher. Esther recognized some of the people that came to see her father from time to time, evenings, in the kitchen. They had a long discussion because some wanted to follow the same route as the Italian trucks, by way of Ciriega Pass, and the others wanted to take the shortest route, through Fenestre Pass. They said it was dangerous to walk behind the Italians, that the Germans would probably go the same way to bomb them.

Then the teacher, Mr. Seligman, stepped up on the edge of the fountain. He seemed troubled and moved, and yet his voice rang out clearly, just as it did when he read books to the children. First he said a few words in French, "Mes amis! Mes amis...Ecoutez-moi;" The hubbub in the square died down and the people who'd started to leave put their suitcases down to listen. Then, in the same strong, clear voice with which he read to the children from *Animals infected with the plague* or excerpts from *Nana*, he recited these lines that remained forever etched in Esther's memory, he pronounced them slowly, as if they were the words of a prayer, and a long time afterward Esther learned that they had bee written by a man named Hayyim Nahman Bialik:

> *Along my tortuous journey*
> *no tenderness have I seen.*
> *I have lost my eternity.*

Next to Esther, Elizabeth wept in silence. The sobs shook her shoulders and her face was frozen in a grimace, and Esther thought it was more terrible then all the screams in the world. She hugged her mother as hard as she could to quell the sobs, as one does with a child.

Already the people were walking toward the top of the square, they went past the fountain as Mr. Seligman looked on. The men walked up in front, followed by the women, the elderly, and the children. They formed a long gray and black troop in the blazing sun, something like a funeral procession.

As she passed in front of the hotel, Esther saw the shape of Mr. Ferne, a stealthy shadow half hidden under a plane tree. With his bowed legs, his long grayish suit coat with sagging pockets, his cap and his goatee, he looked like the caretaker of a cemetery observing a ceremony that didn't really concern him, from a distance. Despite her mother's sadness, despite the worry that knotted in her throat, when Esther saw Mr. Ferne's figure, she felt like laughing. She remembered how he'd hidden when the soldiers teetered up the street carrying the piano. She ran over to him and took his hand. The old man looked at her as if he didn't recognize her. He shook his head and his funny little beard twitched as he repeated, "No, no, go, all of you, go—I can't, I must stay here. Where would I go in the mountains?" Esther squeezed his hand with all her might, she felt tears blurring her eyes. "But the Germans are coming, you have to come with us." Mr. Ferne kept looking at the people walking through the square. "Not at all." He spoke very softly, almost in a whisper. "Not at all. What would they do with an old man like me?" Then he kissed Esther, just once, very quickly, and he stepped away. "Good bye, now. Good bye." Esther ran back to her mother and they began walking with the others up toward the top of the village. When she turned around, Esther no longer saw Mr. Ferne. Maybe he'd already gone back to his piano, in the dark kitchen of the villa. Only a few people remained standing under the arcades of the town hall, people from the village, women wearing their flowered dresses, their aprons. They watched the troop of fugitives already disappearing high up in the village, where the grassy fields and the stands of chestnut trees begin.

Now the people were walking on the road, in the midday sun, there were so many of them that Esther couldn't see the beginning or the end of the troop. There were no more rumbling motors down in the valley, not a sound, only the scuffing of feet on the stony road, and the sound of a river running over shingles.

Esther walked along observing the people around her. She recognized most of them. They were people she'd seen in the streets of the town, at the market, or else afternoons in the square conversing in little groups while the children ran around shouting sharply. There were the old men in long coats with fur collars, wearing black hats from under which poked plaits of gray hair. There was the one they called the hazan, Mr. Yacov, who was walking next to old Eïzik Salanter, carrying his heavy suitcases. Except for Reb Eïzik and Mr. Yacov, Esther didn't know their names. They were the poorer Jewish people, those who'd come from Germany, Poland, Russia, who'd lost everything in the war. When she'd gone into the temple, in the chalet high in the village, Esther had seen them standing around the table with the lit candles, heads veiled with the large white shawls, she'd heard them reciting the words of the book in that mysterious language that was so beautiful, that went straight to the very core of you without your understanding it.

Seeing them now, out in the sun on this rock-strewn road, stooped, walking along slowly in their long, cumbersome coats, Esther felt her heart quickening, as if something painful and inevitable was happening, as if the whole world was walking on that road toward the unknown.

She watched the women and children especially. There were old women she had glimpsed at the back of their kitchens, who never went out except on holidays, or for weddings. Now, dressed in heavy coats, their heads wrapped in black shawls, they moved along the stone road without speaking, their very pale faces squinting in the sun. There were younger women, still slender in spite of the coats and all sorts of packages they were loaded down with, dragging suitcases. They talked amongst one another, some even laughed, as if they were off on a picnic. The children ran before them, wearing sweaters that were too warm, thick leather shoes that they put on only for special occasions. They too were carrying packages, sacks containing bread, fruits, bottles of water. As she walked with them, Esther tried to recall their names, Cécile Grinberg, Meyerl, Gelibter, Sarah and Michel Lubliner, Léa, Amélie Sprecher, Fizas, Jacques Mann, Lazarus, Rivkelé, Robert David, Yachet, Simon Choulevitch, Tal, Rebecca, Pauline, André, Mark, Marie-Antoinette, Lucie, Eliane Salanter...But their names only came back to her with great difficulty because already they were no longer the girls and boys she had known, the ones she used to see at school, the ones who ran shouting through the streets of the village, who bathed naked in the torrents and played war in the bushes. Dressed in clothing that was too large, too heavy, wearing their winter shoes, the girls with their hair beneath scarves, the boys with berets or hats on their heads, they weren't running as fast now, they weren't talking to each other. They seemed like orphans out for a walk, already sad, exhausted, not looking at anything or anyone.

The troop walked through the upper part of the village, past the closed school, the police station. As they went, the inhabitants of the village watched for a moment, standing at their doors or leaning out their windows; silent, like those who were passing by.

For the first time, and it was an aching feeling, Esther realized she wasn't like the people in the village. They could stay home in their houses, they could go on living in this valley, beneath this sky, drink the water from the torrents. They stood there in the doorways, watched at the windows, while she walked past them wearing black clothes and Mario's sheepskin, her head wrapped in the black scarf, her feet sore from the winter shoes, she had to walk with those who, like her, no longer had a home, no longer had the right to the same sky, to the same water. Anger and anxiety rose in her throat, her heart was beating too fast in her chest. She thought of Tristan, of his pale face and his feverish eyes. Mrs. O'Rourke's cool cheek and the hand that had clasped hers for an instant, and Esther's heart had raced because it was the first time Mrs. O'Rourke had spoken to her, and because she'd probably never see her again, ever. She thought of Rachel in the hotel that was now empty. The wind must be blowing in through the open windows and whipping around the large room. For the first time she realized she'd become someone else. Her father could never call her Estrellita again; no one must ever again call her Hélène. There was no sense in looking back, all of that had ceased to exist.

The troop made their way up the rocky road between the grassy fields where Esther used to hide, awaiting her father's return. The torrent crashed below them, the sound of rushing water bounced off the flanks of the mountains. In the sky, the white clouds piled up to the east, making fantastic shapes at the top of the valley, like snowy peaks, like castles. Esther remembered how she used to watch them approaching, stretched out on the flat rocks, still wet with the water from the torrent, feeling the cold droplets shrinking on the skin of her thighs, listening to the music of the water and the buzzing of wasps. She remembered wishing she could follow the clouds because they drifted so freely on the wind, because they floated effortlessly over the mountains, all the way to the sea. She used to imagine everything they saw, the valleys, the rivers, the cities just like anthills, and the large bays where the sea lay shimmering. They were the same clouds today and yet there was something threatening about them. They made a sort of barricade at the mouth of the valley, they shrouded the mountain peaks, they formed a tall, dark, white, insurmountable wall.

Esther held her mother's hand tightly as they walked in step along the road in the long column. Already, the forest had grown denser, the chestnut and oak trees had been replaced by tall pines with almost black needles. Never had Esther followed the torrent up this far. Now you could no longer see the far end of the gorge, or the wall of clouds. Only every now and then, between the tree trunks, the torrent sparkling in the sun. The troop had slowed its pace, struggling up the steep path. The old men, the women carrying small children were already stopping at the side of the road to rest, sitting on rocks or on their suitcases. No one was saying anything. There was the sound of shoes scuffing on the stones and the cries of young children that had a strange ring—a bit muffled by the trees, like the cries of animals. As they walked through the forest, the troop flushed some choughs that flew off a little farther away, screeching. Esther watched the black birds and she recalled what her father had said one day, speaking of Italy. He'd pointed to a crow in the sky, "If you could fly like that bird, you'd be there this very evening." She didn't dare question Elizabeth, ask her, "When will Papa come to join us?" But she held her hand very tightly as they walked along and she shot furtive glances at her, her sharp, pale face, her mouth with pinched lips, her expression, aged by the black scarf on her head that she wore in order to resemble the other women. That too made anger rise in her throat, because she remembered days in summer when Elizabeth put on her beautiful blue dress with the low neckline and her sandals and she brushed her dark black silky hair for a long time to please Esther's father and walk with him to the village square. Esther remembered her mother's long suntanned legs, the smooth skin stretched over her shins, the light shining on her bare shoulders. Now, surely none of that could ever come back, for is it ever possible to retrieve what you've left behind? "Will we come back here with Papa, are we really going away forever?" Esther hadn't asked that after having dressed hurriedly, when she'd picked up the suitcase and left the house, climbing the three narrow steps that led to the street. They walked down the street together till they reached the square and Esther hadn't dared ask her that. But her mother understood; she'd simply made a funny face, shrugging her shoulders, and a little later Esther had seen her wiping her eyes and her nose because she was crying. So then she'd bitten her lip as hard as she could, till it bled, like when she wanted to blot out something bad she'd done.

She hadn't looked at anyone after that, so she wouldn't have to see the sadness in their eyes, so they wouldn't know that she too was thinking about it all. On the stone-strewn road that went up through the forest, the people had spread apart. The younger ones, the men, the young boys, were far ahead; you couldn't even hear their voices calling to one another anymore. Behind them the long procession stretched out. Though they weren't walking fast because of the suitcases that were blistering their hands, Esther and her mother overtook other women, old ones who stumbled over the stones, women carrying babies in their arms, old Jewish men in their extra heavy caftans, leaning on canes. When they came upon them, Esther slowed down to help them, but then her mother would pull her by the arm, in an almost violent way, and it frightened Esther to see the hard expression on her face as they went past those who hung back. As they walked, the women sitting on the side of the path became fewer. Then for a time Esther and her mother walked on completely alone, hearing nothing but the sound of their own footsteps and the faint crashing of the torrent below.

The sun was very close to the ridgeline behind them. The sky had turned pale, almost gray, and in front of them the heavy clouds piled up. Elizabeth had been searching for quite some time and suddenly she caught sight of a sort of clearing around a platform overhanging the torrent. She said, "That's where we'll spend the night." She climbed down a ways till she reached the rocks over the torrent. Never had

Esther seen such a lovely place. Between the rounded masses of the rocks, moss spread making a carpet, and a little higher up to the left there was a little sandy beach where the waves of the torrent plashed quietly. After the struggle up the rocky path and the hot sun, after so much worry and uncertainty, so much weariness, the place looked to Esther like the image of paradise. She ran ahead to lie down on the moss, between the blocks of rock and she closed her eyes. When she reopened them she saw her mother's face in front of her. Elizabeth had washed her arms and face in the torrent, and the faint evening light made a halo around her unfastened hair. "You're so beautiful", whispered Esther. "You should go and wash up too," said Elizabeth, "the water's nice and cool and other people will certainly stop for the night." Esther took off her scarf and her shoes, and went into the ice-cold water till it reached mid calf, lifting her skirt. The cold water slid over her legs, numbing them. She drank some water from her cupped hand, splashed some on her face to soothe the sunburn. The water wet the hem of her dress, the sleeves of her sweater, clung to the sheepskin.

A little later other people did arrive. Many had stopped lower down in another clearing and Esther could hear the children's voices, the women calling. Everyone knew they mustn't light a fire to avoid being spotted by the German army, so they prepared the evening meal as best they could. The women got out the bread and cut it into slices that the children ate as they sat by the torrent. Esther's mother had brought a piece of dried cheese that their landlady had given her and they found it delicious. They also ate some figs and then they went to drink from the torrent, kneeling on the little beach. Before nightfall, they built a shelter with pine branches whose thick needles formed a makeshift a roof.

Night came slowly. In the forest all around, human

voices rang louder. Despite the weariness, Esther wasn't
sleepy. She walked down the torrent following the children's
voices. About a hundred yards farther down, she came upon
a group of little girls playing by the torrent. Although they
were fully dressed, they were in the water up to their thighs
and they were splashing each other and laughing. They were
little Polish girls that had come to the village in the
beginning of summer with their parents, and they spoke
nothing but their own, very foreign and melodious language.
Esther recalled that her father had told her one evening about
a city with a strange name, like the language of the little
girls, Rzeszow, and about the German soldiers that had
burned the houses and turned out all the Jews and locked
them up in stockcars to send them to the camps or to the
forests where even the children had to work until they died.
She was remembering that and standing there watching the
little girls. Now they were here deep in this forest, beside
this torrent, turned away once again, headed for the
unknown, for the mountains where the clouds were
gathering, and yet they seemed as carefree as if they were on
a stroll. Esther walked into the clearing to watch them. Now
the girls were playing tag, running from one tree to the next
with their long black dresses flaring out around them as if
they were dancing. The eldest, who must have been ten or
eleven, had very light eyes and hair, whereas her sisters were
dark. At one point, they noticed Esther. They stopped short.
Together, cautiously, they came nearer, and they pronounced
a few words in their language. Night was falling. Esther
knew she should go back to her mother and yet she couldn't
tear her gaze from the little girl's pale eyes. The others
started playing again.

Their family was gathered near a pine tree, women

dressed in black and men wearing caftans. There was also an old man with a long gray beard whom Esther had seen near the entrance to the temple in the chalet.

The girl took Esther's hand and led her over to the tree. One of the women, smiling, asked her some questions, but all in that strange language. She had a handsome, regular face and her eyes were a very pale green, like those of the little girl. Then she cut a piece of black bread and handed it to Esther. Esther couldn't bring herself to say no, but she felt somewhat ashamed because she'd already eaten cheese and figs without sharing anything. She took the bread and, without a word, ran back to the rock-strewn road and hurried toward the clearing where her mother was waiting for her. Night was already making the trees close in, casting disturbing shadows everywhere. Behind her, she could still hear the voices and laughter of the little girls.

Rain started falling. It made a soft pattering sound on the roofs, a peaceful sound after the rumbling of the trucks and the sound of footsteps. Rachel steps out into the street, in spite of the pitch-black night, she starts walking in the rain, wrapped up snuggly in her mother's long black shawl. When the sound of the Italian trucks had started echoing through the whole valley, she wanted to run straight to the square, but her mother had said, "Don't go! Don't go, please, stay with us!" Her father was sick and Rachel didn't go out. All day long, the noise of the trucks had echoed through the valley, through the mountains. Sometimes the sound was so close that it felt as if the trucks were going to knock down the walls of the house. Afterward, there was the sound of footsteps and maybe that was even more terrifying, that muffled sound, that scurrying. Far into the night people moved up the street, walking away. There were voices, hushed calls, children crying. Rachel stayed awake all night in the dark, sitting on a chair next to the bed where her mother slept. From the other bed in the small room she could hear her father's rapid breathing, his dry asthmatic cough. In the morning, Sunday, everything was very calm. Outside the sun was shining through the slats in the shutters. There were birdcalls in the air, like in summer. But Rachel didn't want to go out, or even open the shutters. She was so tired that she felt nauseous. When her mother got up to get dressed and start cooking, Rachel lay down in the still-warm bed and went to sleep.

Now it is night again, the rain is falling softly on the roofs of the village. When she awoke Rachel didn't really know where she was. For a minute she thought she was in the hotel room with Mondoloni, then she remembered what had happened. Maybe she thought that the carabiniere had been left alone at the hotel and that he too was listening to the rain falling. The Italian soldiers are gone and the mountains are silent again. One day in the hotel room, while she was fixing her hair in front of the mirror, he'd come up to her and looked at her in a funny way. He said, "When the war is over I'll take you to Italy, everywhere, to Rome, to Naples, to Venice, we'll go on a very long journey." That was the day he'd given her the ring with the blue stone.

Rachel is walking through the silent streets. All the shutters are closed. She's thinking about something that makes her heart race, she thinks maybe this is the day, maybe the war is over. When the Americans bombed Genoa, Mondoloni said it was all over; the Italians were going to sign the armistice. The Italian soldiers have fled into the mountains, gone back home, and the town is sleeping soundlessly, like someone who is very weary.

Rachel hurries toward the square. When she arrives in front of the hotel, she'll knock on the shutter, like she always does, and he'll come and open the door. She'll smell his odor, the odor of tobacco, the odor of his body; she'll hear his voice echoing in his chest. She loves it when he talks of Italy. He talks of the cities, of Rome, of Florence, of Venice, he says things in Italian, slowly, as if she could understand. When the war is over, she'll be able to go away, far from this village, far from the spying, gossiping people, boys that throw stones at her, far from the house in ruins; the cold apartment with her coughing father, she'll travel to the cities where there is music in the streets, cafés, cinemas, shops.

She so wishes it were true—right now—that her legs are trembling under her and she has to stop in a doorway with the rainwater running down on her head and making her black scarf stick to her hair.

She's in the street that leads up to the square; she passes the house with the mulberry tree, where Mr. Ferne lives. There's no light coming through the cracks in the shutters, and there's not a sound, the night is very dark. But Rachel is sure the old man is in the house. Listening very closely, she thinks she can hear him talking to himself in his quavering voice. She imagines him asking questions and giving the answers all by himself and it makes her want to laugh.

Now she hears the water rushing into the basin of the fountain. In the square, the trees are lit with a blinding light. Why is there so much light? Isn't there a curfew anymore? Rachel thinks of the sentinels. The carabinieri took a shot at Julie Roussel's husband the night he went to fetch the doctor for the delivery. When Mondoloni talks about the soldiers, he says "*bruti*", lowering his voice in contempt. He doesn't like the Germans. He says they're like animals.

Rachel hesitates at the edge of the square. A bright light is coming from the hotel, it's illuminating the trees and the houses like theatre props. It casts fantastic shadows. But Rachel listens to the water tumbling into the basin and feels reassured. Maybe the carabinieri and the soldiers have decided to celebrate the end of the war. And yet Rachel knows perfectly well now that's not true. The light shining on the square is cold, it makes the raindrops glitter. There's not a sound, not a voice. Everything is silent and empty.

Hugging the balustrade, Rachel approaches the hotel. Between the trunks of the trees, she sees the front of the building. All of the windows are lit up. The shutters are wide open; the door too is open. The light is blinding.

Slowly without understanding yet, Rachel walks up to the hotel. The light is painful, but draws her to it in spite of herself, in spite of her heart that is beating too fast and her trembling legs. She's never seen so much light. The night all around seems even denser, quieter. When Rachel is next to the hotel, she sees the soldier standing by the door. He's standing very still with his rifle in hand, staring straight ahead, as if he wanted to bore a hole in the night with all of that light. Rachel stops. Then, slowly, she backs away to hide. The soldier is a German.

Then she sees trucks stopped, and over in the darkness, the black car of the Gestapo. Rachel backs all the way up to the trees, she flees, runs down the narrow streets to the old house, and her footsteps echo in the silence like the galloping of a horse. Her heart is beating so fast she has a pain in the center of her chest, a burning feeling. For the first time in her life, she's afraid of dying. She would like to run across the mountains, all the way to Italy, all the way to the soldiers' camps in the night, she'd like to hear Mondoloni's voice, smell his body, wrap her arms around his waist. But she comes to the door of the house, she knows it's too late. Now she knows the Germans will come, come to get her and her mother and father too, come to take them far away. She waits a minute for her heart to stop beating so fast and her breathing to slow. She tries to think of the words she'll say to her mother and father, to reassure them, so they won't know right away. She loves them so much she could die, and she didn't even know it.

At dawn, the rain woke them. It was a fine drizzle rustling softly in the pine needles over their heads, mingling with the crashing of the torrent. Drops started coming through the roof of their shelter, ice-cold drops that spattered on their faces. Elizabeth tried to arrange the branches better, but she only succeeded in making it rain in more. So they took their suitcases and, wrapped in their shawls, huddled up at the foot of a larch tree, shivering. The shapes of the trees stood out starkly in the dawn light. A white fog was creeping down the valley. It was so cold that Esther and Elizabeth just sat there hugging each other at the foot of the larch, not wanting to move.

Then the sound of men's voices rang through the forest, they were calling. They had to stand up, wrap up in their half-damp clothing, pick up their suitcases, start out again.

Esther's feet hurt so much that she staggered along the rocky path, keeping her eyes on the shape of her mother in front of her. Other shapes loomed out of the forest like ghosts. Esther hoped to see the little Polish girls behind her. But there were no more children's voices, or laughter. Only, once again, the scuffing of shoes over the stones in the path, and the steady sound of the torrent that was going the other way.

Wrapped in fog, the forest seemed endless. The tops of the trees could no longer be seen, nor the mountains. It was like walking aimlessly, stooping forward, weighed down with the heavy suitcases, stumbling, feet bruised by the sharp-edged stones. Esther and Elizabeth overtook refugees who had started out before dawn and were already exhausted. Old women sitting on their bundles by the path, their faces even paler in the mist. They didn't complain. They waited at the side of the path, sometimes alone, looking resigned.

The path led them right to the torrent, and now they had to wade across it. The fog parted and gave them a glimpse of the slope ahead—covered with dark larches—and the pale blue sky. That raised Elizabeth's spirits and she waded through the torrent holding Esther's hand, then they started up the mountainside without stopping. Higher up on the right there was a huge stone where some people must have spent the night because the grass was trampled all around. Again, Esther heard the choughs calling. But instead of troubling her, the cries made her happy because they meant, "We're here, we're with you!"

Before noon Esther and Elizabeth reached the sanctuary. The valley widened as it led out of the forest and on a ledge looking out over the torrent, they saw the military buildings and the chapel. Esther remembered when Gasparini talked about the Madonna, the statue that was carried up to the sanctuary in summer and brought back down in winter draped in a cloak to keep her warm. It seemed so long ago now; she didn't realize that she was really here. She thought she was going to see the statue in a cave, hidden amidst the trees, surrounded by flowers. She stared at the big ugly buildings that looked like barracks.

Continuing along the path, Esther and her mother reached the ledge. In front of the chapel many people were gathered. The fugitives were already there, those who'd left in the night. Men, young people, women, children and even old people wearing caftans were in the yard, sitting on the ground with their backs against the walls. There were also Italian soldiers from the Fourth Army. They'd set themselves up in one of the buildings. They were sitting outside looking exhausted and, in spite of their uniforms, they too looked like fugitives. Esther looked around for Captain Mondoloni but he wasn't there. He must have gone the other route by way of Ciriega Pass; maybe he'd already crossed into Italy. Rachel wasn't there either.

Esther grasped Elizabeth's hand, "Is this where Papa's coming to join us?" But Elizabeth didn't answer. She put the bags down by the wall of the building and asked Esther to watch them. She went over to talk with some men that were with Mr. Seligman. But they didn't know anything. Esther heard them discussing the way to Berthemont through the pass. They pointed to the other end of the valley, the towering, already dark mountain. Elizabeth came back. Her voice was fretful, weary. She simply said, "We're going to wait here until tomorrow morning. We'll go across tomorrow. He'll join us here." But Esther could tell that she wasn't at all sure.

The fugitives settled down for the night. The Italian soldiers opened the doors to one of the buildings and helped the women carry their suitcases inside. They handed out blankets for the beds and they even brought some hot coffee. Esther didn't know these soldiers. Some were very young, almost children. They said, "The war is over." They were laughing.

After the night spent in the rain, the military building seemed almost luxurious. There weren't enough beds for everyone and Esther and Elizabeth had to share the same bed. Other fugitives were arriving, settling down wherever they could in the dormitory. When there was no more room in the military building, the people went to lie down in the chapel whose doors had been forced open.

The strongest men, along with Mr. Seligman, decided to make it through the pass before nightfall. The wind had blown the clouds away and the high mountains at the other end of the valley were gleaming with snow. Esther was in the courtyard in front of the chapel when the group began climbing up the path above the sanctuary. She watched them go and she would have liked to be with them because they'd be in Italy that very evening. But her mother was too tired to go on and maybe she really was hoping that her father would come that evening.

At the bottom of the slope stood an abandoned cow barn surrounded by wide-open pastures crisscrossed with springs that fed the torrent. Esther thought that her father would come from that direction. She imagined him walking down the mountain, through the pastures with grass up to his waist and jumping from one rock to another to cross the torrent.

The children of the fugitives had already forgotten their weariness. They began playing in the yard of the chapel, or running down the slopes laughing and shouting. Esther watched them and when she realized they'd made her forget to watch for her father to appear at the other end of the valley, she felt a twinge of guilt in her heart. Then the shouts of the children rang out again and her eyes drifted back to watching them. The choughs were still overhead. They were circling in the sky, emitting their own sharp cries, as if they wished to say something to the people.

Then Esther's mother came and sat down beside her, she put her arm around her and hugged her close. She had also spent the whole afternoon keeping an eye on the valley, on the arid black flank of the mountain. She said nothing. Esther asked, "If Papa can't come tonight, will we wait for him here tomorrow?" Elizabeth answered instantly, "No, he said we mustn't wait for him, that we had to keep walking without stopping." "Then he'll come to join us in Italy?" "Yes, sweetheart, he'll join us, he'll come by some other route, he knows all the paths. He might already have gone through Berthemont Pass, with his friends. The Germans are hunting down Jews everywhere, you know. That's why we have to keep walking and not stop." But just like a little earlier, Esther knew her mother was lying, that she was making it all up, just to reassure her. It made something hurt down in the very quick of her body, like when the boys had punched her near the abandoned barn. "What about Rachel?" Esther said all of a sudden. "Are the Germans hunting for her too?" Her mother jumped, as if Esther had said something blasphemous. "Why do you mention Rachel?" Esther said, "Because she's Jewish too." Elizabeth shrugged her shoulders, "She abandoned everything, her parents, everyone. She went off with the Italians." Esther got angry, she said, almost screaming, "No, that's not true! She didn't go off with the Italians! She stayed in the village with her parents." "All right," said Elizabeth coldly, "I suppose she'll be able to fend for herself." They fell silent, both watching the same spot at the far end of the valley, near the edge of the forest. But something was broken, maybe they weren't waiting for anything anymore.

Near the end of the afternoon, the clouds darkened the peaks. Thunder shook the ground with such sharp detonations that some of the fugitives thought it was the beginning of a bombardment and cried out in fear. Rain started falling in large drops. Esther ran for shelter in the chapel. It was so dark she couldn't make anything out and she stumbled over bodies. The fugitives were stretched out on the floor, wrapped in blankets. Others were standing, leaning up against the wall. The left half of the roof had been knocked in with a mortar shell and the rain poured down into the chapel. In spite of the Italians' instructions, candles had been lit on the right side of the altar and the flickering light revealed the shapes and faces of the fugitives. Most of them were old men and women dressed like Russian or Polish people, like the ones Esther had seen during the Shabbat in the chalet. Their faces were drawn with weariness, anxiety.

Near the candles, at the foot of the altar, the old people wrapped in their caftans faced Reb Eïzik Salanter who was reading aloud from a book, his back to the candlelight in order to see better. Leaning up against the cold wall of the chapel, Esther listened once again to the incomprehensible words in that gentle, halting language, never taking her eyes from the old man lit by the candles. Once again, she felt that tingling feeling, as if the unknown voice were speaking to her alone, deep within her. The low, hushing voice was reading the book and the sound of that voice wiped away all of her weariness, her fear, her anger. She no longer thought of the dark slope where her father should have appeared, she stopped thinking of it as a terrifying and deadly ravine, but rather as a very long, very distant path leading to a secret place. Everything was transformed in that room—the mountains with their rumbling thunder, the path disappearing into the gorges—it had all turned into a sort of legend in which the elements were shifting to fit together in a new order.

Outside the rain was coming down hard and the water poured into the chapel through the gaping hole in the roof. The children huddled against their mothers who were rocking gently to the peaceful rhythm of Eïzik Salanter's voice reading the words of the book.

Then the old man stood with the book held open in front

of his face for a long time and he began to chant in a deep, gentle voice that did not waver. So then the men and women and even the little children chanted with him, accompanying him without words, simply repeating the same sound: Aïe, aïe, aïe, aïe!...One of the little Polish girls, the one who had such light-colored eyes and who'd led Esther over to her family, came up to her and took her hand. She'd recognized her in spite of the darkness. In the flashes of lightning, Esther saw her face, as if lit with an inner joy while she chanted with the others, slowly rocking her body back and forth. Esther too, started chanting.

The chant echoed in the chapel, rose above the din of the rain and the thunder. It seemed as if those few candles lit in the candleholders near the altar gave off the same light that was in the temple on the Shabbat evening. Now other people coming from the dormitories of the military complex were entering the chapel. Esther saw her mother standing near the door. Keeping a hold on the young Polish girl's hand, she went up to Elizabeth and ushered her over to the wall where they were standing. Outside, the night was pitch-black, streaked with lightning. Gradually, the chanting stopped. Everyone remained silent, listening to the sound of the rain and the pealing thunder fading away in the valleys. One after the other, the flames of the candles sputtered, died out. No one really knew exactly where he was anymore. Later, Esther crossed the yard in the cold wind and went to bed with Elizabeth and they clung tightly to one another to keep from falling.

At dawn the Italian soldiers took to the road again, followed by the fugitives. The sky was deep blue over the snow-capped mountains. The rocky path wound its way up above the chapel. Slowly, delayed by the children and the old people, the long line inched up the path—tiny black figures in that vast stony landscape.

Now Esther and Elizabeth were crossing an enormous rockslide. Esther had never dreamt of such a landscape. Above her, a chaos of rocks with not a tree, not a blade of grass. The blocks of rock suddenly stopped, balancing on the edge of a precipice. The path was so narrow that stones came loose underfoot and bounced down to the very bottom of the valley. Maybe it was because of the danger, or because of the cold, but no one was talking. Even the small children walked along the narrow path without saying a word. The only sound was that of the torrent hidden down in the valley, the loose stones tumbling down, and people panting heavily.

At one point Esther wanted to put the suitcase down and rest, but her mother took her immediately by the hand with a sort of desperate firmness and forced her to keep walking.

Now disparate groups of fugitives were spread out along the slope. The old men, the women wrapped in their black shawls who had been the last to leave the chapel, were far behind. The mountain ridges already hid them from view. The others, the women with children moved along slowly, not stopping. The path ran along a precipice where a few trees clung precariously. Below her, Esther saw a tall larch, scarred and blackened from lightning, just like a skeleton. On the other end of the valley, the mountain thrust into the sky, bristling with jagged peaks, threatening. Fear existed here, but there was also the beauty of stone glistening in the sunlight, the impenetrable sky. Most frightening of all was what they saw at the other end of the valley, what they'd been walking toward for two days now, the dark blue wall glittering with frost, drowned in a large white cloud that roiled up toward the very center of the sky. It seemed so far away, so inaccessible, that it made Esther's head reel. How could she ever go that far? Was it really possible to reach it?

Or maybe they'd been lied to, maybe all the people would get lost in the glaciers and in the clouds, be swallowed up in the crevices. Farther along, as the path zigzagged up the mountain flank, Esther saw dark birds circling in the sky again but this time they were silent hawks.

All along the path, fugitives were stopped at the foot of the escarpments. Esther recognized some of the women from the chapel. They were haggard with fatigue and hunger; they just sat there on stones by the side of the path, prostrate, blank-eyed. The children stood next to them, motionless, silent. When she went past them, the little girls looked at Esther. There was a strange expression in their eyes, something dark and imploring, as if they wanted to latch onto her with their eyes.

When Esther and Elizabeth reached the lake at the foot of the high mountain, the sun had already slipped behind the clouds; the light was waning. The water in the lake was an icy color, lit by a névé in its center like a mirror. Most of the fugitives were sitting by the side of the lake in the chaotic tumble of rocks, resting. But the healthiest men and women were leaving already, beginning the climb up to the pass, while exhausted groups of women and old people straggled up to the lake one after the other.

Sitting with her back against a rock, sheltered from the gusts of wind, Esther watched the people arriving. Several times Elizabeth got to her feet, "Come on, we have to go, we have to make it across before nightfall." But Esther was searching the path, like the day before, when she was waiting for her father. But it wasn't he that she wanted to see coming up the path. It was old Reb Eïzik Salanter, who'd chanted and read the book in the chapel. She didn't want to leave without him. When her mother got impatient again she said, "Please! Let's wait a little longer." On the steep rocky wall in front of them, the clouds ruffled and parted, revealing for an instant the dark line of the path mingling with a ravine between two sharp peaks, then the edges of the cloud joined again.

Thunder was already rumbling in the deep caves of the peak. Elizabeth was pale, nervous. She walked down to the edge of the lake, walked back again. The fugitives were leaving one after another. Only old women and a few others with young children remained. When she walked up to one of them—a young Polish woman with red hair pushed under a black shawl—Esther saw that she was leaning against a rock weeping silently. Esther touched her shoulder. She would have liked to speak to her, encourage her, but she didn't know how to say anything in her language. So she took a little bread and cheese from the sack of provisions and held them out to her. The young woman looked at her without smiling and she immediately started eating, hunched over on her rock.

Finally a group of fugitives appeared by the lake. Esther recognized Eïzik Salanter and his family. Leaning on his stick, the old man had difficulty walking on the rock-strewn path. The gusts of wind billowed in his caftan and made his beard and hair float away from his head. When she saw him, Esther knew at once that he was at the end of his strength. He sat down by the lake and the men and women accompanying him helped him to stretch out on the ground. His face, looking skyward, was very white, twisted with anxiety. As she went nearer, Esther heard his short wheezing breaths. She just couldn't bear that. She turned away and sought refuge in her mothers arms. "I want to go now," she whispered. But now it was Elizabeth who couldn't take her eyes from the old man lying on the ground.

The light in the sky shifted, turned strangely red. The

rumblings of thunder drew closer. The storm was whirling, huge dark clouds ripped open on the mountains, then later came back together, slipped between the snowy peaks like plumes of smoke. The man who was with Reb Eïzik Salanter suddenly stood up and turned toward Esther and Elizabeth. Without raising his voice, as if he were making a polite remark, he simply said, "The rabbi can't walk, he needs to stay and rest. Go now." He also said that in his own language to the women that were with him. Then, all of the women docilely picked up their bundles and suitcases and started walking toward the pass.

Before entering the ravine leading deep into the mountain, and disappearing in the clouds, Esther stopped to take one last look at Eïzik and his companion, motionless on the edge of the icy lake. They were two black marks amid the rocks.

The path wound up between the sharp peaks. They couldn't see its end. Heavy dark clouds flashing with lightning loomed directly over Esther and her mother. It was frightening, but it was so beautiful that Esther wanted to go higher, closer to the clouds. Patches of fog blushed red, slipped along, tore against the jagged peaks, flowed down through the ravines like ghostly streams. Below Esther and Elizabeth, everything had disappeared. The women and the other fugitives were invisible. They were floating between the heavens and the earth and for the first time Esther could imagine how birds must feel. But there were no more birds here, no more people. They were in a world inhabited only by clouds, the trails of clouds, and lightning.

Mario sometimes used to tell of lightning killing shepherds under trees or in stone cabins. He told Esther that those who entered the death zone heard an odd sound just before being hit by lightning, like a strange buzzing of bees that came from all sides at once and that ran around inside their head and drove them crazy. Now, with heart racing, it was that sound Esther was listening for as she climbed up the long stony path.

Higher up, a fine drizzle began to fall. On their right, perched on the side of the mountain, was a blockhouse. Women and men had taken refuge there, dazed with weariness and chilled to the bone. You could see their silhouettes standing in the doorway to the sinister shelter. But Elizabeth said, "No matter what, we mustn't stop here, we have to get across the border before nightfall." They kept walking, breathless, not thinking of anything. The mist around them was so thick that Esther and her mother thought they were the only ones to have come that far.

Suddenly the sky cleared, showing a large patch of blue. Esther and Elizabeth stopped, lost in amazement. They'd reached the pass. Now Esther remembered the story the village children used to tell, about a window that opened in the sky when the statue of the Virgin fled the mountains. Here it was, a window through which you could see the other side of the world.

In the jumble of rocks between the peaks, the sunlight shone down on the freshly fallen snow. The wind was freezing but Esther didn't feel it any longer. Amongst the rocks, fugitives were sitting and resting, women, old people, children. They weren't talking to each other. Muffled up, backs turned against the wind, they gazed around at the mountain peaks that seemed to be gliding along under the clouds. Most of all, they were gazing out on the other side, at Italy, the slope splotched with patches of snow, the ravines veiled in mist, and the large valley already in night's shadow. Soon everything would be dark, but now that didn't matter anymore. They had made it through, they'd made it through the wall of clouds, the obstacle that so frightened them, they'd overcome the dangers, the fog, the lightning.

Beneath them, in the very place they'd just come from, a red glow flashed inside the thick clouds, the thunder boomed like canon fire. The sun blinked out, the sky clouded over again, more rain began to fall. It was a heavy, cold rain that stung your face and hands, the drops clung to the sheepskin on Esther's chest. She picked up the suitcase; Elizabeth hefted the cloth bag onto her shoulder. The other fugitives stood up, and in the same order as they had come up the pass, men and young people up front, old people and children following in small groups, they began the descent down into the valley already filled with darkness, from which a few white wisps of smoke rose, the remote villages of the Stura, where they believed they would be safe.

Festiona, 1944

It was the long drawn-out winter season. A ribbon of smoke trailed over the lauze roofing stones in Festiona. Afternoons were cold. The sun went down behind the mountains early, the Stura Valley was a pool of shadows. Esther quite liked those shadows, she didn't know why. The smoke that rose from the roofs, that floated along the narrow streets, that wreathed around the Passagieri boarding house, the smoke that shrouded the trees, blotted out the gardens. That was when she'd walk through the deserted streets listening to the sound of her clogs that barely disturbed the cottony silence. There were always some dogs that barked.

All winter long in Festiona, she was alone, alone with Elizabeth. They both worked at the Passagieri boarding house, in exchange for their food and an attic room on the third floor with a French door that opened onto the balcony facing the church. On the steeple, the stopped clock endlessly read ten minutes to four.

Elizabeth standing on the balcony, hanging out sheets, laundry. She wore a sweater over her pinafore, her hands and cheeks were as red as those of a peasant. Washing the kitchen floor with soap and a scrub brush, burning garbage at dawn in the courtyard, peeling vegetables, feeding the rabbits that the restaurant frequently served. But she'd never wanted to kill them. It was Angela, the mistress of the house (people also said she was Mr. Passagieri's mistress), that was in charge of that nasty job and she did it perfunctorily, striking a sharp blow on the neck, turning the skin down, stringing the bloody body up by the feet. The first time she saw that, Esther turned and ran away through the grass till she reached the wide river. "I want to go back to Saint-Martin, I don't want to stay here anymore, he'll never find us here!" Elizabeth had followed her into the bushes, she caught up with her on the bank of the river, breathless, her legs scratched from the brambles. First she slapped Esther, then hugged her; it was the first time she'd ever struck her. "Don't go away, my love, my little star, stay with me; if not, I'll surely die." Esther hated her then, as if it were she who'd wanted it all to happen, who'd put those snow-filled mountains between her and her father, just to break her.

The Passagieri boarding house had very few clients. It was wartime. There were a few traveling salesmen en route for Vinadio, as if they'd lost their way, and three or four peasants from the village below, widowers too old to stay home alone in their kitchens. They talked in the dining room of the restaurant, leaning their elbows on the waxed tablecloth. To help out, Esther set the table, served the soup, the polenta, the wine. They spoke in their melodious language, they said, "wagazza"; they had a funny way of pronouncing the "*r*"s, just like in English. They didn't laugh, but Esther liked them very much, they were so elegant, so discreet.

When Angela went to buy supplies, Esther accompanied her. Angela didn't talk much. She waited at the entrance to the farm for them to bring out the milk, the vegetables, the eggs, sometimes a live rabbit that she carried by the ears. Her varicose ulcer was giving her trouble, she limped, she couldn't wear stockings anymore. Esther stared in horror at the wound that drew flies; at first she thought that it well suited a rabbit-killer. But beneath her outward gruffness,

Angela was very kind and generous. She called Esther "figlia mia". Her eyes were a very bright blue. She was like the grandmother Esther had never known.

In Festiona there was no time, no movement, there were only the gray houses roofed with flat lauze stones where the smoke hovered, the silent gardens, the morning mist that the sun burned off and that came back in the afternoon, roiling through the large valley.

In the evenings, Esther listened to the noises in the little room while waiting for Elizabeth to come home from work. It made her tremble. The dogs barking, answering one another. The clomping clogs of the inmates from the children's home as they came and went from the church. Sometimes the murmuring of prayers. Elizabeth thought she would enroll Esther at the school in the home. But the girl had refused, with no shouting, no tears. "I'll never go there." The home was a large dark two-storied house, with shutters that closed at four o'clock sharp, it lodged about a dozen war orphans and some difficult cases whose parents had placed them there. Both boys and girls were dressed in gray smocks; they were pale, sickly, shifty-eyed. They never left the home except to go to church in the morning and in the evening, and on Sundays to go out for a walk in neat lines, down to the river, supervised by the nuns and a tall man dressed in black who served as a schoolmaster. Esther was so frightened of them that she hid as soon as she heard the sound of their steps echoing in the square and in the streets.

Evenings, Elizabeth gave Esther lessons in the room lit with an oil lamp. The windowpanes of the French door were covered with blue paper because of the bombings. Sometimes they heard the sound of airplanes flying over during the night, very high up. A whining rumble that came from all sides at once, that made your heart beat faster.

Esther clung to her mother, laid her head against her breast. Elizabeth's hands were cold, chapped from doing the wash. "It's nothing Mama, they're going away now."

Sometimes they also heard shots in the night echoing through the whole valley. That was the partisans. Brao said they were called *Giustizia e Libertà*, they came down from the mountains to attack the Germans over by Demonte or else they followed the Stura down to where the bridge crosses the gorge leading to Borgo San Dalmazzo.

Brao was a fifteen-year-old boy, he'd been placed at the children's home, he was one of those difficult cases. He'd run away from home several times, he stole things from farms. He was so thin and frail you'd have thought he was a child of twelve, but Esther thought he was funny. He sneaked away when it was time to go to church and came to see Esther in the courtyard of the boarding house. He spoke a little in French and a lot in signs. Elizabeth didn't want her to see him. She didn't want Esther to speak to anyone, she was afraid of everything, even people who were kind. She said Brao was a hoodlum.

Esther liked to walk with Brao through the fields on the edge of the village. In the morning Brao sneaked away and they struck out together across the fields. The valley was bright with sunshine. Brao knew all the paths, all the shortcuts, and the animal tracks too, wild rabbit runs, the hiding-places of pheasants, the places in between the reeds where you could watch heron and wild duck. Esther remembered Mario, how he used to walk through the wide grassy fields in Saint-Martin hunting vipers. It seemed so long ago now, as if in another country, as if in another life.

With Brao, she went to walk in the riverbed over by Ruà. In spring, when the snow was thawing, the Stura was an enormous river filling the entire bed, carrying mud, tree trunks, tufts of grass ripped from the banks. It was mostly the noise that was stunning, that made you dizzy. The water rushed down, white with swirling eddies, sweeping everything along with it. Esther dreamed about drifting down the river on a raft of branches and grass all the way to the sea and even farther, to the other side of the world. Brao said that if you let the river sweep you along, you'd go all the way to Venice. He pointed eastward, past the mountains and Esther couldn't understand how that water could travel so far without getting lost.

In the Stura river, there were islands. Trees had grown on them, the grass was high. The river separated into several branches, formed bays, headlands, peninsulas. There were clear blue lakes. Crows walked awkwardly on the beaches, then flew off when you came too near, cawing out in hoarse cries that made a shudder run down your spine. There by the river everything was wonderful. Esther could stay there for hours while Brao looked for crayfish. There were all sorts of hiding places.

Esther always thought of her father there. It was as if he were very nearby, somewhere up in the mountains, in the Costa dell'Arp, or in the Pissousa. From up there, he could see her. He couldn't come down because the time wasn't right yet, but he was watching her. Esther felt him looking at her, it was both gentle and strong, a caress, a breath, it mingled with the wind in the trees, with the rhythmic purling of the water on the pebble beaches, even with the cries of the crows.

"If you could fly like that bird, you'd be there this very evening." Then Esther would be with him in Saint-Martin, holding his hand, standing in his shadow, he was so tall he blocked out the summer sunlight.

Winter, then spring, everything was so slow, so long,

like when you're at the back of a cave and you look toward the light. It was because of what was happening down there in Borgo San Dalmazzo. Elizabeth knew, but she never spoke of it. Only once because Esther had gone out on the road with Brao, over to where the river widens out, with all of its branches and islands, and you can barely see the mountains anymore, Elizabeth had come looking for her.

Esther ran into her in Ruà at nightfall, wearing her flowered pinafore and her clogs, her hair hidden under a black scarf like a peasant woman. Elizabeth hugged her very tightly, she was ice-cold. It was the first time that Esther realized her mother was so fragile, as if she'd suddenly grown old. She was ashamed, angry. "Why don't you let me do what I want? I'm sick of this, I want to go away from here, he'll never find us here." She didn't want to say "Papa" anymore; she didn't want to think about that word anymore. She was short of breath, her eyes were filled with tears. It was strange. The fog rolled into the fields, hugged the narrow streets, rose from the river with the night. Elizabeth wrapped her arm tightly around Esther, they walked slowly along, their heads slightly bowed, with all of those beads of fog clinging to their faces.

"They took all the people away, Hélène, do you understand?" Elizabeth spoke slowly, that was why her hands were so cold. The words were slow, calm, and also cold. "They stopped them all on the road, in Borgo San Dalmazzo. They took them all away, even the old women and the small children. They put them on a train, and they'll never come back. They're all going to die."

After that, every time Esther heard the name Borgo San Dalmazzo, she thought of the fog rising from the river, blotting everything out—the faces and the bodies— drowning out the names.

They'd waited in the buildings around the train station. The German soldiers captured them easily as they entered Borgo San Dalmazzo. They were exhausted from the journey, from hunger, from lack of sleep. They'd been walking on rocky paths for days, out in the open. When they came down the narrow valley, the first thing they saw was the church in Entracque, the village rooftops, and they'd stopped, hearts beating wildly. The children just gaped in wonder. They thought they'd made it, that there was nothing left to fear, that the war was over. The valley gleamed in the morning air, the fall colors were already bright, it was a glorious fall, almost inebriating. In the distance, the sound of ringing bells drifted over intermittently, shining flights of pigeons soared over the rooftops. It was like a party.

They started walking again, crossed the village. Dogs barked as they passed, ran after them along the embankments. The children stuck close to their mothers. Standing on their doorsteps, villagers watched them go by. They were older people for the most part, peasants, old women dressed in black. They watched, not saying anything, squinting their eyes against the sun. But there was no hostility, or fear either. As they walked past, some women came up to them, held out loaves of bread, cottage cheese, figs, they said a few words in their language.

The troop moved down the valley to Valdieri, they skirted the town, following the Gesso River. The children stared wide-eyed at the tall buildings lit by the sun, the onion dome of the church, the spire as high as a lighthouse. Here too there were flights of pigeons, tipping up in the sky around the cupolas, bells ringing. Rising plumes of smoke carried the smell of noon meals, dry grasses burning in the fields. The sound of water flowing over shingles in the river, a soft rippling that spoke of the future. They would take the train, they'd travel to Genoa, Livorno, maybe all the way to Rome; they'd take Angello Donati's boat. There was no more war. They could go anywhere; they could start a new life.

When the sun was at its highest point, they stopped by the side of the river to rest. The women doled out the provisions—the dry bread from Saint-Martin and the fresh bread, the cheese, and the figs that the village women in Entracque, in Valdieri, had give them as they passed.

Then maybe it all seemed like an outing to them, simply a picnic in the country, despite the suitcases and the bundles, despite the wounds on their feet, the suffering and the fever burning in the children's eyes. The river sparkled in the sunshine, there were gnats hanging in the air, birds in the trees.

They sat down on the pebble beaches to eat. They listened to the river singing of freedom. The children began to play, running up and down the riverbanks. They made boats with little bits of wood. The men were sitting around smoking and talking. They talked of what they would do over there, on the other side of the mountains, in Genoa, in Livorno. Some spoke of Venice, of Trieste, of the sea they would cross to reach Eretz Israel.

They talked of their land, a farm, a valley. They talked of the city of light, gleaming with its domes and its minarets, in the land where the Jewish people originated. Maybe they dreamt that they'd already arrived and that the domes and towers of Valdieri were at the gates of Jerusalem.

They soon started out again because night was already gathering on the floor of the valley. As they entered Borgo San Dalmazzo on the road to the train station, the soldiers of the Wehrmacht captured them. It all occurred very quickly, before they really knew what was happening. In front of them, at the end of the long, cold, narrow street, stood soldiers wearing green coats. Behind them, trucks advanced slowly with their headlights lit, pushing them forward like a herd. That's how they reached the train station. There, the soldiers had them go into a big building to the right of the station. They all went in, one after the other, until the large rooms were full. Then the Germans closed the doors.

It was night. Voices rang out around the station. There was no light save the glow of the truck headlights. The women sat down on the floor next to their bundles and the children crouched near them. There were children crying, sobs, whispers. The broken windowpanes let the cold night air into the large rooms through wire grates. There was not a piece of furniture, not a bed. At the end of the largest room, the overflowing latrines smelled foul. The night wind blew over the frightened children. Then the youngest ones fell asleep.

Around midnight, they were awakened by the noise of trains pulling in, maneuvering, squeaking, boxcars bumping together, locomotives blowing off steam. There were some whistle calls. The children tried to see what was happening; the youngest started whimpering again. But there were no human voices, only the sounds of machines. They were in the middle of nowhere.

At dawn, the soldiers opened the doors on the side of the railroad tracks and they pushed the men and the women into windowless boxcars painted in camouflage colors. It was cold, the steam from the locomotives hung in phosphorescent clouds. The children clung to their mothers, maybe they said, "Where are we going? Where are they taking us?" Everything was empty, the platforms, the buildings around the station, and the surrounding city. There were only the scattered, ghostly figures of soldiers wearing their long coats, standing in the steam from the trains. Maybe the men dreamt of escaping, all they had to do was forget about the women and children and run across the tracks, jump over the embankment, and disappear into the fields. Dawn was interminable and very silent, no cries and no voices, no birds and no dogs barking, only the low hissing of the locomotives and the screeching of the couplings, then the shrill sound of wheels when they began slipping and scraping on the rails and the train struck out on that journey to nowhere, Turin, Genoa, Ventimiglia, the children hugging their mothers, the acrid smell of sweat and urine, the jolting boxcars, the smoke seeping into the blind cars and the light of dawn showing through the cracks in the door, Toulon, Marseille, Avignon, the clattering of the wheels, the children crying, the muffled voices of women, Lyon, Dijon, Melun, and the silence that followed when the train stopped, and still another cold night, the numbing stillness, Drancy, the long wait, all of those names and all of those faces that were disappearing, as if they'd been brothers and sisters torn from Esther's memory.

The orphans went to the church in Festiona every evening at nightfall. One day, Brao sneaked away and met Esther in the square. "Come on," he said pointing to the church. Esther didn't want to go in. She hated hearing the sound of the children's footsteps, the mechanical drone of prayers. Near the door, there was that strange painting, the Virgin trampling a dragon underfoot. Brao took Esther by the hand and led her into the church. It was like a very dark cave. It smelled of wood polish and tallow. At the back of the church, a tiny light glimmered in the cold on each side of the altar. Esther walked toward the lights as if she could not take her eyes from them.

After a minute, Brao pulled on her arm. He seemed uneasy, he didn't understand. Then Esther took one of the lights and she began to light the candles, one after another. She didn't really know why she was doing it; she wanted to see the light shine, like that evening in Saint-Martin when she'd gone into the chalet high up in the village with all those wavering flames. Now it was the same light, as if time didn't move forward and they were still on the other side, before the barrier of mountains, and the flames were piercing the shadows and looking at you.

It was the eyes of the people back there that were looking at you, the children, the women, Cécile with the scarf over her beautiful black hair. The voices of the men that swelled, boomed out like a thunderstorm, then became very soft and murmuring, and the words of the book in that mysterious language, words that found their way deep inside of you even though you didn't understand them.

With a lit candle in her hand, Esther went around the church lighting other candles wherever she found them, in the corners, in front of the statues, on either side of the altar. Brao remained standing near the door, watching without saying anything but his eyes were shining too. The young girl came and went feverishly, brought other stars of light to life, and now the church was beautifully lit up as if for a celebration. The candles gleamed. They gave off an intense, almost magical heat. It was as if everyone was there again for an instant, she felt the power of their gaze, the children questioning, the women giving their love, she felt the strength in the men's eyes, she heard their deep voices, and that slow rocking of bodies while they chanted, and the whole church vibrating and swaying like a ship.

But it only lasted a brief instant, because suddenly the door of the church opened and the voice of the schoolmaster snapped out. The man dressed in black was holding Brao by the collar of his smock, Brao was shouting, "Elena! Elena!" Esther was ashamed, she should have stayed, helped Brao, but she was frightened and ran away. When she reached the boarding house she closed herself up in the room, but even there, she thought she could hear Brao calling her and the clomping clogs of those cursed orphans walking in step toward the church. Like every evening, they entered the dark cave, they sat on the creaking benches—the girls on the left, the boys with shaved heads on the right—in their old gray smocks with worn elbows, and Brao was with them, his shoulder still sore from the blows he'd taken.

It was the end of summer; everyone knew that the Germans had begun their retreat, that they were headed back northward. Brao talked about it, and so did the people in the restaurant of the Passsagieri boarding house, they talked of the men from *Giutizia e Libertà* and their meeting at La Madonna du Coletto above Festiona. Elizabeth hugged Esther very close, her voice had changed, she wasn't able to explain very well. "We're going home soon, it's all over, we'll be going to France soon." But Esther gave her a hard look. "So, we're leaving tomorrow?" Elizabeth motioned her to be quiet. "No, Hélène, we have to wait, not yet." She was acting as if she didn't understand, as if nothing had happened, as if everything were normal, she didn't even want to say "Esther" anymore, it was a name that frightened her. Esther pulled away from her, left the little room, went down into the courtyard, walked out toward the fields. She felt sick to her stomach, there was a nerve twitching in her chest.

Early the next morning, Esther set out for the Coletto. She began walking on the dirt road. The mountain towered above her, covered with fall's rusted larches. Immediately after passing the last houses of Festiona, the road began winding upward. It was one year ago now that Esther and Elizabeth had walked down that same road coming from Valdieri. It was so long ago, and yet Esther felt like her feet were following in her exact footsteps. It hadn't rained since the beginning of summer. The surface of the road was turning to dust, the stones rolled underfoot, there was a lot of dry grass along the embankment. Esther cut through the bushes instead of following the turns in the road. She climbed without looking back, pulling herself up with the aid of the shrubs. Her heart was pounding heavily in her chest, she felt drops of sweat dampening the back of her dress, stinging her underarms.

There was not a sound in the forest, just the cawing of invisible crows from time to time. The mountain was beautiful and lonely, the morning sun made the needles of the larches shimmer, sharpened the pungent smell of the brush.

Esther was thinking about freedom. *Giustizia e Libertà*. Brao said that they were up there on the top of that mountain. That they met near the chapel. Maybe she could speak with them, maybe they knew something, had news from Saint-Martin. Maybe she could go away with them, cross the mountains and she would find Tristan and Rachel and Judith and all the people in the village again, the old men muffled up in their caftans and the women wearing their long dresses and scarves over their hair. There would be children too, all the children running around the fountain in the square, or bounding down the long street with the stream all the way to the grassy field by the river. But she didn't want to think about all of that. She wanted to go farther than that, take the train to Paris, go out to the ocean, to Brittany maybe. Before, she often used to talk about Brittany with her father, he'd promised to take her there. That was why she was climbing this mountain, to be free, to stop thinking. When she found the people from *Giustizia e Libertà*, she wouldn't have to think about anything anymore, everything would be different.

A little before noon, Esther reached the sanctuary. The

chapel was deserted, the door locked, some of the windowpanes were broken. In the entryway there were the remnants of a fire. Someone had eaten there, maybe spent the night. A few bits of cardboard, some dry twigs were left. Esther climbed up to the fountain above the sanctuary and drank the ice-cold water. Then she sat down to wait. Her heart was beating fast. She was afraid. Everything was so silent, only the light sound of the wind in the larches, but gradually Esther made out other sounds, cracking sounds in the rocks, rustling sounds in the brush, or else the brief passage of an insect, the distant cry of a bird in the undergrowth. The sky was very blue, cloudless, the sun burned down.

All of a sudden, Esther just couldn't wait any longer. She started running, like she'd once done on the road to Roquebillière when Gasparini had taken her to see the wheat harvest and she'd felt an empty feeling—fear of death—creep into her. She ran down the road in the direction of Valdieri till she reached the wide curve from where the whole valley could be seen, and there, she stopped, out of breath. She saw everything lying before her, just as if she were a bird.

The sun shone down on the Valdieri Valley, she recognized every house, every path, all the way out to the village of Entracque, from where she'd come with Elizabeth. It was a wide split that the wind came blowing through.

So then she sat down on the ground by the side of the road and she gazed out into the distance toward the mountains. The sharp peaks clawed the sky, their shadows stretched over the rusted slopes all the way down to the valley. At the most distant point, ice glittered like a jewel.

One year ago, Esther and Elizabeth had come over those mountains with all the people that were fleeing the Germans.

Esther remembered every instant and yet it all seemed so far away, as if in some other life. Everything had changed. Now that which existed on the other side of the mountains had become impossible. Maybe there was nothing left.

It dug out a hole deep inside of her, a window through which the emptiness crept in. That was what she'd seen, she remembered, when she'd come up close to the mountain just before going through the pass. An unreal window in which the sun was shining. But maybe it was only a dream she'd had just before the clouds closed around her and Elizabeth and sunk them into the forgetfulness of Festiona. So the *Giustizia e Libertà* fighters could do nothing for them now, how can shadows be set free?

The sun was sinking down toward the mountain, she could feel the tenebrous march toward night on her face. In the distance stood the mountain everyone called precisely that, Mont Tenebre.

Esther tried not to take her eyes from the far end of the valley, the passage through the ice. The shadows spread gradually, covering the valley, drowning the villages. Now Esther could hear the sounds of life, dogs barking, bells chiming, even children shouting. The smell of smoke drifted up on the wind. It was a day like any other down below. No one was thinking about the war.

Far away, the peak of Gelas seemed to gradually recede into the distance, it floated over the mist, light as a cloud. Esther sat watching, the sun inexorably approached the mountains. She had to slip a sweater over her pinafore because she could already feel the night chill. Brao was probably waiting in the square, it was time for the children from the orphanage to be getting ready to walk to the church. Esther watched the Valdieri Valley for a few more minutes, the sharp crest of the glaciers, as if someone would be walking down from the peaks, following the valley till he reached the smoke-filled villages, a very tall man who would cross the torrents and the grassy fields with his back to the sun, and at long last she would feel his shadow upon her.

Esther

Alon Harbor, December 1947

I'm seventeen years old. I know that I'm going to be leaving
this country forever. I don't know whether I'll reach the other
side or not, but we'll be leaving soon. Mama is leaning
against me, sitting in the sand in the shelter of the broken-
down hut. She's sleeping and I'm waiting. We're wrapped in
a military blanket that Uncle Simon Ruben gave us before
we left. It's a stiff, waterproof American army blanket that
he valued very much. Simon Ruben is Mama's friend, he's
my friend too. He's the one who arranged everything for our
journey. After the war, when we went to Paris without my
father, Simon Ruben took us in. He was a friend of my
father's, he knew him well, and that's why he took us in.
First he put us up in a garage, because he wasn't sure the war
was over and that the Germans weren't coming back. Then,
when he realized it really was over, that there was no reason
to hide anymore, he let us stay in half of an apartment that
he owned on Rue des Gravilliers and in the other half there
was an old blind woman whose name was Mme. d'Aleu, and
that's where we lived. But now there's no money left and we
don't know where to go. There's no place for us anywhere
now. Simon Ruben told Mama that we shouldn't leave
because of the money, but for our lives, so that we could
forget. He said, "Shouldn't we forget that which the earth
has covered over?" He said that, I remember perfectly well,
and I hadn't understood what he meant. He was holding

Mama's hands, he was leaning over the table, his face was very close to Mama's, and he said again, "You must go away to forget! You must forget!" I didn't understand what he meant, what had to be forgotten, what the earth had covered over. Now I know that he meant my father, that's what he was saying, my father had been covered over by the earth, and we just had to forget him. I remember Uncle Simon Ruben, his aged and bloated face so close to Mama. She, so beautiful, pale, and fragile, so young. I remember his face and the shadow of his large eyes with dark black lashes. Even to me, her own child, she seemed young and fragile, just like a little girl. I think she was crying. Alon, we arrived here in the gray of dawn, after having walked in the dark, in the rain, from the train station in Saint-Cyr, walking along listening to the sound of the wind in the forest, a blustering sound, the wind driving us toward the sea. How many hours did we walk in silence, blindly, guided by the thin beam of the flashlight, drenched from the cold rain? Sometimes the rain stopped for a few minutes, we didn't hear the wind anymore. The muddy path wound through the hills, down into valleys. At the break of day, we entered the forest of giant maritime pines at the floor of a valley. The trunks of the trees stood against the dim glow of the sea and it made our hearts leap, as if we were walking in an unexplored land. The man who was our guide gathered everyone together near the ruins of a hut and then he left. Mama sat down on the ground in the sand, complaining about her legs, sniffling a little.

We're waiting in the morning twilight. The wind is blowing in blasts, a cold wind that's trying to get under the shield of our blanket. Mama is cuddled up next to me. She fell asleep almost immediately. I'm sitting very still, to keep from awakening her. I'm so tired.

The train trip from Paris. The cars were packed, there wasn't a single seat left. Mama lay down on the floor on a piece of cardboard in the aisle in front of the door to the toilet, and I remained standing as long as I could to keep an eye on our suitcases. Our two suitcases are wound about with twine to reinforce them. They hold all of our treasures. Our clothing, our toiletries, our books, our pictures, some souvenirs. Mama brought along two kilos of sugar because she says it will surely be in short supply over there. I don't have many clothes. I brought my white cotton summer dress, a pair of gloves, an extra pair of shoes, and above all the books I love, the books my father used to read us sometimes in the evenings after dinner, *Nicholas Nickleby* and *The Adventures of Mr. Pickwick*. They're my favorites. When I feel like crying, or laughing, or thinking about something else, all I have to do is pick one of them up, I open it at random and I immediately find the passage I need.

As for Mama, she only brought one book. Before Mama left, Uncle Simon Ruben gave her the Book of the Beginning, *Sepher Berasith*, that's what it's called. Mama fell asleep on the dirty floor in the aisle of the car, in spite of the jolting couplings and the door to the toilet that was banging next to her head, and the smell...Every now and again someone who needed to use the toilet came down to the end of the aisle. When they saw Mama sleeping on the floor on the piece of cardboard, they turned around and looked elsewhere. But still, there was one person who tried to go in. He stood in front of Mama and said, "Excuse me!" as if she would wake up immediately and get to her feet. She kept on sleeping, so he shouted several times, louder and louder "Excuse me! Excuse me! Excuse me!" Then he leaned down to drag her out of the way. I don't know what came over me then, but I just couldn't stand it, no, that cruel fat man who was going to wake Mama up so he could go to the toilet in peace. I jumped on him and started pummeling him with my fists and scratching him, but I didn't say anything, didn't shout, I had my jaws clenched and there were tears in my eyes. He backed off as if a wildcat had pounced on him; he pushed me away and started yelling in a strange, high-pitched voice, filled with anger and fear, "You haven't heard the last of me! Just wait and see!" And he walked off. So then I lay down on the floor too, next to Mama who hadn't even woken up, and I put my arms around her and I slept a little, it was a sleep filled with noises and jerks that made me feel nauseous.

In Marseille, it was raining. We waited for hours on the huge platform. Mama and I weren't the only ones. There were a lot of people on the platforms, crowded together amidst the luggage. We waited all night long. A cold wind was blowing over the platforms, the rain made rings of fog around the electric lights. People were lying on the ground, leaning against their suitcases. Some were wrapped in blankets from the Red Cross. Some children cried a little, then fell suddenly asleep, overcome with fatigue. Some men dressed in black, Jewish men, talked on endlessly in their language. Talking and smoking, sitting on their luggage, and their voices echoed strangely in the hollowness of the station.

When we'd gotten off the train in Marseille, a little before midnight, no one said anything to us, but a rumor went from one person to the next, down the length of the platform: there would be no train for Toulon till three or four o'clock in the morning. Maybe we would have to spend the whole night waiting on the platform, but what difference did it make? Time had ceased to exist for us. We'd been traveling, been out in the open for so long in a world where time no longer existed.

That's when I saw him on the same platform, under the large clock that looked like a waxen moon. He'd been on the platform of the station in Paris before the train left, so long ago that it seemed like weeks had gone by. He was making his way through the crowd just when the train came into the station in a great fury of hissing steam and screeching brakes. He was tall, thin, and his golden hair and beard made him look like a shepherd. I say that, because now I know that's what his name is, Jacques Berger. So that's what I nicknamed him, the Shepherd.

He was walking against the tide of the crowd glancing around, looking for something, someone, a relative, a friend. When he reached the point where he was almost facing me, his eyes locked on mine for such a long time that I had to turn away and I bent down over my suitcase as if I were looking for something so he wouldn't see me blushing.

I'd forgotten about him, not completely forgotten, but the train, the noise of the couplings, the jolts, and Mama who was sleeping like a sick child by the toilet door, all of that kept me from thinking about anyone at all. G__! I so hate traveling! How can anyone take the train or the boat for pleasure! I would like to spend my whole life in one place, just watching the days go by, the clouds, the birds, dreaming. At the other end of the platform—just like in Paris—the Shepherd in question was standing, as if he were waiting for someone, a relative, a friend. Despite the distance I could see his eyes in the shadow of his brow.

Since we might have to wait on that platform all night long, we needed to get organized. I laid the two suitcases down flat and Mama sat down on the ground, leaning the top part of her body against the suitcases. I planned on doing the same soon. When will it all be over? Today I feel as though I haven't stopped traveling since the day I was born, in trains, in buses, on mountain roads, and also moving from one apartment to another, to Nice, to Saint-Martin, to Berthemont. One day Mama said that all those names were cursed, that we shouldn't ever say them again. Not even think about them again.

The Shepherd spoke to me a little earlier when I was coming back from the toilets in the station. I was walking under the clock and there he was, sitting on his suitcase amidst all the people lying down. Next to him sat the group of Jewish men dressed in black, talking and smoking. He said, "Hello Miss," with his rather deep voice. He said, "It's quite a long wait here on this train platform," and, "you aren't feeling too cold, are you?" with a Parisian accent, I think. I noticed he had a little scar next to his lip, I thought of my father. I don't remember what I said, maybe I walked away without answering, with my head down, because I was so tired, so desperately sleepy. I think I grunted something unpleasant so I could get away faster, settle down with my torso leaning against the suitcase, my legs curled up sideways, as close to Mama as possible. I don't think it ever occurred to me before that she could die.

Nights are long when it's cold and you're waiting for a train. I wasn't able to sleep a single minute, despite the fatigue, despite the emptiness all around me. I kept looking around, as if to make sure that nothing had changed, that everything was still real. I looked at it all, the immense station with its glass dome with the rain streaming down, the platforms stretching away into the night, the halos around the lampposts, and I thought: so here I am. I'm in Marseille, it is the last time in my life that I'll be seeing this. I must never forget it, ever, even if I live to be as old as Mme. d'Aleu, the old blind woman that shared our apartment at 26 Rue des Gavilliers. I must never forget any of it. So, I straightened up a bit, pushing myself up on the old suitcases, and I looked at the bodies stretched out along the platform, against the walls, and the people sitting on the benches, nodding off to sleep, wrapped in their blankets, and they looked like dead skins, cast off piles of clothing. My eyes were burning, there was a dizzy feeling in my head; I could hear the sounds of breathing, heavy, deep, and I felt tears rolling down my cheeks, along my nose, dripping onto the suitcase, without knowing why those tears were coming. Mama shifted slightly in her sleep, she moaned, and I caressed her hair like you do with a child so they won't wake up. A ways off, the clock showed its wan face, its moon face, where the hours went by so slowly: one o'clock, two o'clock, two-thirty. I tried to find the Shepherd at the other end of the platform under the clock, but he'd disappeared. He too had become a dead skin, a cast off piece of rag. So, with my cheek against the suitcase, I thought about everything that had happened, everything that would happen, just like that, slowly, following haphazard paths, like when you write a letter. I thought about my father when he left, the last image I had of him, tall, strong, his gentle face, his very black, curly hair, the look in his eyes, as if he were excusing himself, as if he'd done something foolish. For an instant, he was there, he was kissing me, he was hugging me so tight in his arms I couldn't catch my breath and I was laughing and pushing him away a little. Then he was gone, while I slept, leaving only the image of that grave face, those eyes that were asking forgiveness.

I think of him. Sometimes I pretend that I believe he's the one we're going to see, the one we'll find at the end of this journey. I've been practicing at pretending for a long time, until I believe it. It's hard to explain. It's like the energy that flows between the magnet and the steel pen point. One minute the point moves, quivers. The next minute—so fast you can't even see it—the pen point is stuck to the magnet. I remember when I was ten—it was at the beginning of the war—and we fled Nice to go to Saint-Martin, that summer my father took me down into the valley to see the harvest, maybe it was the very place I went back to three years later with the Gasparini boy. We traveled the whole way in a horse cart and my father helped the farmers cut the wheat and tie it up in sheaves. I stayed close behind him, I breathed in the smell of his sweat. He'd taken off his shirt and I saw the tensed muscles on each side of his back under the white skin, like ropes. All of a sudden, in spite of the sunshine, in spite of the people shouting and the smell of the cut wheat, I knew that it would all come to an end, the thought was very vivid: my father would have to go away, forever, just as we are doing now. I remember, the idea crept up very quietly, hardly making a flutter, then suddenly it swooped down on me, squeezing my heart in its claws, and I couldn't keep on acting as if nothing had happened. Horror-struck, I ran down the path through the wheat, under the blue sky, I ran away as fast as I could. I wasn't able to scream or cry, all I could do was run with all my might, feeling the tight grip crushing my heart, smothering me. My father started running after me, he caught up with me on the road, he swept me up in his arms, tore me off the ground, I remember, and I, I was struggling, he hugged me very hard against his chest, trying to calm my tearless sobbing, my hiccups, stroking my hair and my neck. Afterward, he never asked me a single question, he didn't reprimand me. When people asked him about what had happened, he simply said, nothing, nothing, she was just frightened. But I could see in his eyes that he understood, that he'd felt it too, the passing of that cold shadow, despite the lovely noon light and the golden wheat.

I remember once too, Mama and I went out for a walk one day over by Berthemont, we followed the sulfur stream up above the ruins of the hotel. My father had left ahead of us, he'd met up with the people in the Maquis, it was all very mysterious. There had been an exchange of notes that my father read hastily and then burned immediately, and Mama had gotten dressed hurriedly. She took me by the hand, we walked quickly along the deserted road by the river till we reached the abandoned hotel. First taking a small staircase, then up a narrow path, we began climbing the mountain, Mama was walking fast without getting winded and I had a hard time keeping up with her, but I didn't dare say anything because it was the first time I was going with her. She had that impatient look on her face that I never run across nowadays, her eyes were shining feverishly. Then we walked on a very high slope covered with immense pastures, and the sky was all around us. I had never been up so high, so far away before, and my heart was beating fast, from the effort, from feeling anxious. Afterward we reached the top of the slope and there, at the foot of the peaks, was a vast grassy plain, scattered with shepherd's huts of black drystone. Mama walked over to the closest huts and when we reached them, my father appeared. He was standing in the midst of the tall grasses, he looked like a hunter. His clothes were torn and dirty and he was carrying a rifle slung across his shoulder. I could hardly recognize him because his beard had grown out and his face was suntanned. As usual, he picked me up in his arms and hugged me very hard. And then he and Mama lay down in the grass near the hut and talked. I heard them talking, and laughing, but I stayed a little off to one side. I was playing with pebbles, I remember, tossing them onto the back of my hands like jacks.

I can still hear their voices and laughter that afternoon in the immense sloping pasture with the sky all around us. The clouds were rolling, describing dazzling scrolls on the blue of the sky, and I could hear the laughter and the snatches of my mother and father's voices near me in the grass. And it was then, at that moment, that I realized my father was going to die. The idea dawned on me, and try as I might to push it away it came back, and I could hear his voice, his laughter, I knew that all I had to do was turn around to see them, to see his face, his hair and his beard shining in the sun, his shirt, and the shape of Mama lying next to him. And suddenly I threw myself to the ground and bit my hand to keep from screaming, to keep from crying, and in spite of myself I felt tears slipping out of me, emptiness gnawing in my stomach, making an opening to the outside, emptiness, coldness, and I couldn't stop thinking that he was going to die, that he had to die.

That's what I must forget on this journey, just like Uncle Simon Ruben said, "You must forget, you must go away to forget!"

Here, on the shores of Alon Bay, it all seems so far away, as if it had happened to someone else, in some other world. The strong north wind is blowing in the night and I'm lying very close against Mama, with Uncle Simon Ruben's stiff blanket pulled all the way up to my eyes. It's been so long since I've slept. My whole body aches, my eyes sting. The sound of the sea is reassuring, even if there is a storm. This is the first time I've spent the night by the sea. From the window in the train, as I stood in the aisle next to Mama before we reached Marseille, I saw it for an instant in the twilight, glistening, rippling in the wind. Everyone was over on the same side of the car, trying to get a glimpse of the sea. Later, in the train headed for Bandol, I tried to catch sight of it, my forehead plastered up against the cold window, jostled by the bumps and curves. But there was nothing but darkness, sudden bursts of light, and the far-off lamps dancing like ship-lights in the night.

The train stopped at the station in Cassis and many people got off, men and women muffled up in their coats, some with large umbrellas as if they were going for a walk on the boulevards. I looked out to try and see if the Shepherd had gotten off with them, but he wasn't on the platform. Then the train lumbered slowly away and the people standing on the platform gradually faded into the distance like ghosts, it was sad and a little funny at the same time, like tired birds, buffeted in the wind. Are they going to Jerusalem too? Or maybe they're going to Canada? But there's no way of knowing, you can't ask them. There are people listening, people that want to know, to keep us from leaving. That's what Simon Ruben said when he took us to the platform in the train station, "Don't talk with anyone. Don't ask anyone anything. There are people listening to you." He slipped a piece of paper into The Book of the Beginning, with the name and address of his brother in Nice, Edouard Ruben Furniture, Descente Crotti, that's where we should say we're going if the police stop us. Then we arrived in Saint-Cyr, and everyone got off. A man was waiting for us on the platform of the station. He grouped everyone together who was to embark upon the journey and we began walking down the road, guided by the beam of his flashlight all the way to Alon Harbor.

Now we're on the beach, in the shelter of the broken-down hut, waiting for daybreak. Maybe other people are trying to see, just like I am. They sit up straight, peering out ahead of them, trying to see the light of the ship in the darkness, they search the crashing sound of the sea, listening for the sound of sailor's voices calling out. The giant pines creak and crack in the wind, their needles make the sound of waves cutting past the stem of a boat. The boat that's supposed to be coming is Italian, like Angelo Donati. It's called the *Sette Fratelli*, which means Seven Brothers. The first time I heard that name I thought of the seven children lost in the forest in the tale of Little Tom Thumb. With a name like that it seems nothing can go wrong.

I remember when my father used to talk about Jerusalem, when he would explain all about the city in the evening, like a story before bedtime. He and Mama weren't believers. I mean, they believed in G__, but they didn't believe in the Jewish religion or in any other kind of religion. But when my father spoke of Jerusalem in the days of King David, he told extraordinary tales. I thought it must be the biggest and most beautiful city in the world, not like Paris in any case, because there surely weren't dark streets over there, or dilapidated buildings, or broken drainpipes, or smelly stairwells, or gutters in which armies of rats ran free. When you say Paris, some people think you're lucky—such a beautiful city! But in Jerusalem it was certainly different. What was it like? I had a hard time imagining it, a city like a cloud, with domes and steeples and minarets (my father said there were a lot of minarets), surrounded by hills planted with orange and olive trees, a city that floated over the desert like a mirage, a city in which there was nothing commonplace, nothing dirty, nothing dangerous. A city in which everyone spent his time praying and dreaming.

I don't think I really knew what praying meant back then. Maybe I thought it was like dreaming, when you let secret things creep around you—what you want and love most in the world—just before dropping off to sleep.

Mama often talked about it too. The last days in Paris she lived for that one word alone, Jerusalem. She didn't really talk about the city, or the land, Eretz Israel, but about everything that had once existed over there, about everything that would begin again. For her, it was an open door, that's what she said.

The cold wind is slowly slipping inside of me, going straight through me. It's a wind that isn't coming from the sea, but blowing down from the north, over the hills, it's whistling through the trees. Now the sky is graying, I can see the very tall trunks of the trees and the sky appears between the branches. But the sea still isn't visible. Mama woke up because of the dawn chill. I can feel her body shivering next to mine. I hold her closer to me. I say words to soothe her. Did she hear me? I'd like to talk to her about everything, about the door, tell her it's really a very difficult and slow process, getting through that door. I feel as though she is the child and I, her mother. The journey began so long ago. I can remember each stage, from the very beginning. When we went to live in Paris in Simon Ruben's apartment on Rue des Gravilliers with the old blind woman. That was when I stopped talking, stopped eating, except when Mama fed me with a spoon like a baby. I'd become a baby, I wet the bed every night. Mama put diapers on me that she made from old rags of different colors. There was a void after Saint-Martin, after walking through the mountains to Italy, the long walk all the way to Festiona. Memories came back to me in shreds, like the long wisps of fog trailing over the roofs of the village, and the shadows rising in the valley in winter. Hiding in the room in the Passagieri boarding house, I heard the dogs barking, heard the slow sound of the orphan's footsteps heading toward the dark church every evening, still heard Brao's voice yelling, "Elena!" while the schoolmaster was shoving him around by the shoulder. And the valley that opened all the way out to the icy window, the long rust-colored slopes that I'd searched, the empty paths with only the wind that carried with it the forge-like sounds of the villages, the faint shouts of children, nothing but the wind blowing right into the center of my being, hollowing out the emptiness within. Uncle Simon Ruben tried everything. He tried prayer, he sent for the Rabbi and a doctor to heal the emptiness in me. The only thing he didn't try was the hospital because Mama wouldn't have agreed to that, or to his requesting help from the Social Services either. Those were the terrifying years that I left behind, in the cold shadows, the hallways, and the stairwells of Rue Gravilliers. They are fading away now, slipping by me backwards like the landscape past the train.

Never has a night seemed so long to me. I remember in the old days, before Saint-Martin, I used to wait uneasily for night to come because I thought that was when you could die, I thought that death stole people away in the night. You went to sleep alive and when night faded, you had disappeared. That's how Mme. d'Aleu died one night, leaving her cold white body in the bed, and Uncle Simon Ruben came to help Mama lay out the corpse for the funeral. Mama reassured me, she said that wasn't it at all, death didn't steal people away, it was simply that the body and mind were worn out and they just stopped living, like one goes to sleep. "And what about when someone is killed?" I asked that. I asked that and I was almost shouting and Mama averted her eyes as if she were ashamed at having lied, as if it were her fault. Because she'd also thought immediately of my father and she said, "Those who kill others rob them of their lives, they are like wild animals, they are ruthless." She too was remembering when my father went off into the mountains with his rifle, she was remembering how he disappeared into the tall grasses, never to return again. When adults don't tell the truth they look away because they're afraid that it will show in their eyes. But I was already cured of the emptiness by then, I wasn't afraid of the truth anymore.

Those nights are what I'm thinking about now in the gray light of dawn, as I listen to the sound of the sea on the rocks of Alon Bay. The ship should be coming soon to take us to Jerusalem. Those nights have all melted together, they've blotted out the days. In Saint-Martin the nights crept into my body, left me feeling cold, alone, and frail. Here on the beach with Mama's body lying close to mine and trembling, listening to her breathing mixed with little moaning sounds like a child's, I remember certain nights when we went home to 26 Rue des Gravilliers—the cold, the sound of water in the drainpipes, the creaking sounds coming from the workshops in the courtyard, the voices echoing, and Mama lying next to me in the cold narrow room, holding me close to her body to keep me warm because my life was draining away from me, my life was leaking out into the sheets, into the air, into the walls.

I'm listening, and I think I can hear everyone who is waiting for the boat all around me. They're out there, lying in the sand against the wall of the ruined hut, under the tall pines sheltering us from the strong blustering wind. I don't know who they are; I don't know their names, except for the Shepherd, but that's just what I call him. They're nothing but faces that are barely visible in the semi-darkness, shapes, women muffled up in their coats, old men hunched down under their wide umbrellas. All of them with the same suitcases wound with twine, with the same Red Cross or

American Army blankets. Somewhere amongst them, the Shepherd, alone, still so much like an adolescent. But we mustn't talk to each other; we mustn't know anything. Simon Ruben said so, on the platform of the station. He hugged Mama and I for a long time, he gave us a little money and his blessing. And so, we aren't the only ones to be going through that door. There are others here on this beach, and elsewhere, thousands of others who are waiting for boats that will sail away and never come back. They are sailing for other worlds, for Canada, South America, Africa, to places where perhaps people are waiting for them, where they can start a new life. But for those of us here on Alon beach, who is waiting for us? In Jerusalem, Uncle Simon Ruben would say with a laugh, only the angels are waiting for you. How many doors will we go through? Each time we crest the horizon, it will be like another door. To keep from losing hope, to resist the cold wind, the weariness, we must think about the city that is like a mirage, the city of minarets and domes shining in the sun, the dream city made of stone hovering over the desert. In that city we can surely forget. In that city there are no black walls, there's no black water trickling down, no emptiness or cold, or crushing crowds on the boulevards. We'll be able to live again, find what existed before, the smell of wheat in the valley near Saint-Martin, the water in the streams when the snow melts, the silent afternoons, the summer sky, the footpaths that disappear amidst the high grasses, the sound of the torrent and Tristan's cheek on my chest. I hate traveling, I hate time! It is life before destruction—that's what Jerusalem is. Is it really possible to find that by crossing the seas on the *Sette Fratelli*?

Day is breaking. For the first time, I'm able to think about what's in store for us. Soon the Italian boat will be out there in Alon Harbor, which I'm just now beginning to distinguish. It seems as if I can already feel the rolling of the sea. The sea will take us to that holy city, the wind will push us all the way to the door of the desert. I never spoke of G__ with my father. He didn't want us to talk about it. He had a way of looking at you, very simply and directly, that stopped you from asking questions. Afterwards, when he wasn't there anymore, it no longer mattered. One day Uncle Simon Ruben asked Mama if it wasn't time to start thinking about instruction—he meant religion—to make up for lost time. Mama always refused, without saying no but simply saying we'll see about that later, because it was against my father's wishes. She said it would come in time, when I was old enough to choose. She too believed that religion was a matter of choice. She didn't even want people to call me by my Jewish name, she said, "Hélène" because it was also my name, the name she'd given me. But I called myself by my real name, Esther, I didn't want any other name now. One day my father told me the story of Esther, who was called Hadassa, and had neither father nor mother, and how she had married King Ahasuerus and dared to enter the grand chamber where the king was enthroned to ask him to save her people. And Simon Ruben told me about her, but he said the name of G__ should not be pronounced, or written, and that's why I thought it was a name that was like the sea, an immense name that was impossible to know in its entirety. So now I know it's true, I have to reach the other side, cross the sea, all the way to Eretz Israel and Jerusalem, I have to find that force. I never would have thought it was so huge, I never would have thought it was such a difficult door we had to go through. The fatigue, the cold prevent me from thinking about anything else. All I can think of is this interminable night that is now ending in a gray dawn, and the wind in the giant trees, and the sound of the sea between the sharp rocks. I drop off to sleep just then, lying close to Mama, listening to the wind flapping in the blanket like a sail, listening to the unbroken sound of the waves on the sandy beach. Perhaps I dream that when I open my eyes the ship will be out there on the sparkling sea.

I'm sitting in a cleft in the rocks next to a huge dead tree. I'm on the lookout. Before me, the sea is a blinding blue, it's painful to look at. The gusts of wind whip by overhead. I can hear them coming as they rush over the leaves of the bushes and through the branches of the pines, it makes a liquid sound that blends in with the crashing of the waves on the white rocks. As soon as I woke up this morning, I ran out to the headland in Alon Harbor to get a better view of the sea.

Now the sun is burning my face, burning my eyes. The sea is so beautiful with its slow swell coming from the other side of the world. The waves beat against the coast making a deep-water sound. I'm not thinking of anything now. I look out, my eyes tirelessly scanning the clear line of the horizon, searching the windswept sea, the naked sky. I want to see the Italian boat arrive, I want to be the first, when its stem cuts through the sea toward us. If I don't stay out here at the end of the promontory, at the entrance to Alon Bay, it seems as if the boat won't come. If I turn my eyes away for an instant, it won't see us, it will continue on its way to Marseille.

It has to be coming now, I can feel it. The sea can't be so beautiful, the sky can't have cast off all of the clouds for no reason.

I want to be the first to shout when the boat appears. I didn't say anything to Mama when I left her on the beach still wrapped in the American blanket. No one came with me. I'm the lookout, my eyes are as sure and as sharp as those of the Indians in Gustave Aymard's novels. How I would love my father to be with me right now! Thinking of him, imagining him sitting next to me on the rocks, searching the sparkling sea, makes my heart beat faster and fills me with a sort of dizziness that blurs my vision. Hunger, tiredness might have a little something to do with it too. I haven't slept in so long, haven't really eaten! I feel like I'm going to fall over headfirst into the dizzying black sea. I remember that's exactly how I used to watch the mountain shrouded in clouds where my father should have appeared. Every day in Festiona, I left the room in the boarding house and I went all the way to the top of the village from where I could see the whole valley and the whole mountain, the path coming out, and I looked and looked, so long, so hard, that I felt as if my eyes would bore a hole into the rocky cliff.

But I can't let myself go. I'm the lookout. The others are sitting on the beach waiting in the bend of Alon Bay. When I left this morning Mama pressed my hand in hers without saying a word. The sun had come up and given her new strength. She smiled.

I want to see the Italian boat. I want it to come. The sea is immense, ablaze with light. The high wind rips the foam from the crests of the waves and throws it backward. The powerful rollers are coming from the other side of the world, dashing onto the white rocks, crowding against one another as they funnel into the narrow inlet of Alon Harbor. The blue water eddies inside the bay, sinking into whirlpools. Then it fans out on the shore.

The dead tree trunk is beside me. It's white and smooth as a bone. I'm very fond of that tree. I feel as though I've always known it. It's magic—thanks to it, nothing will happen to us. Insects scurry up the sea-worn trunk, through its roots. Sharpened by the hot sun, the pungent smell of pines drifts over on the wind. The wind keeps blowing, the sea is swirling, I think we're at the end of the earth, at the very limit, at the place where you can't turn back anymore, I think we're all going to die.

Dark cities, trains, fear, war, that's all behind us. Last night when we walked through the hills in the rain guided by the flashlight, we were making our way through the first door. That's why everything was so hard, so tiring. The forest of giant pines at the back of Alon Bay, the sound of the branches cracking in the wind, the cold wind, the rain, and then the tumbled-down wall against which we all huddled like animals gone astray in a tempest.

I open my eyes, the sea and the light burn down into the very center of my body, but it feels good. I breathe in, I'm free. Already the wind, the waves, are whisking me away. The journey has begun.

I spent the whole day wandering around through the rocks on the headland. The sea always at my side, the line of the horizon in my mind. The wind is still blowing, whipping through the bushes, bowing the trunks of the trees. In the rocky recesses, there is holly, sarsaparilla. Near the sea some heather grows with small pink flowers stamped with black centers. The smells, the light, the wind give you a giddy feeling. The sea is churning.

On the beach in Alon Harbor, the emigrants are sitting next to one another eating. For a minute, I sit down next to Mama, without taking my eyes from the line that separates the sky from the sea between the two rocky points. My eyes are burning, my face is on fire. The taste of salt is on my lips. I hurriedly eat the provisions that Mama took from her suitcase, a slice of white bread, a piece of cheese, an apple. I drink a lot of lemonade straight from the bottle. Then I go back to the rocks, to the lookout point, near the dead tree.

The sea is turbulent, ruffed with foam. It changes color constantly. When the clouds stretch over the sky again, it becomes gray, dark, violet, porphyry in fusion.

Now I'm cold. I curl up in the rock shelter. What are the others doing? Are they still waiting? If we lose faith, maybe the boat will turn around, stop struggling against the wind, head back to Italy. My heart is pounding hard and fast, my throat is dry because I know that our life is on the line at this very moment, that the *Sette Fratelli* isn't just any ship. It holds our destiny.

The Shepherd has come to see me in my hideout. It's already evening. Through a hole in the clouds, the sun shoots a harsh beam of light—purplish, as though it were mixed with ash. The Shepherd walks up to me, sits down on the tree trunk, talks to me. I don't listen to what he says at first, I'm too tired to chat. My eyes are burning, water is running from my eyes and nose. The Shepherd thinks I'm crying in discouragement, he sits next to me, puts his arm around my shoulders. It's the first time he's ever done that, I can feel the warmth of his body, see the light making the hairs of his beard shine strangely. I think of Tristan, the smell of his body wet from the river. It's a very old memory, from another life. It's as light as the shiver that is running over my skin. The Shepherd is talking, telling the story of his life, his mother and father taken to Drancy by the Germans, never to return. He says his name out loud, talks about what he will do in Jerusalem, what he would like to study—in America maybe—to become a doctor. He takes my hand and together we walk down to the harbor, down to the stone hut where the people are waiting. When I sit down again next to Mama, it's almost dark.

Little by little, the storm has returned. The clouds have hidden the stars. It's cold, rain is coming down in buckets.

We're wrapped in Uncle Simon Ruben's blanket, our backs against the crumbling wall. The giant pines have started creaking again. I feel a void whirling inside of me, I collapse. How will the boat be able to find us, now that there's no longer a lookout?

The Shepherd awakens me. He's leaning over me, he touches my shoulder, says something, and I must look so drowsy that he makes me get to my feet. Mama is standing too. The Shepherd points out a distant shape advancing on the sea, just in front of the inlet to Alon Harbor, barely visible in the gray light of dawn. It's the *Sette Fratelli*.

No one shouts, no one says anything. One after the other, men, women, children stand up on the beach, still wrapped in their blankets and coats, and gaze out to sea. The ship slowly enters the bay, its sails snapping in the wind. It veers, rolling on the waves that are hitting it broadside.

Just then, the clouds rip open. The sky shines between them and the dawn suddenly illuminates Alon Bay, its white rocks, glitters on the thick needles of the pines. There are sparkles out on the sea. The sails of the ship seem immense, white, almost unreal.

It's so beautiful we all have goosebumps. Mama has knelt down in the sand on the beach and other women do the same, then some men. I too am kneeling in the wet sand and we watch the ship anchor in the middle of the bay. We just watch. We can't speak anymore, can't think, can't anything. On the beach all the women are kneeling. They're praying, or weeping, I can hear their droning voices in the gusts of wind. Behind them, the old Jewish men have remained standing, dressed in their heavy black coats, some leaning on their umbrellas as if they were staffs. They are looking out to sea, their lips are moving too as if they were praying.

For the first time in my life I too am praying. It's within me, I can feel it, deep down inside, in spite of myself. It's in my eyes, in my heart, as if I were outside of my body and could see out beyond the horizon, beyond the sea. And everything I see right now has meaning, it's sweeping me along, casting me into the wind that blows over the sea. I have never felt that before: everything I've lived through, all the weariness, the long march through the mountains, then the horrible years spent in Rue des Gravilliers, the years I didn't even dare go out in the courtyard to see the sky, oppressive ugly years, and tedious—like a long illness, everything is being wiped away here in the glowing light of Alon Bay, with the *Sette Fratelli* drifting in slow circles around its anchor and the large white sails hanging slack and whipping in the wind.

We are all perfectly still, kneeling or standing on the beach, still wrapped in our blankets, numb with cold and sleepiness. We no longer have a past. We are brand new, as if we had just been born, as if we had slept a thousand years— here, on this beach. I say that out loud, the thought came to me in such a powerful flash that my heart is beating so hard I think it will burst. Mama is crying silently, from fatigue, maybe, or from happiness, I feel her body against mine slumping forward, as if she'd been beaten. Maybe she's crying because my father never came down the path where we were waiting for him. She hadn't cried then, even when she realized he would never come. And now there is the emptiness, the emptiness in the form of a boat, sitting still in the middle of the bay, and it's more than she can bear.

Is it a real boat, with men aboard? We look upon it with as much fear as longing, afraid that at any minute it will lift anchor and sail out to sea on the wind, abandoning us on this deserted beach.

So the children start running over the sandy beach,

they've forgotten about being tired, hungry, and cold. They run out to the rocky point waving their arms, shouting, "Hey! Heyo!" Their shrill voices pull me from my daydream.

It really is the *Sette Fratelli*, the ship we've been waiting for, the ship that will take us across the sea, all the way to Jerusalem. Now I remember why I so liked the boat's name, the first time Simon Ruben said it, the "seven brothers". One day, my father and I talked about Jacob's children, who are scattered all over the world. I don't remember all of their names but I loved two of the names because they were full of mystery. One was called Benjamin, the voracious wolf. The other was Zabulon, the sailor. I thought about how he'd disappeared with his ship in a storm one day and the sea had taken him off to another land. There was also Nephtali, the doe, and I fancied that my mother must resemble him because her eyes were so black and so gentle (and I as well, with my elongated eyes, always on the lookout). So maybe it was Zabulon who was coming back today on his ship to take us to the shores of our ancestors, after having roamed the seas for so very many centuries. The Shepherd is next to me, he takes my hand for a minute, without saying anything. His eyes are bright, his throat must be so tight with emotion that he can't talk. But as for me, I suddenly break away, and without waiting another instant, I start running over the beach with the children, and shouting, and waving my arms. The cold wind makes tears run from my eyes, tousles my hair. I know very well that Mama won't approve, but too bad! I have to run, I can't sit still anymore. I too must shout. So I shout whatever comes to mind, I wave my arms and shout to the ship, "Heyo! Zabulon!" The children get the idea too and they shout along with me, "Zabulon! Zabulon! Heyo, Zabulon!" in their shrill voices that sound like the cries of angry birds.

The miracle takes place: a rowboat with two crewmen aboard breaks away from the *Sette Fratelli*. It slips over the calm waters of the harbor and reaches the beach, greeted by the shouts of the children. One of the sailors jumps out. The children fall quiet, a little intimidated. The sailor looks at us for a minute, the women still kneeling, the old Jewish men in black coats, with their umbrellas. He has a red face, red hair matted with salt. The seven brothers are not the children of Jacob.

The storm rises again when we are all in the belly of the ship. From the hatches, I watch the sky changing, the clouds closing back up. The gray sails (seen close up they don't look so white) flap in the wind. They stretch taut, quivering, then fall slack again with sharp snapping sounds as if they were going to rip apart. Despite the engine chugging away in the hold, the *Sette Fratelli* is barely creeping along, it is leaning to one side, leaning so low that everyone has to cling to the frame of the hold to keep from tumbling around. I lie down next to Mama on the planking, my feet jammed up against the suitcases. Most of the passengers are already seasick. In the dim light of the hold, I see their shapes stretched out on the floor, their wan faces. The Shepherd must be sick too because he's disappeared. Those who can are leaning over toward the bottom of the hold, over the water, and are vomiting. Some children are crying in strangely feeble and high-pitched voices that mingle in with the creaking of the hull and the whistling of the wind. There is the sound of voices too, murmurs, entreaties, complaints. I think everyone regrets having been trapped on this boat, this tiny nutshell tossing about on the sea. Mama isn't complaining. When I look at her, she smiles faintly but her face is dirt-colored. She tries to speak, she says, "Star, little star," just like my father used to. But the next minute I have to help her crawl over to the waterway. Then she stretches out afterward and she is cold all over. I press her hand very tightly in mine, the way she used to do when I was sick...Up on the deck, the crewmen are dashing back and forth barefoot in the storm, they're shouting and cursing in Italian, grappling and thrashing about as if curbing a mad horse.

The engine stopped, but I didn't notice it right away. The boat is pitching and rolling so much it's terrifying, and all of a sudden it strikes me that we're going to capsize. I can't stand being shut in with all of this happening. Despite it being strictly forbidden, despite the gale winds and the driving rain, I push open the hatch and stick my head out.

In the dim light of the storm, I see the sea rush toward the boat, explode in a deluge of white spume. The wind has become an invisible monster, it pounds against the sails, jerks at them, leans against the two masts and tips the boat sideways. The wind whirls, it smothers me, forces tears from my eyes. I try to resist so I can watch the sea, so beautiful, so terrifying. One of the sailors motions for me to go back down into the hold. He's a young boy with very black hair, he's the one who helped us get settled in the hold when we boarded. He speaks French. He makes his way toward me, clinging to the rail. He shouts, "Go back down! Go back down! It's dangerous!" I shake my head no, signal to him that I don't want to, that I'll be sick down below, that I'd rather stay on deck. I tell him we're probably going to die and that I want to meet death face to face. He stares at me, "Are you crazy? Get down below or I'll tell the captain." I scream, against the wind, against the deafening roar of the sea, "Leave me alone! We're all going to die! I don't want to go down there!" The young boy points to a dark patch on the sea out in front of the ship. An island. "We're going over there! We're going to wait out the storm! We're not going to die! Now get down below!" The island is straight ahead, less then two hundred meters from us. Already, it is protecting the ship, the wind has stopped pushing against the masts. Water floods over the deck, gushes down the planking, streams from the sails hanging from the yards. Suddenly everything is silent, with the crashing of the sea still echoing in our eardrums. "Then it's true, we're not going to die?" I say that in such a way it makes the young sailor burst out laughing. He pushes me politely toward the hatch just as the other crewmen appear, haggard. Overhead the sky is ablaze. "What's the name of this island? Are we already in Italy?" The young boy simply says, "It's Port-Cros Island, in France, Mademoiselle. This is Port-Man Bay." So I go back down into the belly of the ship. There is a stale smell, I can sense the fear, the anxiety. Groping in the shadows, I look for Mama's body. "It's over now. We've reached Port-Man. It's our first stopover." I say that as if we were on a cruise. I'm exhausted. Now I lay down on the wooden planking too. Mama is next to me, she puts her hand on my forehead. I close my eyes.

We've been in the bay of Port-Man for a day and a night now, not doing anything. The ship is drifting slowly around on its moorings, first in one direction, then in the other. The hold echoes with the sound of tools repairing the engine. Even though the captain (a fat bald man who looks like anything but a seaman) has forbidden it, I go up on deck all the time with the other children. I'm thin, and with my short hair, I believe I can pass for a boy. We go to the poop, amidst the rigging. I sit down and gaze at the black shore of the island under the stormy skies. The coast is so close I'd have no trouble swimming that far. In Port-Man Bay the water is

148

smooth and clear, despite the rainy sky and gusting winds.

The young Italian sailor comes over and sits down beside me. Sometimes he talks to me in Italian, other times in French, or in English mixed with a few Italian words. He tells me his name is Silvio. He offers me an American cigarette. I try smoking it, but it's harsh and sweet and it makes my head spin. Then he takes a bar of chocolate out of his jacket pocket and breaks off a row of squares for me. The chocolate is sweet and bitter at the same time, I don't believe I've ever eaten anything like that before. The boy goes through all of these motions gravely, without smiling, watching the ladder to the bridge where the captain might appear. "Why don't you let people come up on deck?" I ask slowly, staring at him. "It's very uncomfortable down there, it's stuffy and dark. It's inhuman." Silvio seems to think it over. He says, "The captain doesn't like it. He doesn't want anyone to see that there are passengers on board. It's forbidden." I say, "But we're not doing anything wrong. We're going to our country." He puffs nervously on his cigarette. He looks over toward the Island, the dark forest, and the small white beach. He says, "If the customs officers come, they'll stop the ship. We won't be able to leave." He throws his cigarette into the water and gets up, "Now you have to go back down into the hold." I call the other children and we go back inside the boat. In the hold it is hot and dark. There is a din of voices. Mama squeezes my arm, her eyes are glassy. "What were you doing? Whom were you talking to?" The men are talking loudly at the other end of the hold. There is anger or fear in their voices. Mama murmurs, "They say we aren't going any farther, that we've been tricked, that they're going to make us get out here."

We watch the light coming from the hatch all day long, a gray painful light. We can see the clouds going by, shrouds veiling the sky, as if night were falling. Gradually the men fall silent. Up on deck the crewmen stop working. We hear the rain pattering on the hull. I dream that we are far out at sea, in the middle of the Atlantic, and that the two of us are sailing to Canada. Long ago in Saint-Martin, that was where she wanted to go. I remember her talking about Canada in winter—in the little room where I waited wide-eyed in the dark—the snow, the forests, the wooden houses on the banks of endless rivers, the flight of wild geese. That's what I'd like to hear about now. "Tell me about Canada." Mama leans toward me, kisses me. But she doesn't say anything. Maybe she's too tired to think about a country that doesn't exist. Maybe she's forgotten.

During the night the storm starts up again. The waves must be washing over the rocky headland that shields Port-Man, they're crashing against the ship, making it sway and creak and everyone wakes up. We're holding onto the frame to keep from being tossed against the hull. The bundles, the suitcases, other invisible objects slide around and knock against the walls of the ship. We can't hear a single voice, not a human sound on deck, and soon the rumor spreads: the crew has abandoned us, we're alone aboard the ship. Before fear can take root, the men light a storm lantern. Everyone gathers around the lamp, the men on one side, the women and children on the other. I see the faces lit up fantastically, eyes shining. One of the men comes from Poland, his name is Reb Joel. He's tall and thin with beautiful hair and a black beard. Sitting in front of the lamp, he lays a small black box tied with a thong down next to him. He recites strange words in that language I don't understand. He slowly pronounces the words that resound—the rough, long, mellow words—and I recall the voices chanting long ago in the temple in the house in Saint-Martin. No words have ever had that effect on me, like something tingling in my throat, like a memory. "What is he saying?" I ask Mama in a whisper. The men and women are rocking slowly in unison with the movement of the ship in the storm, and Mama is rocking too, watching the flame of the lamp on the floor. "Listen, it's our language now." She says that and I look at her face. The rabbi's words are powerful, they ward off the fear of death. On the planking, the little black leather box shines strangely, as if it encloses some incomprehensible force. The men's and the women's voices join Joel's words and I try to read their lips to understand. What are they saying? I'd like to ask Jacques Berger, but I don't dare go and sit next to him, I might break the spell, and fear would settle back down upon us. They are words that go with the movement of the sea, words that rumble and roll, gentle and powerful words, words of hope and of death, words that are bigger than the world, more powerful than death. When the ship arrived in Alon Bay at dawn, I learned what prayer was. Now I listen to the words of the prayer, the language carries me along on its tide. Reb Joel's words echo through the boat for me as well. I'm not an outsider, I'm not a foreigner. The words sweep me along, take me off to another world, to another life. Now I know, I understand. Joel's words will take us there, all the way to Jerusalem. Even if there is a storm, even if we have been abandoned, we'll reach Jerusalem with the words of the prayer.

The children have gone back to sleep, lying close to their mothers. Grave or melodious voices echo the words of Joel, follow the rhythm of the waves. Perhaps they are commanding the wind, the rain, the night. The flame of the lamp wavers, makes eyes shine. Next to Reb Joel, the little black box gleams oddly, as if the words were coming from it.

I lie back down on the floor. I'm not afraid anymore. Mama's hand runs through my hair, just like in the old days, I hear her voice repeating the words in my ear, the rough mellow words of the prayer. It lulls me off to sleep. Now I'm back in my memories, the oldest memories on earth.

As it was sailing out of Port-Man this morning at dawn, customs officers boarded the *Sette Fratelli*. The sea was calm, nice and smooth after the storm. The ship's engine had been repaired and it was headed out to sea in full sail. I was on deck with several children, watching the deep sea opening out before us. And suddenly, before anyone had time to realize what was happening, the patrol boat appeared. It's powerful stem cut through the sea, it came up alongside of us. For a second, the captain pretended he didn't understand and the *Sette Fratelli*, leaning into the wind, continued cresting the waves as it made its way out to sea. Then the customs officers shouted something from the loud speaker. It was unequivocal.

I watched the patrol boat approach. My heart started beating wildly, I couldn't take my eyes off the men in uniform. The captain gave some orders and the Italian crew broke sail and stopped the engine. Our ship began to drift. Then, following orders, we turned our back on the open sea and headed toward the coast. The still-dark shoreline lies before us. We're not sailing for Jerusalem anymore. The words of the prayer are no longer bearing us along. We're heading for the large port of Toulon where we'll be put in prison.

In the belly of the ship no one is saying anything. The men are sitting in the same place as they were yesterday, like so many ghosts. The children are still sleeping for the most part, their heads lying on their mother's laps. The others have come down from the deck, hair rumpled from the wind. In a corner of the hold near the luggage, the storm lamp has gone dark.

They've shut us up in this large empty room, at the very end of the shipyards in the Arsenal, probably because they couldn't put us in cells with the ordinary prisoners. They gave us cots, blankets. They took all of our papers, money, and anything that could serve as a weapon, even the women's knitting needles and the men's little scissors for trimming their beards. Through the tall barred windows we can see a barren lot covered with cracked cement where tufts of grass wave in the wind. At the end of the lot, there is a high stone wall. If it weren't for that wall, we could see the Mediterranean and dream that we would soon be on our way. Two days after they locked us up in the Arsenal, I wanted so badly to get a glimpse of the sea that I worked out a plan to escape. I didn't tell anyone about it because Mama would be worried and then I wouldn't have had the heart to make a break for it. At lunchtime, three marines enter our room through the door at the far end. Two distribute the rations of soup while the third one stands watch leaning on his rifle. I was able to get near the door without raising any suspicions. When one of the marines handed me the dish full of soup, I dropped it on his feet and escaped, running down the corridor, paying no attention to the shouts behind me. I ran like that, with all my might and I was so fast and so light on my feet that no one could have caught me. At the end of the corridor was the door that opens onto the lot. I ran out into the open air without stopping. I hadn't seen the sunshine in so long it made my head swim and I could feel my heart

pounding in my neck, in my ears. The sky was bright blue—
not a cloud—everything was shining in the cold air. I ran all
the way to the high stone wall looking for a way out. The
cold air was stinging my throat and my nose, making my
eyes water. I stopped for an instant to look over my shoulder.
But it seemed as if no one was following me. The lot was
empty, the high walls shone. It was mealtime and all the
marines must have been in the mess hall. I ran along the wall
without stopping. Suddenly, right in front of me, there was
the huge gate open on both sides and the avenue that led out
to the sea. I went through the gate as quick as an arrow, not
knowing whether there was a guard in the sentry box. I ran
without stopping to catch my breath down to the end of the
avenue where there is a fort and some rocks looking out over
the sea. Now I'm in the brush, hands and legs full of
scratches, jumping from rock to rock. I haven't forgotten
how to do it since Saint-Martin, when I used to go up the
torrent. In a split second I spot the place I'll jump to, the line
of approach I can take, the holes to avoid. Afterward the
rocks get steeper, I have to slow down. I cling to the brush,
climb to the very bottom of the crevices.

When I reach the point just above the sea, the wind is
blowing so hard that I can barely breathe. The wind pushes
me against the rocks, whistles through the brush. I stop in a
hollow in the rocks, and the sea is directly underneath of
me. It's as beautiful as it was in Alon Harbor, a vast fiery
stretch, smooth and hard, with the dark masses of the capes
and peninsulas in the distance. The wind whirls around at
the entrance to my hiding place, it growls and whines like an
animal. Down below, the foam leaps against the rocks,
scatters in the wind. There is nothing here but the wind and
the sea. Never have I felt so free. It makes your head spin, it
makes you shudder. Then I look out to the line of the horizon

as if our ship would appear on the blazing path that the sun is making on the sea. My thoughts carry me to the other side of the world, I've traversed the wind and gone over the sea, I have left behind the black piles of capes and islands where humans dwell, where they imprisoned us. Like a bird, I skim out on the wind over the sea in the sunlight and the salt spray, I've abolished time and distance, I've reached the other side, the place where land and men are free, where everything is truly new. I'd never thought of that before. It's inebriating, because right now I'm not thinking of Simon Ruben anymore, or of Jacques Berger, or even of my mother, I'm no longer thinking of my father who disappeared in the tall grasses up above Berthemont, I'm not thinking of the boat anymore, or of the marines who are looking for me. Only— is anyone really looking for me?

Mightn't I have disappeared forever, suspended in my rocky hiding place, my bird's lair, up over the waves with my eyes fixed on the sea? My heart is beating slowly, I don't feel afraid anymore, I don't feel hungry, or thirsty, I don't feel the weight of the future anymore. I'm free, the freedom of the wind, of light, is now within me. It's the first time.

I stay in my hiding place all day, watching the sun sinking slowly toward the sea. No one comes. I've wanted to be really alone for so long now, without anyone talking next to me. I think of the mountains, the huge valley, the window of ice when I was watching for my father to return. It's the image that I've carried with me wherever I went when I needed to be alone. It's the image that came to me when I was shut up in the dark room on Rue de Gravilliers, it would appear on the wallpaper. I still remember. My father walking through the grass in front of me, and the stone huts where Mama and I came up. The silence, only the sound of the wind in the grass. Their laughter while they were kissing. Just like here, the silence, the wind whistling in the brush, the cloudless sky, and the far end of the vast misty valley and the cones of the peaks sticking up like islands. I kept it all with me, in my head the whole time—in Simon Ruben's garage, in the apartment on Rue des Gravilliers where we never went out, even when Simon Ruben said the Germans wouldn't come back, they would never come back. The mountain was in my head then, the grassy slope that seemed to rise all the way up to the sky, and the valley lost in mist, the thin trails of smoke that drifted up from the villages in the clear air at twilight.

That's what I want to remember, not the horrid sounds, the shots. I am walking along as if in a dream and Mama squeezes my arm. She shouts, "Come on honey, come on, run! Run!" And she drags me by the arm down toward the bottom of the mountain as fast as she can, through the grass that cuts my lips, and I run out in front of her in spite of my trembling knees, with that strange voice of hers in my ears that cracks when she screams, "Run! Run!"

Here in my hiding place, for the first time it seems as though I might never again hear those sounds, those words, as though I'll never see those dream images again, because the wind, the sun, and the sea are inside of me and have washed it all away.

I stay in my hiding place amidst the rocks until the sun almost reaches the horizon and is touching the line of trees on the peninsula across the harbor.

Then I suddenly feel the cold. It settles in with the night. Maybe it's because I'm hungry and thirsty too, because I'm so very weary. I feel as though I haven't stopped walking and running ever since the day we came down from the mountain through the tall grasses that cut my lips and my legs and since that day my heart hasn't stopped beating so hard and so fast, pounding in my chest like a frightened animal. Even in the dark apartment on Rue de Gravilliers, I never stopped walking and running, I never caught my breath. The doctor who came to see me was named Rose, I haven't forgotten his name even though I only saw him once, because I heard Mama and Uncle Simon Ruben saying that extraordinary name, "Mr. Rose said...Mr. Rose went...Mr. Rose thinks..." When he came, when he walked into our shabby apartment, I thought everything would brighten up, start shining. Yet I wasn't really disappointed when I saw that Mr. Rose was a pudgy little bald man, with thick nearsighted glasses. He examined me through my clothing, he felt my neck and my arms and he said I had asthma, that I was too thin. He gave us some eucalyptus tablets for my asthma; he told Mama that I needed to eat meat. Meat! Did he have any idea that all we ate were overripe vegetables that Mama found discarded at the market, and sometimes only peelings? But from then on I had broth made with chicken necks and feet that Mama bought twice a week. After that, I never saw Mr. Rose again.

I think about all of that when night falls in the harbor because it seems like here in this hiding place, I've stopped walking and running for the first time. My heart has finally started beating calmly in my chest, I can breathe with no difficulty, without making my lungs wheeze.

The dogs awakened me before daybreak. The marines found me in my cave, they brought me back to the Arsenal. When I walked into the large room, Mama got up from her bed, she walked over to me, kissed me. She didn't say anything. I couldn't say anything to her either, not why, not that I was sorry. I knew I would never have another day and night like that again. It was still inside of me along with the sea, the wind, the sky. Now they could put me in prison forever.

No one said anything. But the people who'd ignored me up to then now spoke to me in a kind way. The Shepherd came over to sit down beside me, he spoke to me in a polite way that seemed odd. It seemed like years had passed over there in my hiding place in the rocks. We sat there on the floor talking all day long by the tall windows. Reb Joel came over to join us too, he talked about Jerusalem, about the history of our people. I liked it most when he talked about the religion.

Neither my father nor my mother had ever spoken to me about religion. Uncle Simon Ruben talked about the religion sometimes, about ceremonies, holidays, marriages. But for him they were ordinary things, not frightening, not mysterious, just routine. And if I asked him a question about religion, he got angry. He knitted his brow, looking at me askance, and Mama just stood still, as if she felt guilty. It's because my father wasn't a believer, he was a communist, according to what people say. So Uncle Simon Ruben didn't dare send for the Rabbi, and he spoke angrily about the religion.

But when the Shepherd spoke of religion with Reb Joel, he really turned into another person. I loved listening to them and I shot furtive glances in their direction, the Shepherd with his golden hair and beard and Joel with his very white face, his black hair, his slim body. His eyes were a very pale green, like Mario's, I thought he was the one who was truly the shepherd.

It was odd, talking about the religion like that in this large room where we were prisoners. The Shepherd and Joel talked in low voices to avoid disturbing the others, and it was as if we were still prisoners in Egypt, as if we were soon going to leave, and the terrifying voice would echo in the heavens and in the mountains and the light would shine in the desert.

I think I asked stupid questions, because I didn't know anything. My father had never talked to me about all of that. I asked why G__ is ineffable, why he is invisible and hidden, since he created everything on earth. Reb Joel shook his head, saying, "He isn't invisible, he isn't hidden. It is we who are invisible and hidden, it is we who are in the darkness." He said that often, "the darkness". He said that religion is the light, the only light, and that the lives of human beings, their acts, all the grand and magnificent things they build are nothing but darkness. He said, "He who created everything is our father, we are his offspring. Eretz Israel is our birthplace, the place where the first light shone, where the first shades of darkness began."

We were sitting by the window and I was staring at the deep blue sky. "We'll never get to Jerusalem." I said that because I was tired of thinking about it. I wanted to go back to my hiding place in the rocks over the sea. "Maybe Jerusalem doesn't even exist?" The Shepherd shot a furious glance at me. His gentle face was tense with anger. "Why do you say that?" He spoke slowly, but his eyes were bright with impatience. I said, "Maybe it exists, but we'll never get there. The police won't let us leave. We'll have to go back to Paris." The Shepherd said, "Even if they prevent us from leaving today, we'll go tomorrow. And if they prevent us from taking the boat, we'll go on foot, even if we have to walk for a year." He wasn't saying that because he wanted to get away, but because he too wanted to see the land where the religion began, where the first book was written. It made my heart speed up to see the light in his eye. Since he wanted so badly to go to Jerusalem, maybe we really would get there one day.

The days went by like that, long-drawn-out days that we forgot. People said they were going to take us to court and we'd be sent back to Paris. When I saw Mama dejected and sad, sitting on her bed staring at the floor, huddled up in her blanket because of the chill, it broke my heart. I said to her, "Don't be sad, sweet little Mama, you'll see, we'll get out. I have a plan. If they try and put us on a train for Paris, I have a plan, we'll make a getaway." It wasn't true, I didn't have a plan, and ever since my escape, the marines had been keeping a sharp eye on me. "And where would we go? They'd stop us again wherever we went." I squeezed her hands very hard. "You'll see, we'll follow the coast, we'll go to Nice, find Uncle Simon's brother. After that, we'll go to Italy, to Greece, and finally we'll reach Jerusalem." I didn't have the slightest idea which countries you had to cross to get to Eretz Israel, but the Shepherd had mentioned Italy and Greece. Mama was smiling a little. "Dear child! And where would we get the money for the journey?" I said, "Money? That's no problem, we'll work along the way. You'll see, with the two of us, we won't need anyone's help." After talking about it so much, I ended up believing it. If we couldn't find work, I'd sing in the streets and in the courtyards, with my face painted black and I'd wear white gloves like the Minstrels in the streets of London, or else I'd learn how to walk a tightrope and I'd wear a suit covered with sequins and the passersby would throw coins into an old hat and Mama would always be there to keep an eye out because the world is full of bad people. I even pictured the Shepherd walking with us in Italy, and Reb Joel too, with his black clothing and his prayer box. He'd speak to people about the religion, he'd speak of Jerusalem. And people would sit down around him to listen, and they'd give us food and a little money, especially the women and the young girls, because of the Shepherd and his beautiful golden hair.

I had to work out a plan to save us. I spent my nights going over everything in my mind. I thought of every possible trick to escape the marines, the police. Maybe we could throw ourselves into the sea and swim through the waves with some sort of floating devices or on a raft till we got past the Italian border. But Mama didn't know how to swim and I wasn't sure whether the Shepherd did either, or whether Reb Joel would want to jump into the water with his fine black suit and his book.

Come to think of it, he wouldn't want to abandon his family here, leave his people in the hands of enemies who were holding us prisoner. We all had to get away, the old people, the women, the children, everyone who was imprisoned, because they deserved to go to Jerusalem too. Besides, Moses himself wouldn't have abandoned the others to run off to Eretz Israel by himself. That's really what was so difficult.

What I liked most about the large room where we were prisoners were the long afternoons, after the noon meal, when the sun shone on the high windows and burned off some of the cold dampness. The women settled down in the rectangles of light outlined on the gray stone floor, spreading blankets out as if they were carpets, and they chatted while the children played next to them. Their conversations made a strange humming sound like a beehive. The men stayed over at one end of the room, they talked in low voices, smoking and drinking coffee, sitting on the cots, and the sound of their voices made a deeper buzzing, punctuated by exclamations, bursts of laughter.

That's when I liked to listen to the stories that Reb Joel told. He came and sat down with the children on the ground, in the light from one of the windows, and his black hair and clothing shone like silk. At first Joel was only talking to the Shepherd and me, without raising his voice so as not to disturb the others. He opened his black book and read slowly, first in the language that was so beautiful, so rough and mellow, that I'd heard in the temple in Saint-Martin. Then he spoke in French, slowly, searching for words, and sometimes the Shepherd helped him because he didn't speak the language well. Afterwards, Mama came over too and other children, foreign girls and boys who didn't speak our language but who stayed anyway, listening. There was also a young girl whose name was Judith, dressed in rags, always with a flowered scarf on her head, like a peasant. We waited for Reb Joel to start talking and when he began, it was like an inner voice that was saying what we were hearing. He spoke of the law and of religion as if they were the simplest things in the world. In basic terms, he explained what the soul was—comparing it to our shadows—and justice—comparing it to the sunlight, the beauty of children. Then he picked up the Book of the Beginning, the one Uncle Simon Ruben had given Mama before our departure, and he explained what was written there. Nothing was better than the story of the beginning of the world. First he pronounced the words in the divine language, slowly, making each word and each syllable resound, and sometimes we thought we understood just from hearing the words of that language echoing out in the silence of our prison. Because then, everyone stopped the chattering and discussions and even the old men listened, sitting on their cots. They were the words of G__, the words he'd suspended in space before creating the world. Joel pronounced the name slowly in a breath, like this, "Elohim, Elohim, he alone amongst the others, the greatest of all beings, he who is himself and from himself, he who can create..." He read of the first days, in that large room with the rectangles from the windows slowly pivoting on the floor.

"*Thus, in the beginning Elohim created the person heaven, the person earth.*"

I said, "Persons? The heaven and the earth were persons?"

"Yes, persons, the first creatures, in the image of Elohim." He read on, "*For the earth was being formed and darkness was in the void.*" He said, "Elohim used the void, the void is the cement of the earth, of existence."

He resumed, "*And the spirit of the Almighty, Elohim, moved and cast seed over the face of the waters.*" He said, "The spirit, the breath, over the cold water."

He spoke of the sun, of the moon, they were legends. We no longer thought about the darkness in the room, about time making the windows revolve on the floor.

It was wonderful. All of us, Judith, even the younger children understood immediately what his words meant.

He went on reading, "*He, the Almighty, said let there be light. And there was light. He, the Almighty, saw that it was good. He, the Almighty, divided the light from the darkness.*" Joel said, "The light was that which we could know, and the darkness was the cement of the earth. And so, both were given—divided for eternity, and impossible to keep united. On one side, intelligence, on the other, the world..."

"*And, he, the Almighty, called the light IOM, and the darkness he called LAYLA.*" We listened to those names, the most beautiful names we had ever heard. "IOM was like the sea, limitless, filling everything, giving everything. LAYLA was empty, the cement of the earth." I listened to the words of that holy language, echoing out in the prison. "*And it was the end of the day in the west and the dawn in the east. IOM EHED.*"

When Joel said that, Day One, it was like a tingling shiver: the first day, the birth of the world.

"*And he, the Almighty, said let there be a firmament in the midst of the waters. And the Almighty made the firmament dividing the waters below from the waters above. And it was so.*"

"What are the waters below?" I asked. Joel looked at me without answering. Finally he said, "Wait, the book does not speak for no reason. Listen to the rest, "*and he, the Almighty called the firmament SHAMAÏN, the heavens, the waters above, and the night came in the west, the dawn in the east. IOM SHENI.*" He waited a brief instant, then began again, "*And he, the Almighty, said let the waters under the heaven be gathered together unto one place, and let the dry land appear. And it was so.*"

"Why was the water there in the beginning?"

"It was the movement, before immobility, the first movement of life."

I thought about the sea that we must cross. The dry land would begin on the other side. Joel read some more, then he translated, *"And he, the Almighty, called the dry land, ERETZ, and the gathering together of the water he called IAMMIM, endless water, the sea. And the Almighty saw that it was good."*

"What was Eretz like?" I tried to imagine the first lands that emerged from the sea, like the dark islands that I'd seen in the storm from the deck of the *Sette Fratelli.*

"How do you picture it?" Joel turned toward me, then toward the Shepherd, and toward each one of us. And since no one said anything, "You see, it can't be said in words."

He continued, *"He, the Almighty, said let the earth bring forth green grass, herb-yielding seed after its kind to sow upon the earth. And it was so."*

He stopped. "Have you thought about that seed?"

Then he said, "The movement that unites heat and cold, that unites intelligence and the world. The day, the night, the seeds, the water...Everything existed already..."

He read the words of the book, *"And the earth brought forth strong grass, herb-yielding seed after his kind, each herb with its fruit whose seed was in itself, after his kind, and the Almighty saw that it was good. And the evening was in the west and the morning in the east. IOM SHELISHI."*

The voice moves deep within me, it touches my heart, my stomach, it is in my throat and in my eyes. It troubles me so that I move a little off to one side and hide my face in Mama's shawl. Each word is entering me and breaking something. That's the way of the religion. It breaks things inside of you, things that stand in the way of that voice.

Every day, for weeks now in this prison, I've been listening to the voice of the master. Along with the other children, with the men and women, we sit down on the floor, and we listen to the teachings. Now I don't feel like escaping anymore, running off into the sunlight to go and look out upon the sea. What the book says is much more important than what is outside.

Joel read, *"And he, the One, said let there be a light in the firmament of the heaven to divide the day from the night, and lights to represent the future, to measure the passage of time, to measure the changes of living beings."*

"Is that what time was?"

But Joel looked at me without responding. He read on, *"And let them be for lights in the firmament of the heaven to give light upon the earth. And it was so."*

Then he turned to me to answer, "It wasn't time that Elohim gave. It was intelligence, the power to understand. What we call science today. Everything that made it possible for the mechanics of the world to work was in place. Science was the light from the stars..."

No one had talked to me about the stars since my father had pointed them out to me one evening, the summer that he died. The stars that stood still, the shooting stars that slid like droplets over the face of night. That's how he gave me my name, star, little star...

"And he, the One, made two great sister lights, the greater light to rule the day, and the lesser light to rule the night. And all of those named Chochabim, the stars."

Joel closed the Book of the Beginning because night was falling. Silence crept into the room like a cold chill. We stood up, one after the other, and we all went back to our own places. Mama and I went over to sit on my bed near the wall. "Now I know we'll reach Jerusalem." I said that to brighten

Mama's spirits, but also because I believed it. "When we know everything that's in the book, we'll get there." Mama smiled, "That's a good reason to read it." I would have liked to ask Mama why my father had never read the book to me, why he preferred to read me Dickens's novels. Maybe he wanted me to find it on my own, at a point when I'd really need it. Now everything he explained to me, everything they'd taught me in school up to now, became clear and true, it all became easy to understand. It had become real.

The lawyer came to see us in our prison. He arrived early this morning, with a satchel full of papers, and he stayed a good part of the day in the large room, talking with the people. He even ate with us when the marines brought the meal, boiled potatoes and meat. The old Jewish men didn't want to eat the meat because they said it wasn't good, but the women and children ate without paying any attention to them. The Shepherd said that the most important thing was staying alive, so we would have the strength to be free and go to Jerusalem. The lawyer came to talk with Mama too, and with Jacques Berger, and Judith's mother who was with us. The lawyer wasn't such a young man anymore, he wore a gray suit, his hair was well groomed and he had a little mustache. He had a very soft voice and gentle eyes, and Mama was quite pleased to be able to speak with him. He asked Mama some questions about where we'd come from, who we were, and why we'd decided to go to Jerusalem. He wrote down the names and Mama's answers in a school notebook and when he learned that my father had died in the war, because of the Germans, and that he was in the resistance, he wrote it all down carefully in his notebook. He said we couldn't stay here in this prison. He wrote down the names of Jacques Berger and Judith's mother too, and he went over all the papers carefully because they'd been turned over to him at headquarters, before he came. Then he gave each of us our papers back, our identity cards or our passports. People formed a circle around him and he shook

169

everyone's hand. The men and women crowded around him asking him questions, asking when we would be set free, if they were going to send us back to Paris. Those who came from Poland were most anxious to know, the women were all talking at once. So he asked for everyone to be quiet, and he said in a loud voice so that we could all hear, and those who didn't speak French had someone translate his words as he spoke, "My friends, have no fear, my dear friends. Everything will be taken care of, you will soon be allowed to go free. I promise you, you have nothing to fear." The voices around him said, "What about the boat? Can we get back on the boat?" A murmur ran through the crowd at the word boat, and the lawyer had to speak even more loudly, "Yes, friends, you will be able to continue your journey. The boat is ready to sail. Captain Frullo has equipped the ship with the lifeboats that were lacking, and I swear to you...I swear you will be able to resume your journey in a day or two." When the lawyer left, it was already getting dark. He shook hands with everyone again, even the little children.

And he repeated, "Don't worry, my dear friends. Everything will be all right."

We spent the following hours in a sort of exaltation. The women talked and laughed, and at night, the children refused to go to sleep. Maybe it was due to the dry wind that had been blowing for the last few days. The sky was so clear that we could even see at night. I stayed sitting by a window, wrapped in my blanket, and I watched the moon slip between the bars, sink down toward the wall at the end of the barren lot. In the large room, the men were speaking in soft voices. The old religious people were praying.

Now it seemed as if the distance that separated us from the holy city no longer existed, as if that same moon slipping across the sky shone upon Jerusalem, its houses, its olive groves, its domes and minarets. Time no longer existed either. It was the same sky as long ago when Moses waited in the house of the Pharaoh, or when Abraham dreamt about how the sun and the moon, the stars, the water, the earth, and all the animals in the world had been created. Here in the prison of the Arsenal, I knew that we were a part of that time and it made me shiver in fear and made my heart beat faster, like when I listened to the words in the book.

That night, the Shepherd came and sat beside me near the window. He couldn't sleep either. We talked in hushed voices. Gradually, the people around us went to bed and the children fell asleep. We heard the even sound of their breathing, the old men snoring. The Shepherd spoke to me of Jerusalem, the city we would soon be in. He said he would work on a farm, and when he'd saved some money, he'd go to the university, maybe in France, or in Canada. He didn't know anyone over there, he had no friends or relatives. He said that Mama and I could also work in a kibbutz. It was the first time I'd heard anyone speak of that, of the future, of work. I thought of the wheat fields in Roquebillière, and of the men moving forward working their scythes, of the children gathering the fallen ears. My heart was pounding, I felt the hot sun on my face. I was so tired, it seemed as though I'd never stopped waiting in the field up above Festiona, with my eyes on the rocky wall where I could see the end of the path to the pass through which my father had never appeared.

Then I laid my head on Jacques Berger's shoulder and he wrapped his arm around me, just like when I was keeping a lookout for the boat to come, in the rocks in Alon Harbor. I breathed in the smell of his body, the smell of his hair. I felt like going to sleep, finally closing my eyes, and when I opened them again I'd be surrounded by olive trees in the hills of Jerusalem, I'd see the light shining on the rooftops and the minarets.

Mama came over. Without a word, she took me gently by the arm and helped me to my feet, she led me over to my bed near the wall. The Shepherd understood. He stepped away, said good night in a gruff voice and went back over to his bed on the men's side. Mama put me to bed, she wrapped my blanket tightly around me so I wouldn't be cold. I was so tired, I'd never loved Mama so much, because she didn't say anything. She tucked me in with my blanket, just like when I was little, in the attic room in Nice when I used to listen to the weathervane creaking on the corrugated roofs. She kissed me near my ear, just the way I liked her to. Then she lay down herself and I listened to her breathing evenly, without hearing the breathing and snoring of the other people sleeping. I fell asleep while she kept her eyes open in the darkness, looking at me.

The *Sette Fratelli* sailed this morning. The sea is smooth, dark, swarming with seagulls. Now we're allowed to go up on deck as long as we don't get in the way of the crew. The lawyer walked us all the way to the foot of the gangway. He shook each of our hands saying, "Goodbye my friends. Good luck!" Reb Joel in his black suit was the last to board. He asked him humbly what we could do to repay him, but the lawyer shook his hand and said, "Write to me when you arrive." He remained standing on the wharf. Captain Frullo gave the order to cast off. The ship's engine began to rattle louder and we began to sail away. The lawyer was still on the wharf, buffeted by the wind, holding the schoolboy's satchel in his hand. The women and children waved their handkerchiefs and the wharf grew smaller and smaller, with the man's shape hardly visible in the dawn light.

Mama was wrapped in her blanket and shawl, she was already pale due to the rolling of the ship. She watched the coast fade into the distance, the long peninsulas open out. She went into the hold to lie down. We each found the same place we'd had at the beginning of the journey.

Once at sea, dolphins escorted our ship, leaping out in front of the stem. Then the sun came up and the dolphins went off to hide. Tonight we'll be in Italy, in La Spezia.

Standing on the bridge, Esther was looking at the deck of the boat where the passengers were gathered. The weather was marvelous. For the first time in days, the gray clouds had parted and the sun was shining brightly. The sea was a brilliant blue, magnificent. Esther never tired of looking at it.

Last night, the *Sette Fratelli* sailed past Cyprus—all lights out, engines stopped—with only the wind whipping in the sails to speed it along. In the hold, no one was sleeping except the very young children who weren't aware of the danger. Everyone knew that the island was very near, just off the port side, and that English boats were patroling. In Cyprus the English had imprisoned thousands of people— men, women, children—who'd been captured on the sea en route for Eretz Israel. The Shepherd said that if they were captured, the English would surely send them back. They would be kept in a camp and later sent by boat to France, Italy, or Germany or Poland.

Esther hadn't slept all night. The boat slipped silently over the choppy sea, pitching and rolling because of the weight of the wind in the mainsail. Captain Frullo didn't want anyone up on deck. They couldn't light a lamp or even a match for a cigarette. In the hold of the *Sette Fratelli*, it was as dark as an oven. Esther was squeezing her mother's hand very tightly, listening to the purling of the water against the hull, the snapping of the sail. It had been a very long night. It was a night in which every instant counted, like in Festiona, when the Germans were looking for the fugitives in the mountains, or like the night when the Americans had bombed Genoa. But this night was even longer because now they were nearing the end of their journey, after these twenty days at sea. Everyone had waited for so long, prayed, talked, chanted. In the darkness, the voices chanted quietly for a while in their unfamiliar language. Then they had suddenly stopped as if somewhere out at sea, in spite of the distance and the noise of the waves, the English patrols would hear them.

At one point, even though it was forbidden, someone lit a lighter to see what time it was, and the news went from one to the other in German, in Yiddish, then in French, "Midnight...It's midnight. We've passed Cyprus." How did they know that? Esther tried to imagine the island, its high mountains looming at the ship's back, like a grim monster. The passengers started talking again, some laughter rang out. There was the sound of footsteps on the deck, the hatch opened. Silvio, Esther's young Italian friend came down a few steps, "Quiet, not to make noise. The English boats are near." We heard some orders being given up on deck, then the muffled sound of the sail being lowered. With no wind, the ship straightened up, it rocked on the water, taking waves first on one side, then on the next. Where were the English? Esther felt like they were on all sides at once, circling in the sea, searching for the prey that they sensed was there in the darkness.

The ship stayed put for a long time, turning slowly in the wind, tossing on the waves. On deck, there was not another sound. Maybe the Italian crew had left? Maybe they had abandoned ship? Esther was still squeezing her mother's hand. The silence was so heavy that the young children awoke, and they began to cry, and their mothers tried to stifle their cries against their breasts.

The minutes, the seconds drew out, each beat of the heart was separated from the next with a painful wait. After a very long time, once again there was the sound of footsteps on the deck, and the voice of the captain shouted, "*Alza la vela! Alza la vela!*" The wind filled the sail again. We heard the masts creaking, and whirring sounds in the rigging. The ship was moving against the tide, leaning to one side.

Nothing could have seemed more beautiful to Esther. In the darkness, people had started talking again, first in hushed voices, then louder and louder and everyone at the same time, shouting, laughing, singing. The hatch opened up again. Silvio came down with a storm lamp. He said, "We made it through." Everyone shouted and clapped. A little bit later, the engines started up again. The rumbling of the engines seemed like such a sweet tune. Then we lay down on the floor, our heads resting against the bundles readied for our arrival. Esther fell asleep without letting go of Elizabeth's hand, listening to the engine vibrating monotonously in the planking, her eyes staring at the star-shaped flame of the storm lamp.

Before sunrise, she was up on deck. The crew was still asleep. When she opened the hatch, the wind took her breath away. She'd been cooped up in the hold so long that for a second she'd stood there teetering back and forth, not able to move. Then she walked cautiously up to the front of the boat and sat down with the triangle of the jib billowing out before her. She watched day break over the sea from there.

First there was nothing but blue darkness. The stars

wheeling, the dim glow of the galaxy. Light bloomed slowly on the horizon, straight ahead, a splash that swelled and paled the stars. For a few minutes the sky turned gray, and the sea appeared with its shining caps, and the horizon stretching over the world like a fissure. The ship was sailing steadily along, gliding smoothly over the waves with the wind pressing on its sails and the constant whirring of the engine. When the light began, Esther stared at the narrow line of the horizon without blinking, without looking away. Leaning against the rail it seemed as if she and the stem were one, as if it were she who went cutting through the sea, skimming along however she wished, like a bird soaring, she was heading straight for the horizon, trying to be the first to sight the coastline, delicate and light as a cloud, yet very real. She scanned the sea till her eyes hurt.

She remained in that position for hours. Then Silvio touched her shoulder. "Mademoiselle, please." She looked at him, puzzled. The sun was already high in the sky, the sea was ablaze. Silvio helped her walk over to the poop. "The captain won't like it...It's dangerous." He'd said "danzerous", but Esther couldn't laugh. Her face was stiff from the wind, from her scrutinizing the sea so intensely.

"Come along, we'll get you some coffee." But when Esther walked up to the dark hole of the hatchway, she didn't want to go in. She couldn't go down into the hold, smell the fear, the waiting. If she went down there, the shores of Eretz Israel wouldn't appear on the sea. She shook her head and tears rolled down her cheeks. It was the wind and the sunlight that had given birth to those tears, but all of a sudden she felt sobs heaving up in her throat. Silvio looked at her, embarrassed, then he put his arm around her shoulders and had her sit down on the deck in the shade of the ladder to the poop. A minute later he came back with a porcelain cup, "Caffe." She dipped her lip in the scalding liquid. The tears had made her hair stick to her cheeks, her mouth couldn't smile. "Thank you." She would have liked to talk, ask questions, but the words stuck in her throat. The boy saw what was in her eyes. He pointed to the horizon out in front of the bow, "Mezzodì." Then he went back to join the rest of the crew. Esther heard their voices making fun of him.

The passengers came up out of the hold one after the other. The sun was at its zenith, it shone down on the sea, and when the women and children came up on deck they shielded their eyes with their hands. They were all pale, exhausted, blinded as if they'd spent years in the depths of the hold. The men's faces were covered with whiskers, their clothes rumpled. They were wearing hats or caps to protect themselves from the sun and the wind. The women were wrapped in their shawls, some wore coats with fur collars. The old men had slipped on their heavy caftans. One after the other they gathered on the deck at the back of the ship and silently watched the horizon in the east. Reb Joel was there too in his black suit.

The sailors in the wheelhouse had turned on the radio, the music faded in and out, it was the same odd husky voice that Esther had heard one night in the Strait of Messina, Billy Holiday's voice singing the blues.

Elizabeth came up on deck too. Jacques Berger was holding her hand. Her face seemed very pale against her black clothing. Esther would have liked to join her but the crowd of passengers kept her from crossing over to the other side. She climbed up on the ladder to the poop to get a better view. Like everyone else, Elizabeth's eyes were glued on the horizon. Now the sun had started going down on the other side of the ship. The wind had fallen. All of a sudden, without their being aware of how it happened, the coast was there in front of the ship. No one said anything, as if they were afraid of being mistaken. Everyone was watching the gray line that had appeared on the sea, like mist. Above it, large clouds hovered.

The sun sparkled on the waves. The sails of the boat seemed whiter. Then we saw the first birds flying around the ship. Their cries echoed in the silence of the sea that hovered over the people's voices, the rumbling of the engines, over Billie Holiday's voice. Everyone stopped talking to listen to them. Now Esther remembered the black bird that would have flown over the mountains, long ago, the bird her father had pointed out to her. Before nightfall, they too would arrive. They would step down on the beach, free.

Reb Joel came over to the ladder leading up to the poop. He'd carefully combed his beard and hair and his black suit shone in the sun like armor. His face looked tired, anxious, but also energetic, and his eyes were shining just as they had when he read the Book of the Beginning in the prison in France. He came through the crowd, greeting everyone as if he were meeting them again after a long absence. Despite his weary face, his trim figure seemed like that of a young man.

He stopped in front of the ladder and opened the book. Now everyone was turned toward him, no longer staring at the line of land that stretched before the bow of the ship. Captain Frullo came over too and the sailors turned off the radio. In the silence of the sea, Joel's voice rose. He read slowly in that strange mellow language, the language that Adam and Eve had spoken in Paradise, the language that Moses spoke in the wilderness of the Sin Desert. Esther didn't understand, but the words penetrated her, as they had done before, they mingled with her breath. The words shone upon the intensely blue sea, they lit up each part of the boat, even the places that had been dirtied or damaged by the journey, even the stains on the deck or the tears in the sails.

They lit up each face. The women dressed in black, the teenage girls with their flowered scarves, the men, the young children, everyone was listening. Between each phrase in the book, Joel stopped, and we heard the sound of the stem cutting through the water, the rumbling of the motor. The words of the book were as beautiful as the sea, they bore the ship forward toward the cloudy shores of Eretz Israel.

Sitting on the steps of the ladder, Esther listened to the voice, watching the coast grow larger. The words would never be wiped away. They were the same words that Joel had taught in the prison, words that spoke of good and evil, of light and justice, of the birth of man in the world. And today, that's just what it was, it was the beginning. The sea was new. The land had just appeared above the water, the light of the sun was shining for the first time, and up in the sky the birds flew over the ship to lead the way to the shore where they had been born.

After that, everything happened very quickly, like in a dream. The *Sette Fratelli* cast anchor off a large beach at the foot of a line of dark green mountains. Rowboats came out to the ship and unloaded the passengers in small groups. When it was Esther's and Elizabeth's turn, the girl saw the men who were waiting on the beach, the suitcases and the bundles and the women hugging their children to their breasts. Suddenly she was frightened. She went back to the place she'd been sitting, near the ladder to the poop, as if she wanted to sail away with the ship, continue on the journey. Elizabeth was waiting for her, and Jacques Berger was motioning for her to come, but she just sat there, her hand clutching the rungs of the ladder. Finally, Elizabeth came over to her and pulled her over to the rail, and together they climbed down the rope ladder into the rowboat.

A minute later, Esther and Elizabeth were on the beach. The Shepherd was standing next to the suitcases, his red face was drawn with worry, his eyes squinted against the light. In spite of herself, Esther started laughing and immediately afterward she felt tears in her eyes. Her face was burning with fever. She let herself slump down onto the sand, leaning the upper part of her body against her mother's suitcase. She wasn't looking at anything anymore. "It's all over, everything will be all right, Estrellita." Now Elizabeth's voice was calm. Esther felt the slender fingers stroking her hair, matted with salt. Her mother had never called her "little star" before, it was the first time.

Out at sea, the ship was lurching up and down. The chains of the anchors were coming up in fits and starts. On the deck, the Italian sailors were watching the beach. The main sail hung down, slatting in the wind, then suddenly bellied out. The *Sette Fratelli* sailed away. A minute later there was nothing but the dazzling sea in the sunset and the rowboats that were being hauled up on the beach. Esther and Elizabeth walked slowly across the beach with Jacques Berger who was carrying the suitcases. Near the dunes, everyone was waiting, stretched out on the sand. Some had spread out their blankets. Night was falling. The wind was warm, there was a sweet smell in the air, filled with pollen. It made your head swim a little.

It was the light that was beautiful, the light and the white stones. As if she'd never seen anything like it before, as if there had never been anything but darkness. Light, it was the name of the city that she'd been hearing about since she was a small child, the name her father uttered at night so she could take it to sleep with her. The name that had dangled in front of her, in front of Elizabeth, when they walked on the rocky path through the forest on their way to Italy. It was the name she hoped to hear every afternoon in Festiona, waiting and hiding in the grass where her father was supposed to appear. The name was even in the apartment at 26 Rue des Gravilliers, in the dark hallway, the stairwell with water trickling down, the roof full of holes like an old dishrag. It was also the name in the ship flying over the winter sea, the name that shone, that dazzled her, whenever she went up on deck.

Esther went running through the streets of the new part of town where the immigrants had settled. She went up to the top of the hill, lost herself in the pine woods. She walked so far that she could no longer hear a single human sound, only the whistling of the wind in the pine needles, the light flutter of a bird.

The blue sky was dizzying. The stones burned with a white flame. The light was so harsh that tears ran from her eyes. She sat down on the ground with her head on her knees, the collar of her coat pulled up around her ears.

That's where Jacques Berger had found her one

morning, and after that, he went with her every day. Maybe he'd followed her trail, or he'd spied on her from afar when she ran through the streets till she reached the mountain. He called her name, shouting loudly, and she hid behind a bush. Then when he'd gone past, she went back down till she reached an old wall. That's where he caught up with her. They walked through the pines, he was holding her hand. When he kissed her, she let him do it, angling her head to avoid his eyes.

Jacques talked about danger being everywhere, because of the war. He said he was going to fight against Israel's enemies, against the Arabs, against the English. One day he talked about the news of Gandhi's death, he was pale and upset as if it had happened here. Esther heard that, she saw death gleaming in the sky, in the stones, in the pines and the cypresses. Death was gleaming like a light, like salt, underfoot, in every parcel of land.

"We're walking on the dead," Esther said. She was thinking of everyone who had died far away, forgotten, abandoned, all of the people the soldiers of the Wehrmacht tracked through the mountains, through the Stura Valley, the people who had been locked up in the camp in Borgo San Dalmazzo and who'd never come back. She thought of the steep slope under the Coletto, where she'd watched for her father's figure to appear for so long that her eyes got bleary and she passed out. The white stones here gleamed, they were the bones of those who'd disappeared.

Jacques read the black Book of the Beginning and Esther listened to the names of those who had died in this land, those whose bones had turned to stone. She said, "Read me the part Reb Joel was reading on the deck of the boat when we arrived." He read slowly and his soft voice grew loud, intense, it made shivers run up Esther's spine.

"And God spake unto Moses, and said unto him, I am the Eternal: And I appeared unto Abraham, unto Isaac, and unto Jacob, by the name of IAOH, the Lord, but by my spirit was I not known to them. And I have also established my covenant with them, to give them the land of Canaan, the land of their pilgrimage, wherein they were strangers. And I have also heard the groaning of the children of Israel, whom the Egyptians keep in bondage; and I have remembered my covenant. Wherefore say unto the children of Israel, I am the Eternal, and I will bring you out from under the burdens of the Egyptians, and I will rid you of their bondage, and I will redeem you with a stretched out arm, and with great judgments. And I will take you to me for a people, and I will be to you a Lord: and ye shall know that I am IOAH, the Eternal, which bringeth you out from under the burdens of the Egyptians. And I will bring you unto the land, concerning which I did swear to give it to Abraham, to Isaac, and to Jacob; and I will give it you for an heritage."

The words echoed in the mountain silence. Jacques leaned toward Esther, put his arm around her. "What's wrong? Are you cold?" She shook her head but there was a lump in her throat. "Why does there have to be a war? Can't we live in peace?" Jacques said, "It has to be the last war, there must never be any others. Then the words of the book will be realized, we can stay in the land that God has given us."

But the mountain over the city of Haifa was white with bones. The light was not soft. It burned your eyes, it was fierce and violent, and fear was in the wind, in the blue sky, in the sea. "I'm tired, so tired," Esther said. Jacques looked at her, puzzled. The light falling on him, on his blond hair and beard, shining in his pale blue eyes, was softer. She managed to smile. She looked at his large white hand between hers—such very dark, such very tiny hands, the hands of a gypsy. They remained there, stretched out on the rocky slope, breathing in the odor of myrtle and pines, listening to the furtive music of the wind.

When the sun was sinking toward the sea, Jacques took Esther by the hand and they walked through the olive trees, from one terrace to the next until they reached the houses of the new town. The plain lay before them with a few light twists of smoke. Pigeons flew over the rooftops. In the harbor there were new ships, those who'd run the English blockade. Esther and Jacques walked into the streets of the town still holding hands. That is how they became engaged.

On the morning of May 14, people began gathering in Jaffa Square, in front of the Big Mosque, and along the beach. Some had come from the surrounding farms just for a few hours. Many, like Esther, Elizabeth, and Jacques Berger came with their suitcases to begin the journey. The teenage boys and girls formed noisy groups. Some indigent women with young children sought shelter under the pines. The sun was already shining brightly. Like the poor people, Elizabeth and Esther settled down on the beach near the old town. Everyone was waiting silently without really knowing what was going to happen. Today was the day everything was going to begin, that's what people said. Trucks were going to take everyone to Jerusalem.

Now other families were arriving on the beach. Most of them were people from central Europe clad in black. They sat down on the dunes near the road and waited, gazing patiently at the sea. Only the children and teenagers couldn't sit still. They roamed the beach, calling out to one another. A few of them had brought along musical instruments, an accordion, a guitar, a harmonica. From time to time a clamor of song arose.

No one was thinking about what was going to happen, about that day. It was like being outside of time, hovering over the earth. That was what that day was like, with no beginning or end. When the trucks had come into the immigrant's camp in Haifa, it was still dark. Esther and Elizabeth were sleeping in their clothes with their packed suitcases next to them. In a second they'd climbed up into the truck. As for Jacques, he'd gotten into a truck carrying only men, all armed in case they were attacked on the road. When the trucks entered Tel-Aviv the sun was up. That's why the day didn't seem to have a beginning.

When the trucks rolled into the city, they passed a convoy going in the opposite direction, toward Haifa. All the men climbed out onto the road to watch the convoy. They shouted and clapped. Jacques came looking for Esther. His eyes were bright with excitement. He said, "They're English soldiers who are leaving. We're free!" The English armored vehicles moved slowly along the dusty road and High Commissioner Cunningham's car was in the middle of the convoy. They drove past the men and women and disappeared in a cloud of dust driving off toward the cruiser *Euryalus* that awaited them.

Now, the people on the beach began to eat—bread, olives, fruit. The teenagers had roasted two sheep over driftwood fires, and they handed out pieces of the browned meat all around. One of the boys walked up to Esther, he held out the plate with the pieces of meat to her. Esther served herself and so did Elizabeth, and Jacques took a piece as well. The boy was twelve or thirteen. He had a handsome suntanned face, curly hair, and huge black eyes as shiny as jasper. In French, Esther asked him, "What's your name?" But he didn't understand. Jacques translated. "Yohanan." He walked away to hand out more pieces of meat to the families waiting on the beach.

When they finished eating, they washed their hands with sand and seawater. Jacques Berger took out the Book of the Beginning and began to read slowly—translating as he went along—the *Beha' alote'ha*, the passage that tells of the light that hung in the sky like a meteor until morning, and the cloud that covered the tent of the tabernacle, and guided Moses' people in the desert. Esther listened to the mysterious remote words and they echoed strangely there on that beach, beneath the sky, facing the deep blue sea, with the scattered groups of immigrants sitting and waiting, the children playing in the sand, the music of the harmonica that was coming from who knows where, and the smell of smoke. Esther thought about the lights she'd seen in Saint-Martin the first time she'd gone into the chalet, the candles lit in the dimness, and old Eïzik Salanter wearing his white shawl reading the words of that rough and mellow language that she didn't understand.

Just before four o'clock Esther and Jacques walked over to the museum in the old part of town. They walked along with the crowd, the teenagers, the children. Around the museum stood armed soldiers and militiamen too, wearing armbands. The main avenue was packed with people and everything was silent. Those who were just arriving stopped, waited, not making a sound, not talking. Some men and some women got out of a car and went into the museum. Standing on her tiptoes and looking over the heads, Esther saw a little man dressed in black with the face of an old herdsman framed by a thick mass of white hair. Then a loudspeaker strung up in the garden of the old building began to emit a slightly hoarse, husky voice and everyone held their breath to listen to what it was saying, even those who didn't understand Hebrew. Leaning toward Esther, Jacques translated, "Israel is the birthplace of the Jewish people, it is here that their religion, their independence, their culture were born...For the Jewish people and for the entire universe, it is here that the Book was written so that it should be given to the world..." Jacques stopped translating because he couldn't get the words out anymore. When the voice suddenly fell silent, everything was quiet for a moment and then a chant began to resound, first in the distance, then getting nearer and nearer, spreading to the entire street, the neighboring streets, so far out that the whole world must have heard it. Esther wasn't chanting because she'd never learned the words, but she couldn't swallow and her eyes were filled with tears. There was another silence and the loudspeaker again sounded with the faint, drawn-out voice of old Rabbi Maimon giving his blessing. Jacques leaned back toward Esther, "Israel exists, the State of Israel has been proclaimed." Above the museum the flag was raised on the pole, with the blue star fluttering in the sky.

The teenagers ran through the streets singing. Hands joined, farandoles formed, serpentining. A hand caught Esther's, she too was running till she was breathless through unknown streets, her hand clasping that of a young girl wearing a striped sailor's jersey. On top of all her weariness, this was intoxicating, mad. Jacques also ran down the dazzling streets, being drawn close to Esther, then swept away again. There was music and singing everywhere.

In a café near the beach, they sat down to rest, have a cup of coffee, a beer. The girl with the striped jersey was called Myriam, and another, Alexia. The boys introduced themselves too, Samuel, Ivan, David. They spoke only Yiddish, German, a little English. They drank and smoked and laughed, trying to talk to one another like that, groping for words. Jacques held Esther close to him, stroked her hair. He was a little drunk.

They started roaming the streets again. Despite the preparations for the Shabbat, the young people continued to dance, make music. When night fell, they went back to the beach, to the spot where the pine trees grew in clay soil amidst the rocks jutting out into the sea. The boys collected wood and pine needles and they made a fire in the rocks just to watch the light. They sat there around the fire, not talking much, listening to the crackling flames, tossing more twigs on from time to time. Never had they seen such a beautiful light, in the night, with the wind blowing in from the sea.

When the fire went out, they stretched out between the trees on the pine needles. Esther felt the earth turning slowly beneath her, like a raft drifting on the water. She felt Jacques' body against hers, she heard his breathing. She also heard the sound of the other couples, their bodies crunching the pine needles and breaking the twigs. The Shepherd's lips sought hers. She felt his body trembling. She sat up, "Come on, we have to go back and join Mama." They walked for a while without saying anything. Then Esther took Jacques' hand and they ran down to the end of the beach stumbling over the sand. They found Elizabeth wrapped up in her old blanket, leaning against the suitcases. When they got back, she simply said, "It's time to sleep." And she lay down on the sand.

Two days later Esther and Elizabeth were in the bed of a truck headed for Jerusalem. The convoy consisting of six trucks and an American Jeep moved slowly along the rutted road, through the arid hills to the east of Ramla. In the first two trucks were the armed men, and Jacques Berger was with them. The four trucks in the rear carried the women and children. When Esther drew the tarpaulin aside she saw only dust and the bright headlights of the truck behind them. At times the dust cleared a little and she caught a glimpse of the hills, the ravines, a few houses. The wind was cold, the sky an immutable blue. And yet the war was there, all around them. According to the news some Jewish farmers had been murdered in the Ataroth settlement. In Tel-Aviv, before they left, Jacques had read General Shealtiel's declaration that was pasted on the wall to Esther: "The enemy now looks toward Jerusalem, the eternal home of our eternal people. It will be a savage, merciless, battle with no retreat. Our destiny will be victory or extermination. We will fight to the last man for our survival and for our capital." The Arab army under the command of John Bagot Glubb and King Abdallah had bombed the road between Tel-Aviv and Haifa. The Egyptians had crossed the border, they were marching to join the troops on the western shore of the Dead Sea.

Even so, no one in the trucks was afraid. They were still feeling light-headed from hearing the proclamation of the State of Israel, the chain dance through the sun-drenched streets, the songs, the delightful evening on the beach amidst the pines.

People said that now the English were gone, everything would work out fine. Others said that the war was only just beginning, that it would be the Third World War. But Elizabeth didn't want to hear any of that. She too felt the giddiness, the joy, now that the end of their journey was so near. Her eyes shone, she talked, even laughed like she hadn't done in ages. Esther looked at her regular features framed by the black scarf and thought she looked very young, very pretty.

During the long hours when everyone was waiting to leave, Elizabeth was the one who'd spoken of Jerusalem, the temples, the mosques, the bright domes, the gardens and the fountains. She spoke about it as if she'd already seen it, and maybe she really had seen it in her dreams. The city was the most beautiful place in the world, a place where every wish came true, where there could be no war because all of the people the world over who'd been plundered and driven out, all of the people who'd wandered the earth with no homeland, could live there in peace.

The caravan of trucks entered a forest of pines and cedars through which clear streams ran. The convoy stopped in the village of Latrun and the soldiers and immigrants got out to freshen up. There was a fountain and a washtub, the water gurgled out peacefully. The women washed the dust from their faces and arms, the children splashed each other laughing. Esther took a long drink of the cold water, it was delicious. There were bees hanging in the air. The streets of the village were deserted, silent. At times, they could hear something like the rumbling of a storm far away in the mountains.

While the women and children drank, the men stood at the entrance to each street, rifles in hand. The silence was odd, menacing. Esther remembered the day she and Elizabeth had walked into the square in Saint-Martin where everyone was gathering before their departure, the old men in their black coats, the women with black scarves knotted tightly around their faces, the children who were running around innocently, and on that day too there had been the very same silence. Only the rumbling, like thunder.

The convoy struck out again. Farther along, the road ran through narrow passes strewn with boulders where night had already set in. The trucks slowed down. Esther drew back the tarpaulin and saw a column of refugees. A woman sitting next to her leaned over. "Arabs". That was all she said. The refugees were walking on the side of the road, passing the trucks. There were about a hundred of them, maybe more, just women and young children. Dressed in tatters, barefoot, rags wrapped around their heads, the women turned their faces aside as they passed through the cloud of dust. Some were carrying bundles on their heads. Others had suitcases, boxes tied up with string. One old woman even had a rickety stroller loaded with disparate objects. The trucks had stopped and the refugees walked slowly past, turning away their faces with blank looks. There was a heavy, deathly silence weighing on those faces, like so many masks of dust and stone. Only the children looked back with fear in their eyes.

Esther climbed down from the truck, she walked over to the group, trying to understand. The women turned away, some shouted harsh words at her in their language. Suddenly a very young woman broke away from the crowd. She walked toward Esther. Her face was pale and haggard, her dress covered with dust, she was wearing a large scarf over her head. Esther saw that the straps of her sandals were broken. The girl walked up close enough to touch Esther.

There was a strange gleam in her eyes, but she didn't speak, she didn't ask anything. For a long moment she stood still with her hand resting on Esther's arm as if she were going to say something. Then she pulled a blank notebook with a black cardboard cover out of her pocket and on the first page in the top right-hand corner she wrote her name, in capital letters like this: N E J M A. She handed the notebook and the pencil to Esther, so that she too would write down her name. She stood there for a moment longer, hugging the notebook to her breast, as if it were the most important thing in the world. Finally, without saying a word, she went back toward the group of refugees who were already walking away. Esther took a step toward her, to call her, to hold her back, but it was too late. It was time to get back into the truck. The convoy set out again, surrounded by a cloud of dust. But Esther couldn't rid her mind of Nejma's face, her eyes, her hand lying on her arm, the deliberate solemnity of her gestures as she extended the notebook where she had written her name. She couldn't forget the women's faces, their averted eyes, the fear on the children's faces, or the heavy silence over the land, in the shadows of the ravines, around the fountain. "Where are they going?" she'd asked the question to Elizabeth. The woman who had drawn back the tarpaulin looked at her without answering. "Where are they going?" Esther repeated. The woman shrugged her shoulders, maybe because she didn't understand. Another woman dressed in black with a very pale face responded, "To Iraq." She said it in a callous way and Esther didn't dare ask her anything else. The road had been gutted during the war, the dust made a yellow halo under the tarpaulin of the truck. Elizabeth held Esther's hand tightly in her own, just as she had long ago on the path to Festiona. The woman also said, looking at Esther as if she were trying to read her thoughts, "No one is innocent, they're the mothers and wives of the men who are killing us." Esther said, "But what about the children?" Those eyes wide with fear had been etched in her mind, she knew nothing could erase their faces."

In the evening, the convoy reached the gates of Jerusalem. The trucks stopped in a large square. There were no soldiers or armed people around, only women and children who were waiting by other trucks. The sun was fading, but the city still shone. Esther and Elizabeth climbed down with their suitcases. They didn't know where to go. Jacques Berger had already left for the center of town. The thunder-like rumbling was very near, the earth shook with each explosion, they could see fires glowing. Before Esther and Elizabeth stood the walls of the city, the hills covered with narrow-windowed houses, and maybe the fabulous outlines of the mosques and temples. In the copper-colored sky, a large billow of black smoke rose from the center, spread out, formed a threatening cloud from which the night took root.

Nejma

Nour Chams Camp, summer 1948

This is a memoir of our life in the Nour Chams Camp, as I, Nejma, have decided to record it in remembrance of Saadi Abou Talib, the Baddawi, and our aunt, Aamma Houriya. Also in remembrance of my mother, Fatma, whom I never knew, and of my father, Ahmad.

Does the sun not shine for us all? That question runs endlessly through my mind day in and day out. The man who asked it over a year ago now is dead. He's buried at the top of the hill overlooking the camp. The children dug a hole in the earth with their hoes, picking out the stones and throwing them into two equal piles on either side, then they lowered him in, covered with a worn sheet they had sewn together themselves but which was too short, and it was a queer sight to see the old man's stiff body under that sheet with his bare feet sticking out, being lowered into the grave. His sons pushed the dirt in with their hoes, and the younger children helped with their feet. Then they placed the larger stones on top, so the stray dogs wouldn't be able to dig up the grave. I was thinking of the stories that our aunt used to tell us on rainy days, about ghouls, about hungry wolves that ate the dead. Aamma Houriya loved to tell terrifying stories when the sky grew dark, stories of devils and spirits. When Old Nas died, that was what I thought of, even before feeling sad, the sound of Aamma Houriya's voice telling a

197

story mingling with the sound of the falling rain.

When the soldiers came to his home to bring him to the camp, that's what the old man had said to them, and afterward he never ceased repeating that same question. The soldiers probably hadn't understood. And if they had understood, maybe it would have made them laugh, "Does the sun not shine for us all?"

Our camp had more than its share of sun that summer when the earth cracked and the wells ran dry one after the other. Old Nas died at the end of summer, when rations started running low. Then people waited for hours on the rocky hill above the camp for the truck from the United Nations to come, because from up there you have the best view of the road to Tulkarm.

You could tell far in advance when the truck was coming because from the top of that hill you could clearly see the cloud of dust in the west, over toward Zeïta. So then the children started shouting and chanting. They shouted and chanted the same words over and over again: "Flour!...Flour!...Milk!...Flour!" Then they went running down the hill to the entrance of the camp banging on empty jerricans or old tin cans with their sticks, and they made such a racket that the elderly people cursed them and all the stray dogs started barking. Old Nas, from atop his hill can still hear them today, he's the first to know that the trucks bringing flour, oil, milk, dried meat are coming. Maybe if he had gone up on top of the rocky hill with the children he wouldn't have died. But down at the bottom of the hill, in the streets of the camp, there were sounds coming from all sides, sounds of despairing people—that's what he heard, and that's what broke his heart, and that's why he didn't want to go on living. He died a little more each day, like a plant shriveling up.

The rumors first came from Janin, and then they spread through all the camps, Fariaa, Balata, Askar: the United Nations was abandoning us, they were going to stop giving us food and medicine, and we were all going to die. First the old men would die, because they are the weakest, then the old women and the children that had just been weaned, pregnant women, people sick with fever. After that, the young people would die, even the strongest and the most courageous of the young men. They would become like the dry brush in the desert, standing spindly against the winds, they would die. That's what the foreigners decided, so we would disappear from the face of the earth forever.

Hassan and Saïd, Old Nas's two sons, were strong and manly, they were tall with muscular legs and brown faces from working in the fields, their eyes were bright as flames. But the rumor crept into them, the whispering voices, when they buried their father wrapped in his sheet on top of the rocky hill. So now they don't even wait for the foreigners' trucks to come anymore. Maybe they hate them. Maybe they're ashamed to have become what they are, like beggars pleading for their food at the gates to the city.

The Nour Chams Camp is sinking little by little into misery. When we first came in the United Nation's tarpaulined truck, we didn't know that this place would be our new home. We all thought that it was just for a day or two, before taking to the road again. Just until the bombing and the fighting in the cities ended, and then the foreigners gave each of us a plot of land, a vegetable garden to cultivate, a house where we could start living as we had before. Old Nas's sons had a farm in Tulkarm. They left everything behind, the livestock, the tools, and even their reserves of grain, oil, and their women left their cooking utensils, their linens, because they too thought they were only leaving for a day or two, just long enough for things to calm down. Old Nas's sons had asked the goat-herder who lived near them, and who wasn't part of the convoy that was being displaced, to watch over the house while they were gone, not to let anyone steal the chickens and make sure the goats and cows had water. In payment, they gave him the oldest goat in the herd, the one that was sterile and whose teats had dried up. When they climbed into the truck, the old Bedouin shepherd had stood there and watched them go, his narrow eyes like two slits on his face, with the old goat tied to a rope trying to nibble at a newspaper on the road. That was the last image they'd brought with them from the home in which they were born, then the truck drove off, blotting it all out in a cloud of dust.

I look out over the camp from up on the rocky hill, sitting on a large stone not far from the place where Old Nas is buried. Was he thinking of this hill when he used to say, "Does the sun not shine for us all?" Here the sun beats down interminably on the vast stretch of the desert, the sunlight is so intense that the other hills, over by Yaabad and Janin, ripple and seem to move forward like ocean waves.

Down below, the alleys of the camp lie in impeccably straight lines. Each day, it has slowly become our prison, and who knows if it shan't be our cemetery? On the arid rocky plain, bordered in the east by the dry wadi, the Nour Chams Camp makes a large dark smear, the color of rust and mud, at the end of the dusty road. I love to sit up here in the afternoon silence and imagine the rooftops of Akka—all the different sorts of flat roofs, domes, high towers, the ancient walls overlooking the sea where you could watch the seagulls gliding on the wind and the thin crescent sails of the fishing boats. Now I realize that all of that will never again be a part of our lives. Akka—Arab soldiers in tatters, heads bleeding, legs wrapped in rags that served as bandages, unarmed, their faces sunken with hunger and thirst, some of them no more than children whom exhaustion and the war had already turned into men; and the throngs of women, young children, cripples that stretched out all the way to the horizon. When they arrived at the walls of Akka, they didn't have the courage to enter the gates of the town so they simply lay down on the ground in the olive groves waiting to be given water and bread, a little buttermilk. That was in the spring, and they told of what had happened in Haifa, they told of the fighting in the narrow streets, how it spread through the covered market in the old part of town, and of all the bodies lying face down on the ground. So the people had walked toward Akka following the sea, on the immense sandy beach, all day long in the burning sun and wind, until they reached the walls of our city.

I remember, that evening I wandered out alone, wearing a very long dress, covered with veils, I stooped over and carried a walking stick so I would look like an old woman searching for a little food, because people in town said there were bandits hiding among the fugitives, and that they raped young girls. At the gates to the city, I saw all those people lying on the ground, amid the thorn bushes and the olive trees, like thousands of beggars. They were exhausted, but they weren't sleeping. Their eyes were wide with fever, with thirst. Some of them had managed to make little fires that were glowing here and there in the dim twilight on the beach, shining on their vanquished faces. Old men, women, children. As far as the eye could see on the beach and in the dunes, all those people strewn about as if they'd been flung down upon the earth. They didn't complain, they didn't say anything. And the silence was more terrifying than cries or laments. Every now and again the whimpering of a child arose, then stopped. And the sound of the sea on the shore, the long waves rolling placidly in, washing up against the beached skiffs.

I walked around amongst those bodies for quite some time, and I felt so much pity that I forgot to feign the gait of an old beggar-woman. Then all of a sudden, I just couldn't bear it any longer. I went back to town. At the gates, an armed man tried to bar my way. He asked me roughly, "Where are you going?" I told him my name and my father's address. He shone a flashlight in my face. Then he laughed at me, asking what a girl of my age was doing out alone. I walked away without answering him. I felt ashamed, because of everything I'd seen.

After that, I heard the spitting of gunfire around the city, canons firing that rocked the earth night and day when the Druze began battling the Haganah just before summer. Then the fighting men left for the war and Ahmad, my father, went with them, marching northward. He entrusted the house to me, gave me his blessing, and he left. He too thought he would soon be back, but he never came home. Later, I learned that he'd been killed in the bombing of Nahariyya.

Then the tarpaulined trucks came to take the civilians away to a safe place. The soldiers came, they moved into our house, and I was put into a truck.

The convoys of trucks drove through the gates of Akka and those who were left behind looked on. The trucks drove off in all directions, toward Kantara, toward Nabaith, or else toward Gaza in the south, or Tulkarm, Janin, Ramallah. Some of them, they say, even went as far as Salt, and Amman, on the other side of the Jordan River. Neither Aamma Houriya nor I had any idea where we were going.

We didn't know we were to join the throngs of bodies flung to the ground that I had seen one day at the foot of the ramparts.

The Nour Chams Camp is undoubtedly the very end of the world because it seems to me that beyond this point there can be nothing else, there is no hope left. The days begin adding up. They are just like the fine dust that comes from nowhere, invisible and intangible, that covers everything, your clothing, the roofs of the tents, your hair and even your skin, I can feel the weight of that dust, it mingles with the water I drink, I can taste it in my food and on my tongue when I awake in the morning.

There are three wells in Nour Chams, three holes dug into the dry riverbed, edged with circles of flat stones and covered with old boards. At the break of day, when the sun is still hidden behind the hills and the sky is immense and pure, I take the buckets down to fetch the still-muddy water. Already, the uninterrupted lines of women and children are filing toward the wells. In the beginning, when we first came to the camp, the sounds of voices, of laughter still rang out, as if it could have been anywhere in the world, a place where there were no wars or prisons. The women exchanged bits of news with each other, spread rumors, invented stories, as if nothing mattered, as if they were simply on a trip and they would soon be going back home.

They said, "Where are you from?" And the clear voices pronounced the names of the places where they were born, where they'd been married, where their children were also born, Qalqiliya, Jaffa, Qaqun, Shafa Amr, and the names of the people they'd known, the old streets of Akka, of Al-Quds, of Nablus. Hamza, who lived near the Malkpela cave,

Malika, the mother of the cobbler who kept a stall near the Rabbi Yokhanan synagogue, and Aïsha who had three daughters and lived next to the big Christian church, near the citadel where Glubb Pasha had set up his canons. I listened to those names, Moukhalid, Jebzz, Kaisariyeh, Tantourah, Yajour, Djaara, Nazira, Djitt, Ludd, Ramleh, Kafr Saba, Ras al-Aïn, Asqalan, Gazza, Tabariya, Rounaneh, Araara, all those names that had a peculiar ring in the cold air around the wells, as if they already belonged to another world.

Aamma Houriya was too tired to be able to go down to the wells and listen to the names. So when I came back with the two buckets of water, I set them down in front of the door to our shack and I told her everything I'd heard, even the names that I wasn't familiar with. She listened to it all nodding her head as if it had some deep meaning that I couldn't understand. I had an exceptionally good memory.

That was in the beginning, because later, little by little, the sound of the voices died away as the water in the wells grew scarcer and muddier. Then you had to let the water settle in the buckets for an hour or two before pouring it into the water jars, tilting the bucket carefully so that the silt stayed at the bottom. So every morning the sun would rise over a land that gradually grew more bitter, red, scorched, with wispy thorn bushes and those acacias incapable of providing shade, the dry valley of the wadi, the houses of planks and cardboard, the torn tents, the makeshift shelters of car fenders, oil drums, bits of tires attached with wire that served as roofs. Everyone watched, every morning, as the sun appeared over the hills after the morning prayer, everyone but old Leyla, whose very destiny was written in her name, for she was blind and her white eyes could not see the sun. She remained sitting on a large rock in front of her cave, mumbling prayers or insults, waiting for someone to bring her some food and water, and everyone knew that the day people forgot about her she would die. Her sons had all been killed in the war, during the storming of Haifa, and she was alone in the world.

Little by little, even the children stopped running and shouting and fighting around the camp. Now they stayed near the shacks, sitting listlessly in the shade on the dusty ground, half-starved and looking like dogs, shifting positions according to the movement of the sun. Except when the time for food distribution came around, when the sun was at its highest point.

I watched them then and they were the mirror of my own weakness, my own decline. For many of them— especially the poorest ones, the orphans with no mother or father, or those who had fled the coastal villages under the bombs, penniless, with no provisions—the ordinary faces of childhood seemed already wilted with incomprehensible old-age. Scrawny little girls with stooped shoulders, their bodies floating in dresses that were too big for them, young boys half-naked, with bowed legs, huge knees, dark gray ash-colored skin, scalps mottled with ringworm, eyes devoured by gnats. I watched the faces especially, stared at them intently because I didn't want to see them: the expression that I couldn't fathom, that empty look, distant, strange, lit by the glow of fever. When I walked aimlessly, haphazardly, through the streets of Nour Chams, keeping close to the rows of houses, the walls of tarpaper, of old planks, I saw children's faces everywhere, I was haunted by those vacant faraway looks. And, as if in a mirror, I saw my own face, not that of a sixteen-year-old girl, a veiled beauty that the impatient eyes of young men sought, but the face of an old wrinkled women, wilted and glowering with misery, desiccated by approaching death.

Wherever I went in the camp, that was the face I saw, my face, and my emaciated hands with the bulging veins, and the wispy shadow of my body, slipping along like a ghost. The others either averted their eyes or stared at me without blinking, from the darkness of their *tarh* like from the back of a cave, saying nothing, but with a sort of crazed muteness.

Now, even at the wells, the women had stopped talking. They no longer complained, they no longer pronounced the names of towns and people that had disappeared. With the summer drought, the water was even lower in the wells and the bucket thrown in at the end of a rope scraped the muddy, almost black bottom.

Water had become so scarce that we couldn't wash ourselves anymore, or wash our cloths. The children's clothes were blotched with excrement, with food, with dirt, and the women's dresses had become stiff with grime, like tree bark.

The old women, with blackened faces and matted hair, gave off a smell of carrion that made me nauseous. At the time, we shared our house with an old peasant woman from the coast (from Zarqaà). The odor of the old woman had become so unbearable for me that I'd taken to sleeping outdoors, in the dust, rolled up in an old piece of canvas.

The only time I felt good was when I could get away from the camp. Early in the morning, I climbed up to the top of the rocky hill until I reached Old Nas's grave. One day on the path I saw an animal die of thirst for the first time. It was the old white she-dog that belonged to Saïd, Old Nas's younger son. I knew the dog because the old man had taken a liking to her near the end of his life, and she often lay down next to him, her front paws stretched out on the ground and her head held up. I don't believe she had a name, but she followed the old man everywhere he went. When he died, the dog followed him all the way to the grave on top of the hill and she didn't come back down till the next day. Since then, every morning she went up to the top of the hill and came back down at nightfall. But water had become precious, and when I ran across her that morning she was dying. She was panting so hard that I could hear her all the way down at the bottom of the path. Lying amid the thorn bushes in the light of the rising sun, she was thin, flaccid and looked simply like a light spot on the ground. I went over to her, got close enough to touch her, but she didn't recognize me. She was already at death's door, glassy-eyed, her body shaken with tremors, her swollen black tongue hanging out of her mouth. I stayed beside her till the end, sitting on the ground as the sunlight grew blindingly bright. I thought about what Old Nas used to endlessly repeat, like a song, "Does the sun not shine for us all?" Then the sun was high in the sky, scorching the hopeless earth, scorching the faces of the children, beating down ruthlessly on the dying dog's coat. I had never felt like that before, as if there were a sort of curse, a merciless force in the light that shone on a world where life is broken and lost, where each new day takes something from the day that precedes it, where suffering is immovable, blind, impossible to understand, like the mumblings of Old Leyla in her cave.

That's why Saadi Abou Talib, the Baddawi, the man who would later become my husband and who did not know how to read or write, having learned that I'd been to school in al-Jazzar, asked me to describe everything that we endure in the Nour Chams Camp, so that the world would know, and no one would ever forget. And I listened to him, and that's why I wrote of our life, day after day, in the school notebooks that I'd brought with me. Before he left for the north from where he never returned, my father, Ahmad, had wanted me to learn to read and write, just as if I were a boy, so that I could learn the suras of the Book, and do sums and solve problems in geometry like any boy can. Had he imagined that one day I would use my writing skills to fill up the notebooks with my memories? I think he would have approved, and that's why I listened to what Saadi the Baddawi said to me.

I'm writing for her too, for her, Esther Grève, the girl who wrote her name at the top of the first page in my notebook on the road to Latrun Spring, in the hopes that she will one day read all of this and come to see me. She came that day, and I saw my destiny in her face. We were united for a brief moment, as if we had always been meant to meet each other. When I've finished writing these notebooks, I'll give them to one of the United Nations soldiers and ask him to take them to her, wherever she is. That's why I have the strength to write, despite the loneliness and the madness all around.

I spoke of the death of the white she-dog, of her unremitting suffering as the sun rose implacably in the sky over the rocky hill, because it was the fist time that I'd seen death. I had already seen dead men and women, lying on their mats in very clean, very white rooms, in the old days in Akka; the dead seemed to be sleeping, covered with the very white and very clean sheet that would be sewn closed around them; their eyelids had dark marks on them, their lips were held closed with a fine thread that ran around their chin and was lost in their hair. That was how my Aunt Raïssa and my Grandfather Mohammad were—cold, still, looking a little uncomfortable in death as if they weren't quite used to it yet. Then there were the coffins that were put in the graves, heads toward the south, and the work of the gravediggers, the strident laments of the professional mourners. There had been no mystery surrounding Old Nas's death, he was the first to go, like a lamp being blown out, and all I had seen of him was the shape wrapped in the old sheet that was too short and his two bare feet tilting down toward the deep earth.

But the white she-dog had really died, I saw the frantic terror in her gaze, her glassy eyes, I heard the effort of her breathing that did not want to cease, I felt the very long and painful tremor under my hand; and then the cold silence of her body, while the sun shone ruthlessly upon her dusty coat. Then I realized that death had entered our camp. Now, it would take the other animals, and the men, women, and children, one after the other. I ran through the bushes all the way up to the top of the hill, from where you can see the road to Attil, to Tulkarm, the hills of Janin, the dark patch marking the dry wadi, everything that had become part of our world and kept us prisoners. Why were we here? Why didn't we leave, make our way over those hills to the west, till we reached the sea that might save us?

Most of the residents of the Nour Chams Camp came from the mountains. They had lived in those red valleys strewn with thorny trees, over which goat herds driven by a child slowly roamed. That is all they knew, they had never seen the sea. Amma Houriya wasn't even interested in it.

But I was born in Akka, facing the sea, that's where I grew up, on the beach to the south of the city, swimming in the waves that came all the way up to the ramparts by the English fort, or else below the walls of the French fort, watching the fishermen's pointed sails, striving to be the first among all the children to recognize his father's boat. It seemed to me that if I could just look at the sea again, death wouldn't matter anymore, it would no longer have a hold on me or on Aamma Houriya. Then the sun wouldn't be so ruthless anymore, days wouldn't take the life out of the days that had come before. Now all of that was denied to me.

When the foreign soldiers made us climb up in the tarpaulined trucks to bring us out here, out to the ends of the earth, to this place from which you can go no farther, I realized that I would never again see the things I loved. Where are the sails of the boats gliding over the sea in the morning, surrounded by seagulls and pelicans?

In the children's eyes, as they crouch in the dark shacks, motionless, like stray dogs that no one takes any notice of, I saw my own old-age, my own death. My sunken wrinkled face with dull skin, my hair that had once been so lovely, that flowed down to the small of my back like a silk cloak, had become this dirty bushy mass, full of dust and sticks, crawling with lice, and my body had become slight, my blackened hands and feet had veins bulging like the hands and feet of old women.

It's been a long time since anyone in Nour Chams has had a mirror. The soldiers took everything that might have been used as a weapon when they searched our bags— knives, scissors, but also mirrors. Were they afraid we would hurt them? Or did they think we would use them against ourselves?

I never really thought about mirrors before. It was a natural thing to be able to see my face. Now I know that without mirrors we are different, we're not really the same. Maybe the soldiers who took them away knew that? Maybe they had noticed us looking worriedly at other people's faces, as if we were trying to see in them what we had become, trying to remember ourselves, trying to remember our own names.

Every day, every week that went by in Nour Chams, brought more men, more women, more children to the camp.

Now I remember how our Aunt Houriya came to the camp. Even though she was no blood relation of mine and she arrived a few days after I did along with the refugees from al-Quds, I called her my aunt because I loved her as if she were a true relative. She'd come, just as I had, in a United Nations tarpaulined truck. Her only belonging was a sewing machine. Since she had no place to live, I took her into the shack of wooden planks where I was living alone, in the part of the camp that was at the foot of the rocky hill. When she got down from the truck—the last person to get off—the impression I got of her was the one that always remained with me, right up to the end—dignified, composed, amid all of us already exhausted from the hardships. She had a reassuring silhouette, standing nice and straight on the dusty ground. She was draped in a traditional garment, the long *galabieh* of light-colored cloth, the black *shirwal*, her face covered with a white veil, wearing sandals encrusted with copper on her feet. The newcomers gathered their bundles together and started walking toward the center of the camp to find shelter from the sun, a place to live. The foreigners' truck went back to Tulkarm in a cloud of dust. She stood there beside her sewing machine, very still, as if she were waiting for another truck that would take her still farther. Then, amongst the youngsters that were staring at her, she chose me, maybe because I was the oldest. She said to me, "Show me the way, my child." That's what she said, she'd used the word *benti*, my child, and I think that's why I called her Aamma, aunt, as if she'd come to Nour Chams to see me, as if I had been waiting for her.

When she took off her veil in the shack, I liked her face straight away. Her skin was a dark copper color and there was a strange gleam in her sea-green eyes, as if they held a special light, something peaceful and disquieting at the same time. Maybe she was able to see beyond things, beyond people, like certain blind persons can.

Aamma moved into the shack where I was living alone. She put down the sewing machine wrapped in a few rags to protect it from the dust. She chose the part of the house nearest the door. She slept on the ground rolled up in a sheet that she would pull over her head and disappear into completely. During the day, when she had finished making the food, she sometimes used her sewing machine to repair people's clothing, and they paid her with whatever they could, food, cigarettes, but never money, because in our camp money was of no use at all. She did that for as long as she had thread. The women brought her bread, sugar, tea or sometimes olives. But sometimes they had nothing to give her but thanks, and that was enough.

Nights were especially wonderful, because of the stories. Sometimes, just like that, without our knowing why, at the end of the afternoon, when the sun went down and disappeared behind the mist gathering in the west, in the direction of the sea, or on the contrary, when the wind swept the clouds away and the sky was resplendent, with the crescent moon hanging in the night like a saber, Aamma Houriya began to tell a Djinn story. She knew, she felt it in her bones, that it was the right evening to tell the tale. She sat down in front of me, and her eyes shone out eerily as she said, "Listen, I'm going to tell you a Djinn story." She knew all about the Djenoune, she'd seen them, like red flames dancing on the desert at night. You never saw them in the daytime, they hid in the bright sunlight. But at night, they appeared. They lived in cities, like human cities, with towers and ramparts, cities with ornamental lakes and gardens. She alone knew where those cities were, and she even promised to take me there when the war was over.

So, she started to tell a story. She sat down in the doorway to our shack, facing outward, not wearing a veil, because she wasn't telling the story just for me. I sat inside the house, in the shadows, very close to her so I could hear her voice.

Then the neighbor children arrived, one after the other. They passed the word on from one to another, and they sat down in front of the house in the dust, or they remained standing, leaning against the wall of boards. When Aamma Houriya started telling a Djinn story, she had a different voice, a new voice. It wasn't her everyday voice anymore, but one that was more hushed, deeper, that forced us to keep quiet in order to hear her better. Evenings, there was not a sound in the camp. Her voice was like a murmur, but we could hear every word, and we didn't forget them.

Aamma Houriya's face changed too, gradually. To hear better, I stretched out on the floor near the door, and I watched her face come to life. Her eyes shone even more, shot out sparks. She mimed expressions, she showed her frightened face, her angry face, her jealous face. She mimicked voices, deep and muffled, or sharp, strident, and even whimpering. Her hands made motions, as if she were dancing, making her copper bracelets jangle. But the rest of her body was motionless, sitting with her legs crossed in the doorway.

The stories Aamma Houriya told us, sitting in the dust in front of the shack as the light grew softer, were beautiful tales. They were stories that frightened us, about men who turn into wolves when they cross a river, or about dead people who come up out of their graves to breathe. Stories of spirits, of ghost cities lost somewhere in the desert, and travelers who go astray and happen to enter one of those cities, and never come back. Stories about a Djinn who marries a woman, or of a Djenna who captures a man and drags him to her house high in the mountains. When the desert wind blows, an evil Djinn enters the bodies of children and makes them lose their minds, makes them climb up on the roofs of houses as if they were birds, or makes them jump into deep wells as if they were toads.

She also told us stories of the evil eye. When Bayrut, the sorceress, bewitches the mother of a young child and makes her believe she is her aunt.

The young woman turns her back for a minute and Bayrut takes the child and puts a large stone wrapped in blankets in its place in the cradle, then she cooks the child and serves the baby to its own mother for dinner. Then Aamma showed us how we could resist the evil eye, by putting our hands in front of our faces and writing the name of God on our forehead. She showed us how to scare witches away, by blowing on a pinch of sand in the open palm of our hands. She also told stories of Aïsha the African, who was black and cruel—disguised as a slave, she ate the hearts of children to remain immortal. When Aamma Houriya took me by the hand and had me sit down next to her in front of the house, asking, "What will I tell you about tonight?" I immediately answered, "A story about old immortal Aïsha!"

I forgot who I was, where I was, I forgot about the three dry wells, the miserable hovels where men and women slept on the ground, awaiting the night, awaiting the unknown; I forgot about the starving children that stood watch on top of the rocky hill, waiting for the United Nations supply trucks to come, and who cried out when they saw the approaching cloud of dust, "Bread! Flour! Milk! Flour!" And the hard, bitter bread that was distributed in rations of two slices per person a day, and sometimes only one slice. I forgot about the sores that covered the children's bodies, the fleabites, the scabs from lice, the crevasses in their heels, their hair falling out by the handful, the conjunctivitis burning their eyelids.

Aamma Houriya didn't always tell us stories to frighten us. When she saw we were at the breaking point, that the children were exhausted and their faces were sunken from hunger, and that the scorching sun was unbearable, she said, "Today is a day for a water story, a garden story, a story of a city with fountains that sing and gardens full of birds."

Her voice was softer, her eyes shone with a gayer light and she began her story:

"Long ago you know, the earth wasn't what it is today. Both the Djenoune and human beings inhabited the earth. The earth was like a vast garden, surrounded by a magical river that flowed in both directions. On one side, it flowed to the west, on the other, it flowed to the east. And this place was so beautiful that it was called *Firdous*, or paradise. And you know, from what I've heard, it wasn't very far from here. It was on the seashore, very near the city of Akka. Today there is still a small village that goes by that name, paradise, and they say that the inhabitants of that village are all descendants of the Djenoune. Whether that is the truth, or a lie, I can't really say. In any case, eternal spring reigned in that garden, it was filled with flowers and fruits, fountains that never ran dry, and the inhabitants were never in want of food. They lived on fruit, honey, and herbs, for they did not know the taste of flesh. In the middle of the vast garden there was a magnificent cloud-colored palace, and the Djenoune lived in that palace, because they were the masters of the land, God had entrusted it to them. In those days, the Djenoune were kind, they never tried to harm anyone. Men, women and children lived in the garden around the palace. The air was so balmy, the sun so clement, that they had no need of houses to protect themselves, and winter never came and it was never cold. And now children, I am going to tell you how it was all lost. For the place where that garden once stood, the land so sweetly named, Firdous, paradise, the garden filled with flowers and trees, where fountains and birds sang endlessly, the garden where human beings lived in peace and ate nothing but fruit and honey, is now the dry earth, the rough bare earth, with not a tree, not a flower, and humans in that land have become so vicious that they wage a ruthless and cruel war, abandoned by the Djenoune.

Aamma Houriya stopped talking. We remained very still, waiting for the rest of the story. It was while she was telling that story, I recall, that the young Baddawi, Saadi Abou Talib came into the camp for the first time. He squatted down on his heels, a little off to one side, to listen to what our aunt was telling us. On that day Aamma Houriya was silent for a long time, so that we could hear our hearts beating, the soft sounds coming from other houses before nightfall, the babbling of babies, the barking of dogs. She knew the value of silence.

She went on: "You know, it was the water that was the most beautiful thing in that garden. It was like nothing you've ever seen, or tasted, or dreamt of, such clear water, so cool and pure that those who drank of it enjoyed eternal youth, they never grew old, they never died. Streams ran through the garden, winding their way to the wide river that flowed around the garden in both directions, from west to east and from east to west. That's what the world was like in those days. And it would still be like that, and we too would be in that garden today, in the shade of the trees—right now as I speak to you—listening to the music of fountains and the song of birds if it hadn't been that the Djenoune, the masters of the land, got angry at the humans and dried up all the springs, and poured salt in the wide river that turned into what it is today, an endless, bitter expanse."

Houriya paused again for a moment. We watched the sky growing slowly darker. Wisps of smoke twirled up here and there between the roofs of the shacks, but they were deceptive and illusory, we knew that. The old women had lit fires to boil some water, but they had nothing but a few herbs to throw into it, and a few roots that they'd pulled up in the hills. Some had nothing at all to cook, but they lit a fire out of habit, as if they could feed themselves on smoke like the spirits in the stories that Aamma Houriya told us. She continued her tale, and all of a sudden my heart started beating faster because I realized that it was really our story she was telling, the garden, the paradise that we had lost when the Djenoune had punished us with their anger.

"Why did the Djenoune get angry with the humans, why did they destroy the garden where we could have continued to live in eternal spring? Some say that it is because of a woman, because she wanted to enter the palace of the Djenoune, and to do so, she made the humans believe that they were as powerful as the Djenoune, and that they could easily throw them out of the palace, since they were more numerous. Others say that it was because of two brothers, one was named Souad and the other Safi. They were born of the same father, but of different mothers, and because of this they hated each other. Each son wanted to have the part of the garden that belonged to the other. They say that even as young children they fought each other with their bare hands and the Djenoune laughed at them scuffling like two young rams tumbling around in the dust. Then they grew older and they fought with sticks and stones, and the Djenoune continued to laugh and make fun of them from up on the walls of their palace, near the clouds, saying they were like monkeys. But they became adults and the battle continued, now they used swords and rifles. The two men were equally strong and cunning. They inflicted cruel wounds on one another, their blood ran on the ground, but neither would admit he was beaten. The Djenoune still watched them from up on the walls of their palace, and they said, "let them fight and exhaust their strength, then they can become friends." But that is when an old woman intervened, they say she was a witch with a black face, dressed in rags, and it might well have been Aïsha, because she was very old, and she knew all the secrets of the Djenoune. One after the other, the two brothers went to consult her, they promised her piles of gold if she would assure their victory. The old slave rummaged through her bags and gave each of them a present. To Souad, the elder, she gave a small cage which held a wild red beast that shone curiously in the night, and no one had ever seen anything like it in that garden. To the second young man, whose name was Safi, she gave a large leather bag that held an invisible and powerful cloud. For in those days, neither fire nor wind existed in the garden. So the two brothers, who were at the height of their enmity, threw their evil presents at one another, without giving it a thought. When the man with the small cage opened it, the wild red beast bounded out and immediately engulfed the trees and grasses and became immense. Then the other brother opened his leather bag and the wind came roaring out upon the raging flames and changed them into a gigantic wildfire that set the whole garden ablaze. The red flames burned everything up, the trees, the birds, and all the humans that were in the garden except for a few that found refuge in the wide river. Then, from their palace surrounded with black smoke, the Djenoune were no longer laughing. They said, "May God's curse be upon all mankind, and its future generations." And they left the devastated garden forever. And before they left they dried up all the springs and all the fountains, to be sure that nothing would grow upon that land, then they flung down a huge mountain of salt that shattered and spilled into the river. That is how the garden of *Firdous* became this arid desert and the wide river that ran around the garden became bitter and stopped flowing in both directions. And that's the end of my story. Since that day, the Djenoune have hated human beings and they have still not forgiven them, and Aïsha, the immortal slave woman, continues to roam this land, giving arms and death to those who listen to her words. God forbid that she should ever cross our path, children."

Night had fallen, Aamma Houriya stood up and walked over to the well to say her prayers, and each of the children returned to his own house. Stretched out in my place on the floor next to the door, I could still hear Aamma Houriya's voice, as light and even as her breathing. I smelled the odor of smoke in the sky, the odor of hunger, and I thought: how long will mankind be abandoned by the Djenoune?

Roumiya arrived at the Nour Chams Camp at the end of summer. She was already more than six months pregnant when she came. She was a very young woman, nearly a girl, with a very white face lined with fatigue, but there was still something childlike about her face, something that was accentuated by her blonde hair pulled into two even braids and her cool water-colored eyes that looked at you with a kind of frightened innocence, the way certain animals do.

Aamma Houriya had immediately taken the girl under her wing. She brought her over to our house and moved her into the spot left by the old woman who had found shelter elsewhere. Roumiya was one of the Deir Yassin survivors. Roumiya's husband had been killed there, just as her mother and father had been, and her parents-in-law too. The foreign soldiers found her wandering around on the road and took her to a military hospital because they thought she was mad. As a matter of fact, maybe Roumiya really had gone mad, because ever since that day she'd taken to sitting for hours in a corner, not moving, not saying a word. The soldiers took her around to the camps near Jerusalem, to Jalazoun, to Mousakar, to Deir Ammar, then to Tulkarm, to Balata. And that is how she ended up coming to the end of the road, all the way out to our camp.

When she first came to our place, she didn't want to take her veil off, even in the house. She would sit near the doorway, absolutely still, wrapped in her long, dust-covered veil that reached down to her knees, and stare out with blank eyes. The children that lived around us said she was crazy, and when they walked past the door, or met her on the path near the entrance to the camp, they blew a little dust out of the hollow of their hand to ward off the evil spirits.

They spoke of her in whispers, saying *"habla, habla,"* she's gone mad, and they also said *"khayfi,"* she's been frightened, because her eyes were fixed and dilated like the eyes of a startled animal, but in truth, it was the children who were afraid. We always thought of her a bit like that, khayfi. But Aamma Houriya knew how to get through to her. She tamed Roumiya bit by bit each day. In the beginning, she brought her a bowl of porridge with Klim milk, just like she would for a child, and she ran her finger, moistened with saliva, over the girl's dry lips to make her start eating. She spoke to her gently, caressed her, and little by little Roumiya awakened, came back to life. I can remember the first time she took her veil off, her white face shone out in the light, her delicate nose, her childish mouth, the blue tattoo-marks on her cheeks and on her chin, and especially her hair, long, thick, full of copper and gold highlights. Never had I seen hair so lovely, and I understood why they'd given her that name, Roumiya, for she was not of our race.

For a brief moment, fear stopped shining in her eyes. She looked at us, at Aamma Houriya and me, but she didn't say anything, didn't smile. She hardly ever spoke, just a few words, to ask for some water or some bread, or else she would suddenly spout off a sentence that she didn't understand, and that didn't make any sense to us either.

At times I would get fed up with her, with her blank stare, and I'd go up on the rocky hill, up where Old Nas was buried, up where the Baddawi now lived in a hut he had built out of branches and stones. I stood over with the other children, as though I were looking for the supply trucks to come. Maybe it was Roumiya's beauty that drove me away, her silent beauty, her eyes that seemed to be looking through everything and draining it of all meaning.

When the sun climbed toward the highest point in the sky, and the walls of our house threw off heat like the walls of a furnace, Aamma Houriya bathed Roumiya's body with a towel soaked in water. Every morning, she went to fetch water at the well, because water was scarce and all mud-colored, and it needed to be left standing for a long time. It was her cooking and drinking ration, and Aamma Houriya used it to wash the young woman's belly, but no one else knew anything about it. Aamma Houriya said that the unborn child shouldn't be deprived of water, for he already lived, he could hear the sound of water running over the skin, he could feel its freshness, like rain. Aamma Houriya had strange ideas, it was like the stories she told, once you understood them, everything seemed so much clearer, so much more real.

When the sun reached the highest point in the sky and nothing stirred in the camp, with the heat encompassing the rough board and tarpaper shacks like flames in a furnace, Aamma Houriya hung her veil up in the doorway and it made a blue shade. Docilely, Roumiya allowed herself to be completely undressed. She was waiting for the water that came trickling down from the towel. Aamma Houriya's nimble fingers washed each part of her body, the nape of her neck, her shoulders, the small of her back. Her long braids twirled around on her back like wet snakes. And then Roumiya stretched out on her back and Aamma let the water run down over her breasts, onto her dilated stomach. At first I would leave, take a walk outside to avoid seeing all of that, I'd go teetering around in the blinding light. Afterwards, I stayed, almost in spite of myself, because there was something powerful, something incomprehensible and real, in the gestures of the old woman, like a slow ceremony, a prayer. Roumiya's enormous belly bulged up below the dark dress rolled up under her chin, just like a moon, white, streaked with pink in the blue half-light. Aamma's hands were strong, they twisted the towel over her skin, and the water tumbled down, making its secret sound in the cave-like house. I watched the young woman, I saw her belly, her breasts, her head thrown back with closed eyes, and I felt sweat running down my forehead, my back, making my hair stick to my cheeks. In our house, like a secret hidden amidst the heat and drought outdoors, all I could hear was the sound of water trickling onto Roumiya's skin, her slow breathing and Aamma Houriya's voice humming a wordless lullaby, just a faint murmuring, a drawn out droning sound that she interrupted each time she dipped the towel into the bucket.

It all lasted an eternity, such a long time that when Aamma Houriya finished bathing Roumiya, the girl had fallen asleep under the veils darkening in spots on her damp belly.

Outside the sun was still dazzling. The camp was heavy with dust, with silence. Before nightfall, I was up on top of the hill, my ears filled with the sounds of water and the droning voice of the old woman. Perhaps I had stopped seeing the camp through the same eyes. It was as if everything had changed, as if I had just arrived, as if I were unfamiliar with the stones, the dark houses, the horizon obstructed by the hills, the dried-up valley scattered with scorched trees where the sea never comes.

We've been prisoners in this camp for such a long time. It's difficult for me to recall what it was like before, in Akka. The sea, the smell of the sea, the cry of the gulls. The fishing boats slipping across the bay at dawn. The call to prayer at dusk, in the twilight, as I walked through the olive groves by the ramparts. Birds flew up, lazy turtledoves, silver-winged pigeons suddenly crossing the sky, turning, tilting up, flying off in the opposite direction. In the gardens, the blackbirds twittered anxiously as night approached. I've lost all of that now.

Here, night comes swiftly, there is no call, no prayer, no birds. The blank sky changes color, reddens, and then the night rises from the depths of the ravines. In the spring, when I first arrived, nights were hot. The heat of the sun blew down from the rocky hills late into the night. Now it is autumn, nights are cold. No sooner does the sun disappear behind the hills than you feel a chill rising from the earth. People cover themselves as best they can, with the blankets that the United Nations distributed, with dirty cloaks, with sheets. Wood has become so scarce that we don't light fires at night anymore. Everything is dark, silent, freezing. We've been abandoned, far from the world, far from all life. I've never felt like this before. Very quickly, stars appear in the sky, making their beautiful patterns. I can remember long ago, I was walking on the beach with my father, and the patterns that the stars made seemed familiar to me. They were like the lights of unexplored cities hanging in the sky. Now their pale, cold light makes our camp seem even darker, even more abandoned. On nights when the moon is round, the stray dogs bark. "Death is passing," says Aamma Houriya. In the morning, the men take the bodies of dogs that have died in the night and throw them far from the camp.

Children also cry in the night. I feel a shudder running all through my body. When morning comes, shall they go looking for the bodies of children who have died in the night?

The Baddawi, the one they call Saadi, went to live up on the rocky hill near the place where old Nas is buried over a year ago now. Not far from the grave he built a shelter from old branches and a piece of canvas. He stays up there all day and all night long, almost without moving, staring at the road to Tulkarm. The children go up to see him every morning and together they keep watch on the road by which the supply truck will be arriving. But when the truck comes, he doesn't go down. He sits up there by his shelter, as though it were none of his concern. He never comes to get his share. Sometimes he's so hungry that he comes halfway down the hill and since our house is the first one he finds, he just stands there a few feet away. Aamma Houriya takes a little bread or a chickpea cake of her own making, she lays it on a stone, and then goes back into her house. Saadi approaches, his eyes fixed steadily on mine with a kind of hardened timidity that makes my heart race. The dogs roaming about in the hills around the camp have that same cast to their eyes. The Baddawi is the only one who isn't afraid of the dogs. Up there on the hill he speaks to them. That's what the children say, and when Aamma Houriya heard that, she said he was simple-minded and that was why our camp was protected.

Every morning, I went up to the top of the hill to watch

the United Nations truck arrive. That's what I'd say. But it was also to see the Baddawi sitting on the stone in front of his hut of branches, wrapped in his woolen cloak. His hair was long and unkempt, but he had the face of a young, still-beardless boy, with just a thin mustache. When I walked up to him, he looked at me, and I saw the color of his eyes, the same as those of stray dogs. He only came down from the hill to drink at the well. He waited in line, and when his turn came, he dipped the water out of the bucket with his hand, and he drank nothing more until evening. The girls made fun of him, but they were a little frightened of him too. They said that he hid in the bushes to spy on them when they went to urinate. They said that he tried to drag one girl off, and that she bit him. But that's just a lot of gossip.

Sometimes, when Aamma Houriya told a Djinn story, he came to listen. He didn't sit with the children. He sat a little apart, his head bent down toward the ground, listening. Aamma Houriya said that he's alone in the world, that he hasn't any family left. But no one knows where he's from, or how he happened to come out here to the end of the road, to Nour Chams. Perhaps he was here before everyone else, with a herd of goats, and he just stayed on when his animals died, not knowing where else to go. Maybe he was born here.

He came up to me, talked to me. He spoke in a gentle voice, with an accent I'd never heard before. Aamma Houriya said that he speaks like the people of the desert, like a Baddawi. That's why we call him that. He looked at me with his yellow eyes. He asked me who I was, where I came from. When I spoke to him of Akka and of the sea, he wanted to know what the sea was like. He'd never seen it. All he had ever seen was the great salt lake, and the immense valley of Ghor, and al-Moujib, where he said the palaces of the Djenoune were. And then I told him about what I had seen, the steady waves that come to die breaking against the walls of the city, the trees washed up on the beach, and at dawn, the sailboats slipping through the mist amid the flapping flight of pelicans. The smell of the sea, the taste of salt, the wind, the sun sinking into the sea every evening, right up to its very last spark. I loved the way he listened, his arms crossed over his cloak, his bare feet planted squarely on the ground.

I didn't talk the way Aamma Houriya did, because I didn't know any tales. I could only talk about what I'd seen. And he in turn spoke of what he knew, the mountains where he kept the herds near the great salt lake, walking day after day along the underground rivers that run beneath the sand, gnawing at herbs and bushes, with as sole companions the dogs running out ahead of him, the nomad campsites, the smell of fires burning, women's voices, his brothers from afar with other herds meeting there, and then striking out again.

When I spoke to him, or when he spoke to me, children came to listen. Their eyes were wide with fever, their hair all matted, their dark skin shone through the rags of their clothing. But we were just like them, I, the girl from the city by the sea, and he, the Baddawi, nothing set us apart anymore, we all had the same stray-dog eyes. We talked every evening when twilight soothed the scorch of day, watching the thin wisps of smoke floating up from the camp, and then nothing seemed hopeless anymore. We could get away, be free again.

After that I didn't go to wait for the supply truck anymore, either. Up on top of the hill, sitting by Saadi, I saw the cloud of dust far away on the Tulkarm road, and I heard the riotous cries of the children chanting: "Flour!... Milk!...Flour!"

So Aamma Houriya had to go down for our rations. And I just sat there listening to Saadi, trying to remember even more about what it was like, long ago, on the beach in Akka when I waited for the fishing boats to come in, and tried to catch sight of my father's boat first.

Aamma scolded me: "The Baddawi has put a spell on you! I'll take a stick to him!" She was making fun of me.

The war is so far away. Nothing ever happens. At first the children played with pieces of wood, imitating the sounds of rifle shots, or else they threw stones, lying flat on the ground, as if they were grenades. Now they don't even do that anymore. They've forgotten how. "Why don't we leave this place? Why don't we go back home?" They used to ask that too, and now they can't remember. Their mothers and fathers avert their faces.

There is a kind of film clouding the men's eyes. It makes them look foggy, their gaze is shallow, unrecognizable. There's no more hatred, no anger, no more tears, or desire, or restlessness. Maybe it's because water is so very scarce, water, the sweet side of life. And so there is this milky film, just like in the eyes of the white she-dog when it started to die. That's why I love Saadi's eyes. The water hasn't gone out of his eyes. His yellow irises shine out like those of the dogs roaming about in the hills around the camp. He's laughing, but to himself, without moving his lips, with his eyes only. It's very plain to see.

Sometimes he talks about the war. He says that when it's all over, he'll go south, down by the great salt lake, to the valley of his birth. He'll go in search of his father, his brothers, his uncles and his aunts. He thinks that he'll find them and that one day he can go back to walking with the herd along the invisible rivers again.

He says names that I've never heard before, names as distant as stars: Suweima, Suweili, Basha, Safut, Madasa, Kamak, and Wadi al-Sirr, the river of the secret, where everyone goes in the end. Out there, according to him, the land is so harsh, and the wind so strong, that men are swept along like bits of dust. When the wind rises, the herd walks toward the River Jordan, and sometimes even beyond, all the way to the great city of al-Quds, the one the Hebrews call Jerusalem. When the wind dies down, the herd returns to the desert. He says, just like old Nas did: Does the land not belong to everyone? Does the sun not shine for us all? His face is young, but his eyes are very knowing. He isn't a prisoner at the Nour Chams camp. He can go whenever he likes, cross the hills, go to those golden and pearl-colored cities where, Aamma Houriya says kings once lived who ruled even the Djenoune, to Baghdad, to Isfahan, to Basra.

One night I was so sick I was burning up inside. It felt like a stone were lying on my chest. I left the shack. Outside everything was calm. Aamma Houriya was sleeping wrapped up in her sheet by the door, but Roumiya wasn't asleep. Her eyes were wide open. I could see her chest rising and falling as she breathed but she didn't say anything when I went past her.

I saw the stars. Little by little everything started shining brightly in the dark, shining with a hard, painful light. The air was hot, the wind seemed to come blowing down from the mouth of an oven. Yet no one was outside. Even the dogs were hiding.

I looked at the straight lines of the alleys in the camp, the tarred roofs of the houses, the pieces of sheet metal rattling in the wind. It was as if everyone were dead, as if everything had disappeared, forever. I don't know why I did it: suddenly, I was afraid, I was in so much pain because of the weight on my chest, because of the fever that was burning inside of me, all the way down to the bone. So I started running down the alleys of the camp, not knowing where I was going, and shouting: "Wake up! Wake up!" At first my voice wouldn't come out of my throat, I only let out a hoarse cry that ripped through me, a crazed cry. It echoed out oddly in the sleepy camp and soon the dogs started barking, one, then another, then all the dogs around the camp and all the way up into the invisible hills. And I just kept running down the alleys, barefoot in the dust, with that burning feeling in my throat and in my body, the pain that didn't want to loosen its grip. I shouted to everyone, to all the plank and sheet metal houses, to all the tents, to all the cardboard shacks: "Wake up! Wake up!" People started coming out. Men appeared, women draped in their coats despite the heat. I was running and could distinctly hear what they were saying, the same thing they'd said when Roumiya arrived: "She's crazy, she's gone crazy." The children woke up, the older ones ran along with me, the others were crying in the dark. But I couldn't stop anymore. I ran and ran through the camp, going through the same streets time and again, first over by the hill, then down toward the wells, and along the barbed wire fencing that the foreigners had put around the wells and I could hear my breath wheezing in my lungs, I could hear my heart pounding, I could feel the heat of the sun on my face, on my chest. I was shouting in a voice that was no longer my own: "Wake up! Prepare yourselves!"

Then all of a sudden I couldn't catch my breath. I fell to the ground near the barbed wire. I couldn't move anymore, couldn't speak. The people walked up to me, women, children. I could hear the sound of their footsteps, I could clearly hear their breathing, their words. Someone brought some water in a metal goblet, the water ran into my mouth, over my cheek, like blood. I made out Aamma's face, very near to me. I pronounced her name. She was there, her soft hand lying on my forehead. She was murmuring words that I didn't understand. Then I realized they were prayers and I felt the Djenoune moving away from me, abandoning me. Suddenly, I felt empty, terribly weak.

I was able to walk, leaning on Aamma's arm. Stretched out on the mat in our house, I heard the sound of the voices fading away. The dogs kept barking for a long time and I fell asleep before they did.

When I went up to the top of the rocky hill in the morning, Saadi came up to me and said, "Come on, I want to talk to you." It was still early, there weren't any children out yet. I noticed that Saadi had changed. He'd washed his face and hands down at the wells at prayer time, and even though his clothes were torn, they were clean. He held my hand very tightly in his and his eyes were filled with a brightness I had never seen. He said, "Nejma, I heard your voice last night. I wasn't sleeping when you started calling to us. I realized you had received the message from God. No one heard you, but I heard your call and that's why I have prepared myself."

I wanted to pull my hand away and leave, but he was holding it so fast that I couldn't escape. The hill was deserted, silent, the camp was far away. I was afraid, and the fear was mingling with a feeling I didn't understand. He said, "I want you to come with me. We're going to cross the river, till we reach the valley of my birth, al-Moujib. You'll be my wife and we will have sons, God willing." He was speaking without haste and a sort of joy lit his eyes. That's what attracted and frightened me at the same time. "If you like we can even leave today. We'll take some bread, a little water, and we'll cross the mountains." He was pointing eastward, toward the hills still in darkness.

The sky was blank, the sun was beginning its ascent. The earth was shining with new freshness. Below, at the bottom of the hill, stood the camp like a dark smear from which a few trails of smoke arose. You could see the shapes

232

of women near the wells, children running in the dust.

"Talk to me Nejma. All you have to do is say yes and we'll go today. No one can keep us here." I said, "It can't be, Saadi. I can't go away with you." His eyes darkened, he let go of my hand and sat down on a rock. I sat next to him. I could hear my heart beating hard in my chest, because I wanted to go. I began to talk so I could stop listening to my heart. I talked about Aamma Houriya, about Roumiya and the child that was going to be born. I talked about my city, Akka, to which I had to return. He listened without responding, looking out at the vast valley, the camp, so like a prison with those people coming and going along the alleys like ants, busying themselves around the wells. He said, "I thought I'd understood your call, the call that God sent you last night." He said that in a calm voice, but he was sad and I felt tears in my eyes, and my heart started racing again because I wanted to go away. Now I took his hands in mine, his fingers that were so very long and thin and the pale marks of his nails against his black skin. I felt the blood running through his hands. "Maybe one day I'll go away, Saadi. But I can't leave now. Are you angry with me?" He looked at me, smiling, and his eyes were bright again. "So that was the message that God sent you? Then I will stay too."

We walked a little ways on the hilltop. When we came up in front of his shelter, I saw he'd prepared a bundle for the road. Food wrapped in a piece of cloth and a bottle of water attached with a string. "When the war is over, I'll take you to our house, in Akka. There are lots of fountains there, we won't need to take water with us."

He unwrapped the bundle and we sat down on the ground to eat a little bread. The sunlight was burning off the morning freshness. We heard the bustling of the camp, the children who were coming up. There was even the swift flight of a bird, letting out sharp cries. We both burst out laughing because it had been so long since we'd seen a bird. I lay my head on Saadi's shoulder. I listened to his halting, melodious voice speaking about the valley where he followed the flock with his brothers along the underground river of al-Moujib.

After that came the winter and life became difficult in Nour Chams. We had been in the camp for almost two years now. The supply truck came less and less frequently, twice a week, or even only once. A whole week went by without the truck coming to the camp. There were rumors of war, people said terrible things. They said that in Al-Quds, the old part of the city had burned down and that the Arab soldiers threw burning tires into the cellars and the stores. Refugees came in the truck, men, women, children with distraught faces. They weren't poor peasants anymore like in the beginning. They were richer people from Haifa, Jaffa, shopkeepers, lawyers, even a dentist. When they climbed out of the truck the ragged children from the camp swarmed around them, chanting, "Foulous! Foulous!" They followed the newcomers until they gave up a few coins. But the new refugees didn't know where to go in the camp. Some slept out in the open with their suitcases piled up at their feet, wrapped in their blankets. For them, the truck had brought cigarettes, tea, Marie biscuits. The truck drivers sold it all to them in secret, while the poor people were waiting in line to get their rations of flour, Klim milk, dried meat.

When the newcomers got out of the truck, people gathered around, asked them questions. "Where are you from? What news have you brought? Is it true that Jerusalem is burning? Does anyone know my father, old Serays, who lives on the road to Aïn Karim? You, did you happen to see my brother? He lives in the largest house in Suleïman, the one with a furniture store? What about my drapery store, facing the Gate of Damas, was it spared? And my pottery store near the Omar Mosque? And what's become of my house in al-Aksa, a lovely white house with two palm trees in front of the door, Mehdi Abu Tarash's house? Have you heard anything about my neighborhood, near the train station? Is it true that the English bombed it?" The newcomers advanced through the questions, dazed by the journey, blinking their eyes because of the dust, their fine clothes already stained with sweat, and gradually the questions stopped, silence returned. The inhabitants of the camp fell away as they passed, still trying to read an answer to their questions in the blank eyes, the slumped shoulders, in the children's faces glistening with fear like a feverish sweat.

That was when the first city-dwellers arrived, fleeing the bombs. Their money was worthless here. In vain, they had handed out bills by the fistful all along the road. To pay for a pass, for the right to stay just a little longer in their home, for a seat in the tarpaulined truck that brought them to the camp at the end of the road.

Then the rations got even skimpier because of all the people that had come into the camp. Death struck everywhere now. When I went to the wells in the morning, the passageway between the barbed wire fences was scattered with the cadavers of dogs. Those still alive, growling like wild beasts, fought over the remains. The children could no longer wander far from the houses for fear of being devoured by the dogs. When I went up to the top of the stone hill to see Saadi, I had to carry a stick to ward off the dogs. He wasn't afraid. He wanted to stay up there. His eyes were still bright and he took me by the hand to talk with me and his voice was gentle. But I didn't stay very long anymore. Roumiya was on the verge of giving birth and I didn't want to be far from her when it happened.

Aamma Houriya was worn out. She couldn't bathe Roumiya any longer. Now the wells were almost dry, in spite of the rains. Those who were last to throw their bucket in brought up only mud. You had to wait all night for the water to reappear at the bottom of the wells.

The only food was oatmeal mixed with Klim milk. The able-bodied men, the young boys of ten or twelve, and even the women, left one after another. They went northward toward Lebanon, or eastward in the direction of Jordan. People said they were going to join the Fedayeen, the martyrs. They were called the *aïdoune*, the revenants, because one day they would return. Saadi didn't want to go to war, he didn't want to be a revenant. He was waiting for me to go away with him to the valley of his childhood, to al-Moujib, on the far side of the vast salt lake.

Roumiya hardly went out of the house anymore, only to go to the bathroom in the ravine outside the camp. She only went with me, or sometimes Aamma Houriya accompanied her as she teetered along the path holding her belly in her hands.

It was there, in the ravine that the pains started. I was up on top of the hill because it was early in the morning and the sun was very low, lighting the land through the mist. It was a time for the Djenoune, a time that the red flames might be dancing near the well in Zikhron Yaacov, as Aamma Houriya had seen just before the English came.

I heard a sharp cry, a cry that pierced the dawn silence. I left Saadi and started running down the hill, cutting my bare

feet on the sharp stones. The cry had come only once and I
stopped short, trying to guess where it had come from. When
I entered our house I saw the sheets thrown to one side. The
jar of water that I'd filled at daybreak was still full.
Instinctively, I went toward the ravine. My heart was racing
because the scream had lodged inside of me, I knew it was
time, Roumiya was going to give birth. I ran through the
brush toward the ravine. I heard her voice again. She wasn't
screaming, she was moaning, groaning louder and louder,
then stopping as if to catch her breath. When I went into the
ravine, I saw her. She was lying on the ground with her knees
up, wrapped in her blue veil, her head covered. Aamma
Houriya was sitting next to her, caressing her, talking to her.
The ravine was still in shadow. The night chill attenuated the
smell of urine and excrements. Aamma Houriya lifted her
head. For the first time I saw an expression of helplessness
on her face. Her eyes were blurred with tears. She said, "We
have to carry her. She can't walk." I was going to go for help
but Roumiya pulled the veil from her face, she sat up. Her
child's face was twisted with pain and anxiety. Her hair was
damp with sweat. She said, "I want to stay here. Help me."
Then the moans started again, punctuated by the
contractions of her uterus. I just stood before her unable to
move, unable to think. Aamma Houriya snapped at me, "Go
get some water, the sheets!" And since I didn't move, "Hurry
up! She's started labor." So I started running with the sound
of my blood roaring in my ears and my breath whistling in
my throat. In the house I took the sheets, the jar of water,
and because I was in such a hurry, the water was slopping
out of the jug and drenching my dress. The children were
following me. When I got to the entrance of the ravine I told
them to go away. But they stayed, they scaled up the sides of
the ravine to watch. I threw stones at them. They backed

away, then they returned.

Roumiya was suffering a great deal, lying on the ground. I helped Aamma lift her up to wrap her in the sheet. Her dress was soaked from the waters and on her bloated white stomach the contractions looked like waves on the surface of the sea. I'd never seen that before. It was terrifying and beautiful at the same time. Roumiya wasn't at all the same, her face had changed. Thrown backwards, looking up at the bright sky, her face seemed like a mask, as if some other person were beneath it. Mouth open, Roumiya was panting. Now and again whimpering sounds that were no longer her voice rose from her throat. I ventured a little closer. With a dampened cloth I put water on her face. She opened her eyes, she looked at me as if she didn't recognize me. She murmured, "It hurts, it hurts." I wrung the cloth over her lips so she could drink.

The wave came back on her belly, went all the way up to her face. She arched her body backwards, pinched her lips closed as if to prevent her voice from coming out, but the wave was still swelling and the moan slipped out, became a scream, then broke, became a panting breath. Aamma Houriya had placed her hands on Roumiya's belly, and she pushed with all of her weight, as hard as if she were trying to push the dirt from a piece of laundry on the edge of the washtub. I looked on in terror, the grimacing face of the old woman as she mauled Roumiya's belly, I felt as though I were witnessing a crime.

Suddenly the wave started moving faster. Roumiya arched up high, heels dug into the sand, shoulders against the stones in the ravine, face turned toward the sun. With a supernatural scream she pushed the child out of her body, then slowly fell back to the ground. So now there was that shape, that being covered with blood and placenta wearing a living cord around its body, which Aamma Houriya had taken and started to wash and that suddenly started to let out it's first cry.

I looked at Roumiya stretched out, her dress pulled up on her belly, bruised from Aamma's fists, her swollen breasts with purple tips. I felt nauseous, profoundly dizzy. When Aamma Houriya finished washing the baby, she cut the cord with a stone, knotted the wound on the child's belly. For the first time she looked at me with a peaceful face. She showed me the baby, tiny, wrinkled, "It's a girl! A very pretty girl!" She said that in a relaxed voice as if she'd found the baby in a basket. She lay it down gently on its mother's breast where milk was already dribbling out. Then she covered them with a clean sheet and sat down next to them humming. Now the sun was rising in the sky. The women began to come into the ravine. The men and the children kept their distance on the slopes of the ravine. The flies whirled overhead. Aamma Houriya seemed to suddenly remember the horrid smell. "We'd better be getting home." Some women brought a blanket. Five of them together lifted Roumiya holding her baby tightly to her breast, and they carried her away slowly like a princess.

Life had changed now that the baby was in our house. Despite the lack of food and water there was new hope for us. Even the neighbors felt it. Every morning they came to our door, they brought a present, sugar, clean linen, a little powdered milk they'd taken from their rations. The old women who had nothing to offer brought dead branches for the fire, roots, fragrant herbs.

Roumiya had changed too since the birth of the baby. She no longer had that foreign look in her eyes, she stopped hiding behind her veil. She'd given her daughter the name of Loula because it was the first time. Al-marra al-loula. And I thought it was true—here in our miserable camp where the world had cast us, far from everything. Now there was a heart in the camp, there was a center, and it was in our house.

Aamma Houriya never tired of telling all the women who came to visit about the birth, as if it were a miracle. She said, "Just think, I took Roumiya to the ravine so she could go to the bathroom just before sunrise. And God willed that the child be born there in that ravine, as if to show that the most beautiful thing can appear in the most vile place, amidst the refuse." She elaborated upon that theme infinitely, and it became a legend that the women spread around through the grapevine. The women stuck their heads into the house, holding their veils in place, to get a glimpse of the wondrous thing, Roumiya sitting down giving her milk to Loula. And it was true, the legend that Aamma Houriya had invented enveloped her in a special kind of light, with her clean white dress, her long blond hair hanging over her shoulders, and that baby sucking at her breast. Something was truly going to begin, it was the first time.

It was in winter when our camp became desperate, hungry, abandoned. The children and the old men were dying from fever and illnesses caused by the well water. It was mostly in the lower part of the camp where the newcomers had settled. Saadi could see the people burying the dead from up on the hill. There were no coffins, the bodies were wrapped in an old sheet, without even sewing it up, and a hole was hurriedly dug on the side of the hill with a few big rocks on top to keep the stray dogs from digging them up. But we wanted to think that it was all happening far away and that, thanks to Loula, nothing like that could happen to us.

It was cold now. At night the wind blew over the stony land, burned your eyelids, numbed your limbs. Sometimes it rained and I listened to the sound of the water running over the planks and tarpaper. In spite of our hardships, to me it seemed as fine as if we were in a house with nice high dry walls and a pool in the courtyard where the rain would be making its music. To catch the rain, Aamma put all the receptacles she could find under the rainspouts—pots, jars, empty powdered milk cans, and even an old car hood that the children found in the riverbed. So I listened to the rain tinkling in all the receptacles and I was feeling as joyful as I did in the old days, in my house, when I listened to the water cascading down over the roof and onto the tiles of the courtyard, and watering the orange trees in pots that my father had planted. It was a sound that made me feel like crying too, because it spoke to me, it told me that nothing would ever again be like it was before, and that I would never see my home again, or my father, or the neighbors, or anything I used to know.

Aamma Houriya came to sit down beside me as if she sensed my sadness. She spoke to me gently, maybe she told me a Djinn story, and I leaned against her, but without letting myself be too heavy because she was weak from all the privations. Earlier in the evening when the rain had started falling she had joked, "Now this old plant will turn green again." But I knew that the rain wouldn't bring back her strength. She was so pale and thin, and she coughed constantly.

Now it was Roumiya who took care of her. Aamma looked after the baby wrapped in cloths, she sung it lullabies.

The United Nations truck hadn't been back for a long time. The children went into the hills looking for roots, leaves, and myrtle fruit to eat. Saadi knew the desert well. He knew how to trap prey, small birds and jerboas that he roasted and shared with us. I never would have thought I could take so much pleasure in eating such tiny creatures. He also brought back wild berries, arbutus, that he gathered far away, beyond the hills. When he brought his harvest tied in a scrap of cloth that he laid ceremoniously on the flat rock in front of the door, we pounced on the fruit to eat and suck them avidly and he teased us in a placating voice, "Don't bite your fingers. Don't eat the rocks."

Something strange was going on between the Badawi and Roumiya. She, who used to look away when Saadi came near the house, now pulled her veil over her face as if to hide but her clear eyes stared at the young man. In the morning when I came back from the wells I didn't have to go up on the hill to find Saadi. He was there, sitting on the flat rock next to the house. He didn't speak to anyone, he stayed a little off to one side, as if he were waiting for someone. Now I couldn't take his hand in mine anymore, or put my head on his shoulder to listen to him. He spoke to me with the same soft and melodious voice, but I knew it was no longer me he was waiting for. It was Roumiya's silhouette hidden in the shadow of the house, Roumiya and her long hair through which Aamma Houriya was running a fine comb, Roumiya who was breast-feeding her baby, or who was fixing the meal with flour and oil. At times they talked to each other. Roumiya sat on the doorstep, wrapped in her blue veil, and Saadi sat on the other side of the door and they talked, they laughed.

So then I'd go up on top of the hill, carrying my stick to ward off the dogs. There were no more children up there, I kept a lookout for the supply truck by myself. The sunlight was blinding, the wind blew up clouds of dust in the valley. In the distance the horizon was gray, blue, intangible. I could imagine I was by the sea, on the beach in the dusk and I was watching for the fishing boats, to be the first to see the one I knew so well, with its red sail and, on its keel, the green star of my name that accompanied my father.

One morning a stranger came into our camp escorted by soldiers. I was up on the hilltop standing watch when the large cloud of dust rose on the road to Zeïta, and I realized it wasn't the food trucks. My heart started pounding with fear because I thought they were soldiers coming to kill us.

When the convoy came into the camp everyone was hiding because they were afraid. Then the men came out of the cabins and the women and children came with them. I ran down the hill.

The trucks and the cars stopped at the entrance to the

camp and some men and women got out, soldiers, doctors, nurses. Some were taking pictures or talking with the men, handing out candy to the children.

I moved up through the crowd to hear what they were saying. The men in white spoke in English and I only caught one or two words that I understood. "What are they saying?" a woman asked worriedly. In her arms was a child with an emaciated face, its head balding with ringworm. "They are doctors, they've come to treat the sick." I said that to reassure her. But she kept watching them, her face half-hidden behind her veil, and repeated, "What are they saying?"

Among the soldiers was a very tall, slender, elegant foreigner dressed in gray. While all the others were wearing helmets, he was bareheaded. He had a gentle, slightly red face, he would lean his head to one side to listen to what the doctors were saying to him. I thought he was the boss of the foreigners and I inched closer to see him better. I wanted to go up to him, I wanted to talk to him, tell him all that we were suffering, the children who died here every night, whom we buried in the morning at the foot of the hill, the weeping of women that droned from one end of the camp to the other, so that you had to plug up your ears and run up the hill to keep form hearing them.

When they started walking through the streets with the soldiers my heart started beating very fast. I ran toward them shamelessly, despite my torn dress and tangled hair and my dirt-stained face. The soldiers didn't see me right away because they were keeping their eyes to the side in case someone wanted to attack them. But he, the tall man with light-colored clothes, saw me and stopped walking—his eyes fixed on me, as if he were questioning me. I could see his gentle face, reddened from the sun, his silver hair. The soldiers stopped me, held me back, they were squeezing my arms so hard it hurt. I realized I'd never reach the boss, that I wouldn't be able to talk to him, so I shouted the only words I knew in English, "Good morning sir! Good morning sir!" I was shouting that with all my might and I wanted him to understand with only those words what I wanted to tell him. But the soldiers pulled me away and the group of men in white and the nurses walked on. He, their boss, turned back toward me, he looked at me smiling, he said something I didn't understand but I think it was simply, "Good morning," and all the people walked on with him. I saw him walking away through the camp, his tall light-colored shape, his head tilted to one side. I went back to join the others, the women, the children. I was so tired from what I'd done that I didn't feel the pain in my arms, or even the bitter disappointment of not having been able to say anything.

I went back to our house. Aamma Houriya was lying under the blanket. I saw how pale and thin she was. She asked me if the food truck had finally come and, to comfort her, I told her that the truck had brought everything, bread, oil, milk, dried meat. I also told her about the doctors and nurses, the medicine. Aamma Houriya said, "That's good. That's good." She remained there, lying on the floor under the blanket, her head resting on a stone.

Sickness came to the camp in spite of the doctors' visit. Death was no longer furtive, carrying off old men and children in the night, a cold feeling that crept into the bodies of the weaker people and snuffed out the warmth of life. It was a plague that roamed the alleys of the camp sowing death in broad daylight, every minute, even amongst the most able-bodied men.

It had all started with the rats that we saw dying in the narrow streets of the camp right out in the sunlight as if they'd been chased from the ravines. At first the children played with the dead rats and the women picked them up with a stick and threw them a little further away. Aamma Houriya said that they should be burned, but there was no gasoline or wood to make a bonfire.

The rats had come from all sides. At night we could hear them running over the roofs of the houses, their claws made little screeching sounds on the sheet metal and the planks.

It was death they were fleeing. In the morning when I went out at dawn to fetch water for the day, the ground around the wells was strewn with dead rats. Even the stray dogs didn't touch them.

The children died first, those who had played with the dead rats. Word spread through the camp because children— the brothers or friends of those who died—ran through the camp shouting. Their shrill voices echoing the terrible, incredible words that even they didn't understand, like the names of demons, "*Habouba!...Kahoula!...*" The cries of the children reverberated like the cawing of sinister birds in the still afternoon air. I came out into the burning sun, I walked through the alleys of the camp. It was deserted. Everything seemed sleepy, yet death was everywhere. In the north end of the camp—where the newcomers were, the rich people from al-Quds, Jaffa, Haifa, who'd fled the war—some people were gathered in front of a house. One of the men was dressed like an Englishman, but his clothing was torn and soiled. He was the dentist from Haifa. He was the one who had welcomed the doctors and the boss of the foreigners into the camp. I'd seen him with the soldiers. He'd watched me when I'd run up to them to try and talk with the man in light-colored clothes.

He was standing in front of the house with a handkerchief over his face. Next to him, women were crying, collapsed on the ground, their veils over their mouths and noses. In the darkness of the house the body of a young boy was stretched out on the floor. The skin on his chest and stomach had dark blue marks on it and there were terrifying splotches on his face and all the way down to the palms of his hands.

The sun beat down in the cloudless sky, the rocky hills around the camp shimmered in the heat. I remember that I walked slowly through the streets, barefoot in the dust, listening to the sounds that came from the houses. I could hear my heart thumping and there was silence all around in that blinding light as if death had spread over the entire world. In the houses, people hid in the shadows. I couldn't hear their voices but I knew that here and there other women, men, were sick with the plague, and were burning with fever and moaning with pain because of the swollen, hard glands under their arms, in their neck, in their groin. I thought of Aamma Houriya and I was sure that the fatal marks had already appeared on her body. I felt nauseous. I couldn't go home. Despite the heat, I climbed the stony slope up to the top of the hill all the way up to Old Nas's grave.

There were no more children up there, and the Baddawi wasn't in his shelter of branches. No one waited for the food truck to arrive anymore. The plague would wipe out every living person in Nour Chams. Perhaps it had even infected the whole earth, a scourge that the Djenoune sent to mankind, as God had commanded, so they would stop making war; and then when they were all dead and the sand of the desert had covered their bones, the Djenoune would come back, they would reign once again in their palace overlooking the garden of paradise.

I waited all day long in the shade of the scorched shrubs, hoping for I know not what. Hoping maybe that Saadi would come. But ever since he'd been living next to our house he never came up to the grave any more. When he left, it was for several days to hunt hares or partridges in the mountains to the east or to the north in Bédus, the place where he said there were the ruins of a Djenoune palace, just like in the valley of his childhood.

All day long I kept a lookout from atop the hill, waiting for the figure of a man, a child, listening to the distant voices of the women.

Before sunset, I came back down, because of the wild dogs that came out at night. In the dark house, it wasn't Aamma who was sick. It was Roumiya. Stretched out on her sheet on the floor, the sickness was already upon her. Her face was swollen with fever, her eyes were bloodshot. She was breathing rapidly, making a painful noise, and her body shook with tremors, in waves. Near her, Aamma Houriya sat in silence. Wrapped in her blue veil she just stared at her without moving. Baby Loula wasn't there. Aamma had entrusted her to a neighbor. From time to time, as I'd done in the ravine when Roumiya was giving birth, Aamma dipped a cloth into the water jug and slowly wrung it over the young women's face. The water ran over her lips, wetting her neck and hair. Already, Roumiya's eyes no longer saw. She could no longer hear, she didn't even feel the water running over her chapped lips.

All that night Aamma Houriya remained sitting next to Roumiya. Outside the moon was full, magnificent, alone in the middle of the blue-black sky. To keep from hearing the sound of her breathing, I slept outside, wrapped in my blanket, my head resting on the flat stone in front of the door. At daybreak Saadi arrived. He was bringing back some partridges, wild dates. Standing in front of the doorway to our house, leaning on a staff, he seemed very tall, thin. His dark face shone like metal.

Saadi went into the house and I strained to listen to the silence, as I had in the streets of the camp. He came back out, he took a few steps, and he sat down near the door, broken with fatigue. The dead birds and the dates scattered in the dust. I went into the house. Aamma Houriya was sitting in the same place, the wet cloth still in her hand. In the shadows I saw Roumiya's body, her face cocked backward, her eyes closed, her blond hair wet around her shoulders. She looked as if she were asleep. I thought about when she arrived at the camp, so long ago it seemed, so very long ago. There was the silence of death and I felt not a single tear in my eyes. But this was a death like in wartime, it froze everything around Roumiya. Her face wasn't marked by the disease. It was very white, with two dark circles around the eyes. I'll never be able to forget that face. As I was just standing there, very still, next to the door, Aamma Houriya looked at me. Her eyes were hard. In a voice I'd never heard before, almost hateful, she said, "Go away, get out of here. Take the child and go. We're all going to die." She lay down on the floor next to Roumiya. She too, closed her eyes, as if she were going to go to sleep. So I dropped my head and I left.

In the neighbor's house, I made a bundle with some bread, some flour, some matches, salt, several cans of Klim milk for Loula. I also packed my notebooks in which I'd written about my life each day. It was all I was taking from the camp. Saadi had kept his bottle of water ready. Then I tied the baby on my back with a veil, I took the bundle and walked out of the camp on the road the supply trucks came down.

The sun was still low, just touching the edge of the hills, but the horizon was already shimmering. At one point I turned around to look at the camp. Saadi, by my side, said nothing. His gaze was hard through the narrow slits of his eyes. He put his hand on my shoulder and led me away down the road.

They walked every day from sun-up to noon, southward through the arid hills. When the Klim milk was finished, Nejma said they had to find milk or the child would die. Tulkarm was occupied by soldiers. From up on an outcrop, Saadi stood watch all day long, not moving, like he used to do up on the rocky hill by Old Nas's grave. His eyes were so sharp that he could make out the barbed wire closing off the town, and the hidden machine guns stationed under the rocks. On the other side there was the black line of the railroad running through the fertile fields, and even farther off, the smoke of Moukhalid harbor and the stretch of sea, dark and unreal.

When he came back Nejma listened especially to that: the sea, distant, inaccessible. She lay down in the shade of a tree to give Loula a bottle in which she'd mixed the last spoonfuls of powdered milk. After drinking it, the child started whining. Saadi left again.

She waited for him there by the tree for the rest of the day, then during the cold night and even the next day, almost without moving, except to go to the bathroom, changing places to follow the shade of the tree. There was only a little sugar water left for Loula and some Marie biscuits. If Saadi didn't come back, they would surely die.

The baby was suffering from thirst, from the heat. In spite of the cloths she was wrapped in, her skin was sun burnt, her lips were swollen. To soothe her, Nejma sang the songs of her childhood, but she couldn't remember the words very well. She was just waiting there, her eyes staring into space, listening to Loula's breathing that sounded odd in the silence of the hills.

Several times she saw shadows passing, and her heart quickened because she thought it was Saadi coming back. But it was people who were fleeing Tulkarm, heading southward also. They went past without suspecting that Nejma was there, without hearing Loula whimpering in the night. The second evening, after Nejma had said her prayer and run her hand over her face and the child's because she was preparing to die, Saadi came. He came up to the tree without a sound, he said to Nejma, "Come and see." His voice was impatient. He helped Nejma walk. "Come quick." Lower down, Nejma saw two pale shapes tied to a shrub: a goat and her kid. She felt a sudden surge of joy like she hadn't known since her childhood. She ran toward the beasts that bolted. The goat pulled at its tie struggling, and the kid began to run through the brush. Nejma laid the baby on the ground, she approached the goat with one of the last of the English biscuits in the palm of her hand. When the goat had been calmed down, Nejma tried to milk her, but her hands had no strength.

The Badawi milked the goat into a metal dish. The swollen teats squirted out fragrant thick milk. Immediately Nejma poured the warm milk into the bottle and took it to Loula. The baby drank without catching its breath, then she fell asleep and Nejma laid her at the foot of the tree. There was some milk left over. Saadi drank first and Nejma drank too, straight from the plate. The warm, salty milk ran into her throat, spreading its warmth deep down in her body. "It's good." For the first time, Nejma was feeling hopeful again. "Now we won't have to die." She said that in a low voice, to herself. Saadi looked at her without answering.

Night came and they lay down on the ground with Loula between them. Nejma listened to the kid goat stumbling over the stones in the night, and the sound of his head butting against his mother when he nursed. The stars shone in the dark sky. Nejma hadn't looked at them for a long time. They were beautiful in the south. They weren't the same as the ones that shone over the camp.

The cold settled in. Nejma took the Baddawi's hand and he came close to her, lifting himself over the baby's sleeping body. With her head lying against his chest, Nejma felt his throbbing life, breathed in his odor. They remained like that for a long time without moving, eyes open in the dark. Desire rose in the boy's body, he unfastened his clothing. Nejma felt dizzy, she began to tremble. "Are you afraid?" asked Saadi, but gently, not mocking her. She clasped her body to his, wrapping her arms and legs around him pressing her chest against him. She was breathing rapidly, as if she'd been running. There were no thoughts in her, only the cold night outside, the shining stars, and Saadi's burning body, his penis tearing her as it entered.

They walked each day a little farther southward, through the hills, catching a glimpse of the dark line of the sea from time to time. Then they followed the course of the dried up rivers till they reached Djemmal. The goat and its kid followed them, drank the same well water, ate the same roots. Every morning and every evening after Loula had had her fill, they drank the warm milk that gave them strength. Saadi showed Nejma how to squeeze the swollen teats and make the milk spurt out.

They ate arbutus, berries from myrtle shrubs. They didn't go into the cities, for fear of the soldiers. War was everywhere. The rumbling of cannons rolled in the distance like thunder, but they never saw any combat. In some places, tumbled-down houses, carcasses of horses and donkeys, craters from shells in the ground. One day as they were approaching Azzoun in the mountains, suddenly there was a terrifying noise in the sky. Saadi and Nejma froze as the planes passed and their shadows sped over the earth. The Constellations crossed the sky slowly, describing a half circle that Nejma and Saadi seemed to be the center of. Meanwhile the goat and its kid fled into the brush. When the planes disappeared over the horizon, Nejma was trembling so hard that she had to sit down on the ground, hugging the child who was crying. "It's nothing," said Saadi. "They're heading southward, toward Jerusalem." But they'd never before seen planes that close.

He ran to catch the goat. To get hold of the rope, he had to be cunning and get downwind as if he were hunting a hare.

Then they walked in the direction of Haouarah, toward the East. At nightfall they arrived in the valley of Azzoun. They settled down on the bank of the river, under the acacias. The evening was cool, the wind rustled in the leaves, there were bats in the sky. Set back a little ways from the river, an abandoned olive grove gave off a peaceful smell. Here, with the slow flow of the river water, the smell of the trees, the sound of the wind in the acacias and the dwarf palms, one forgot about hunger, thirst, the war, everything that killed women and children, that forced people far from their homes, and the disease that made splotches on adolescent's faces and bodies, that had burned up Roumiya's body. Nejma could hear Aamma Houriya's voice saying, "Go away! Get out of here. We're all going to die."

Saadi went to wash in the river before the prayer. He turned toward the valley of his childhood, al-Moujib, and he touched the sand of the beach with his forehead. When night had completely fallen, he took off his clothes and he went into the river. He swam for a while against the current.

Nejma came to join him. She kept her sherwal on and, clasping the baby against her breast, she went into the river. The cold water enveloped her, made whirlpools around her back. Loula screamed, but Nejma spoke to her softly, and the water made her want to laugh. In the starlight the river shimmered between its dark banks. The wind was coming in gusts, whooshing through the leaves of the acacias.

When Nejma came out, Saadi had already milked the goat. He gave the warm bottle to Loula. Then they took turns drinking straight from the metal plate. Nejma wanted to light a fire to keep warm, but Saadi was afraid it would catch the soldiers' attention. They ate myrtle berries, wild figs, and some bitter olives. The child was already sleeping, wrapped in Nejma's veil in a hollow in the sand.

Saadi and Nejma lay down in their clothing. They listened to the sound of the wind in the leaves of the acacias, the unbroken rippling of the water in the valley. Saadi leaned over Nejma's face, brushed his lips against her. She tasted the warmth of his breath ecstatically. When he penetrated her, she no longer felt any pain. She wrapped her arms and legs tightly around his body, her hands were around his neck. She heard her breath growing stronger and her heart thudding faster and faster.

They set up a more permanent camp on the floor of the valley where the river formed a deep pool as blue as the sea that the birds came skimming over. On the banks there were acacias, tamarisks, wild olives. In one of the hills over the valley Saadi discovered the ruins of a farm, a few high walls of stone and of pisé, what was left of a burned roof. The fire had consumed everything around the farm, all the way out to the corral. Nejma didn't want to go in. She said it was the house of dead people. Saadi shut the goats in the corral, and built a shelter out of branches a little lower down on the riverbank.

The days were long and fine there in that valley. Mornings, Nejma watched the sunlight appearing in the cleft of the hills over the river. The water shone like a glittering path between the still-dark banks. The sky grew lighter and the rocky hills emerged from the night. Nejma walked over to the pool leaving Loula asleep in her veils under the lean-to. She washed her body, her face, her hair, facing the sun. When she'd finished the prayer, she lit a fire with the dead branches Saadi had gathered. In the plate she boiled white salsify, wild carrots, and other bitter, sour roots that she wasn't familiar with. They lit fires only at dawn because Saadi said the airplanes couldn't see them in the mist. Nejma thought that maybe the war was over and everyone was dead in the camps, in Tulkarm, in Nour Chams. Maybe the soldiers had gone back home.

When Loula finished her bottle, Nejma sat with her in the shade of the tamarisks. She watched the water flowing into the deep pool: it had been so long since she'd felt such peace. She could dream, with her eyes half shut, of the sea rolling over the rocks, of the cries of seagulls when the fishing boats neared the jetty.

Saadi went looking for food. Barefoot, wearing his woolen robe, his face and hair hidden under his long white scarf, he roamed the rocky hills searching for roots and myrtle berries. One day he found a beehive hanging from the branches of an acacia, like a fruit born of the sun itself. He lit a fire with dried leaves until the smoke made the bees come out. Then he climbed the tree and broke open the hive to take the honeycomb. Nejma had delighted in eating the thick honey mixed with the cells and even Loula sucked on the comb.

That's how the days passed from sunrise to sunset with nothing but the steady sound of the river, Loula's cries and tears, the soft bleating of the goat and her kid. Saadi called Nejma "my wife", and it made her laugh. Most of all, she loved evening time, when everything was finished. Saadi turned toward the night for God's call, then he went to sit down beside Nejma and they talked while Loula fell asleep. It was as if no one else were alive in the world, as if they were the first, or the last, it was the same thing. Bats appeared in the gray sky and took their turn at skimming over the deep pool of water, hunting mosquitoes. Saadi and Nejma drank the still-warm goat's milk, took turns dipping their lips into the metal plate. The stars shone before them in the cleft in the hills, the cold night wind began making its sound in the tamarisk leaves.

Later, when it was very cold, Saadi leaned tenderly over Nejma's lips and she drank in his life-breath. It was such an ardent moment that it seemed as if she'd never lived for anything but that, when their bodies became one, when their breath, their sweat, mingled and everything around them disappeared. And still later, when Nejma felt sleep numbing her senses, Saadi recited a poem, a chant, almost in a whisper, very close to her ear, which spoke of his native valley, of his mother and father, his brothers, the herds he led toward the valley where the great river flowed. He chanted that for her and for himself, then he too lay down, wrapped in his cloak.

One night they were awakened by people who were approaching: shadows walked along the riverside, stopped at the pool. Saadi was alert, ready to defend himself. Then they heard children crying. They were fugitives like themselves, walking at night and hiding during the day. At daybreak Nejma went down to the river, carrying Loula in her veil. She saw the newcomers: only women and children coming from the camps in Attil, Tulkarm, Kalansaoueh, or else from the coastal cities of Jaffa, Moujalid, or Tantourah. The women had horrible stories to tell, villages destroyed, burned, babies killed, men imprisoned or fleeing into the mountains and the women and children on the roads, carrying large bundles of food on their heads. Those who'd been lucky had taken trucks to Iraq. There were soldiers everywhere; they wandered the roads in armored vehicles, they were heading for al-Quds and even farther, to the salt lake.

The old women chanted, invoking the names of their sons who'd been killed. Some of them called to Saadi, "And what about you? Why aren't you fighting? Why are you fleeing with the women instead of taking up your rifle?" Saadi didn't answer. When the women saw that Nejma was holding a baby, they stopped their invectives. "Is it your son?" They drew the veil away and saw that it was a girl. Nejma lied, "It's my first daughter. Her name is Loula, the first time." The women burst out laughing. "So you had the child the first time you slept with him!"

Saadi wanted to leave. He said now others would come and the soldiers would take them away. He said it calmly. He found it only natural to leave. Ever since he was a child he'd never stopped packing his bags and walking through the desert behind his herds. But Nejma looked around sadly. It was the first place she'd been able to live without thinking of the war. It was like in the old days in Akka, at the foot of the ramparts when she looked out to sea and there was no need of the future.

They left at daybreak, herding the goat and her kid in front of them, walking up the valley until the river became a torrent of clear water flowing over the rocks. One morning as they came to the summit of a mountain, not far from Haouarah, Saadi showed Nejma a green shadow on the horizon. "That's al-Ghor, the great river."

To avoid the cliffs, they took the southern path toward Yassouf Loublan, Djidjiliah. Then eastward again till they reached Mejdel. Saadi worriedly watched the wide valley. Clouds of dust rose in the air. "The soldiers are already down there." But Nejma couldn't see them. Conjunctivitis blurred her vision. She was so tired that she fell asleep on the ground without even hearing the child crying.

They slept in the ruins of Samra before going down toward the river. Upon awakening in the morning, Saadi saw that the kid goat was dead. The goat stood next to it, nudging it with her horns, not understanding. Saadi dug a hole in the earth, he buried the kid. So that stray dogs wouldn't dig it up, he put stones from the roman ruins over the grave. Then he milked the goat. But the chapped teats gave but a little milk mixed with blood.

Before evening they reached the great river. The muddy water ran through the valley amidst tall trees. Everywhere around the riverbanks there were traces of men, tanks, blownout tires, footprints too, excrement.

They walked southward, toward al-Riha, the border. At dusk they met other fugitives. This time they were men coming from Amman. They were thin, sunburned, in rags. Some walked barefoot. They spoke of camps where people were dying of hunger and fever. So many children died that their bodies had to be thrown into dried up canals. Those who had the strength went northward, heading for the whiteman's land, Lebanon, heading for Damascus.

Saadi and Nejma crossed the river before dark on the bridge guarded by King Abdallah's soldiers. They spent the whole night on the riverbank. The heat was subterranean, as if there were a fire burning deep underground. When day broke, Nejma saw the Sea of Lot, the great salt lake for the first time. Strange blue, white clouds hovered over the water by the cliffs. Near the shore, in the place where the water from the river ran into the sea, yellow foam created a barrier that quivered in the wind. Nejma stared at the sea with her stinging eyes. The sun wasn't up in the sky yet, but already the wind was blowing hot. Saadi pointed southward, to the mountains faded with mist. "That's al-Moujib, the valley of my childhood." His clothes were in tatters, his bare feet were wounded from the stones and, under his long white scarf, his face was shriveled and black. He looked at Nejma and Loula who was whimpering with her mouth stuck to the veil looking for a breast to suck. "We'll never make it to al-Moujib. We'll never see the palace of the Djenoune. Maybe they've gone too." He said that in a calm voice, but tears ran from his eyes, made streaks on his cheeks and dampened the edge of his dusty scarf.

On the bridge the women, the children, were beginning to cross over. The refugees walked along the road toward the east, toward Salt, toward the camps in Amman, in Wadi- al-Sirr, Madaba, Djebel Hussein. The dust under their feet made a gray cloud that the wind lifted into a whirl. From time to time the tarpaulined trucks of soldiers passed on the road, headlights on. Saadi tied the goat's rope around his wrist and he put his right arm around his wife's shoulders. Together they began walking down the road to Amman, they tread in the steps of those who went before them. The sun shone high in the sky, it shone for everyone. The road had no end.

Child of the Sun

Ramat Yohanan 1950

I'd found a brother, it was Yohanan, the boy who had given us some mutton to eat on the beach when we'd first arrived. He had a very gentle face with the same laughing eyes and black curly hair that gypsies have. When we arrived at the kibbutz, he was the one who showed us the houses, the stables, the tower, the water tanks. I walked out to the edge of the fields with him. I saw a pond sparkling from between the apple trees and on the hilltop on the other side of the prairie, Druze houses.

Yohanan still spoke nothing but Hungarian, with a few words of English now. But it didn't matter. We spoke to each other with our hands, I read his eyes. I'm not sure if he recognized us. He was sharp and nimble, he ran through the brush, always accompanied by his dog. He made a wide detour and came back toward me panting. He laughed at the slightest thing. He was the shepherd. Every day at dawn he left with the herd of goats and sheep. He took the animals out to graze on the other side of the prairie, near the hills. In the bag slung over his shoulder he carried bread, fruit, cheese and something to drink. At times I brought him a hot meal. I walked through the apple orchards and when I reached the prairie, I would listen for the sound of the sheep to locate the herd.

We came to the Ramat Yohanan kibbutz in the beginning

of winter. Jacques had been sent to fight on the Syrian border, near Tiberias. Whenever he was on leave he came back with friends in an old, dented-up green Packard with a smashed windshield. We went to the seaside together, walked through the streets of Haifa, looked at the shops. Or else we went to Mount Carmel and just sat under the pines. The sun shone down on the sea, the wind rustled in the needles of the trees, a sharp smell of sap filled the air. In the evening he came with me to the camp, we listened to music, jazz records. In the dining hall, Yohanan played the accordion, sitting on a stool in the middle of the room. The light from the electric bulb shone on his black hair. The women danced, strange dances that made you giddy. I danced with Jacques, drank white wine from his glass, laid my head on his shoulder. Then we went for a walk outside, not saying anything. We held each other's hand, like lovesick kids. I could feel the warmth, breathe in the smell of his body, I'll never forget that.

We were to be married. Jacques said that it wasn't important; it was only a ceremony to please my mother. In the spring when he came back from the army.

When his leave was up, he went back in the car with his friends driving toward the border. He didn't want me to go there. He said it was too dangerous. It would be several weeks before I'd see him again. I'd recall the smell of his body. Nora was the one who lent us the room so we could make love. I didn't want my mother to know. She didn't ask any questions, but I think she knew.

Nights were mellow, the color of dark velvet. We could hear insects fluttering everywhere. On Shabbat nights, snatches of accordion music drifted in and out, like a breath. After lovemaking, I would put my ear to Jacques' chest, listen to his heart beating. I thought we were merely children, so remote, so full of dreams. I thought it would all last forever. The blue night, the song of insects, the music, the warmth of our bodies joined on the narrow cot, the drowsiness hanging over us. Or sometimes we would talk, smoking cigarettes. Jacques wanted to study medicine. We would go to Canada, to Montreal, or maybe Vancouver. We would leave when Jacques finished his military service. We would get married, and we would leave. The wine went to our heads.

The fields were vast. Work consisted in pulling up young beet sprouts, leaving only one every twelve inches. Boys and girls worked together, wearing the same pants and shirts of coarse canvas and some thick-soled boots. In the morning the fields were brittle from the night chill. A milky vapor snagged on the trees, on the hills. The workers moved along in a crouch picking the pale beet stems. Then the sun rose over the horizon, the sky turned a very raw blue. The furrows in the fields were filled with young people making a chattering sound like birds. From time to time swarms of sparrows suddenly flushed in front of us.

Elizabeth stayed at the camp. She'd been assigned to the laundry room to wash and repair the work clothes. She felt too old to stay out-of-doors all day long. But for Esther, it was rough and magnificent. She never tired of feeling the sun burning on her face, her hands, her shoulders through the cloth of the shirt. She worked with Nora. They moved up the furrows at the same speed, filling gunnysacks with the sprouts they'd uprooted. At first they talked, joking about waddling like ducks. Sometimes they stopped to rest, sitting in the mud, sharing a cigarette. But at the end of the day they were so tired they couldn't walk anymore. Their numb legs would no longer hold them up. They finished the job scooting around on the seat of their pants. Around four o'clock, Esther went back to the room, she lay down on her bed while her mother went to dinner. When she woke up, it was morning, a new day was beginning.

She carried the burn of the sun on her body. It was for all of those wasted, dull years. Nora too was burned, outrageously so. Sometimes she lay down on the ground, her arms spread wide, eyes closed, for such a long time that Esther had to shake her, make her get up. "Don't do that, you're going to get sick." When there was no work in the fields, Esther and Nora went over by the hills to take the shepherd his meal. As soon as he saw them coming, Yohanan took out his harmonica and played the same tunes he did on the accordion, Hungarian dances. The children from the village arrived, they climbed down through the rocks on the hill, approaching timidly. They were so poor, their clothing ragged, you could see their dark skin through the holes in their robes. When they saw Esther and Nora, they were halfway reassured, they came down a little farther, they sat down on the stones to listen to Yohanan play the harmonica.

Esther took the food from the bag, bread, apples, bananas. She offered them the fruit, shared out the bread. The bolder ones, the boys, took the food without saying anything, and backed away to the rocks. Esther went over to the little girls, climbed up the rocks to them, she tried to talk to them—a few Arab words she'd learned at the camp: *houbs, aatani, koul*! It made the children laugh, they repeated the words as if they were in a foreign language.

Then some men came. They wore the long white robe of the Druzes, they had white handkerchiefs on their heads that hung down on their necks. They stayed up high on the crest of the hill, their silhouettes rising against the sky like birds. Yohanan stopped playing, he motioned them to come. But the men did not move closer. One day Esther ventured up through the rocks to them. She took bread and fruit that she gave to the women. It was silent, frightening. She gave them the food, then she went back to join Nora and Yohanan. The following days the children came down as soon as the flock reached the foot of the hill. One of the women came down with them, she was around Esther's age, she was wearing a long sky-blue robe and gold threads ran through her hair. She held out a jug of wine. Esther wet her lips, the wine was cool, light, a bit sour. Yohanan took a drink in turn, and Nora drank too. Then the young woman retrieved the jug and went back up through the rocks to the top of the hill. That was all—the silence, the children's eyes, the taste of wine in the mouth, the bright sun. That's also why Esther thought that everything should last forever, as if nothing had ever existed before, as if her father would appear and he too would walk through the rocks up on the hilltop. When the sun was nearing the horizon, almost touching the haze out at sea, Yohanan rounded up his animals. He whistled to the dog, took up the crook, and the sheep and goats started walking toward the center of the prairie where the pond sparkled between the trees.

Sometimes in the afternoon, when the sun was declining, Esther went to sit with Nora in the groves of avocado trees. The leafy shade was nice and cool and they sat there for a long time talking and smoking, or else Esther went to sleep, her head resting on Nora's hip. The grove was up high, you could see the whole valley from there. In the distance, the dark hills near Tiberias and the light patches of the Arab villages. Further off still was the border where Jacques was fighting. At night there were mortar flashes sometimes, like the flashing of a storm, but you never heard any rumbling.

Nora was Italian. She was from Livorno, her mother, father, and little sister had disappeared, the fascists had taken them away. The day that the militia came for them, she was at a friend's house and she'd survived during the war because she'd remained hidden in a cellar. "Look, Esther, there's blood everywhere." She said strange things. There was a lost look in her eyes, a bitter fold on each side of her mouth. When she wasn't wearing work clothes, she dressed in black like a Sicilian woman. "Do you see the blood shining on the pebbles?" She would lift up flat rocks, she liked to uncover scorpions. They fled over the powdery dirt between the avocado trees seeking another shelter. Nora picked them up between two twigs without harming them, she inspected the swollen poison gland, the erect stinger. She said she could tame them, teach them tricks.

She worked in the beet fields with Esther, she would immediately spot any spiders hiding under stems. She took them off gently with a blade of grass, put them down a little farther off so they wouldn't be harmed. In her room, she let spiders weave their webs on the ceiling. It made odd gray stars that oscillated in a draft. The first time Jacques went into her room, he started back in disgust. He wanted to sweep the webs away but Esther had stopped him, "You can't do that, they're her friends." Jacques got used to it. He thought Nora was a bit mad too. But it didn't matter. "At any rate," he said, "you have to be a bit mad to do what we're doing here."

One day while Nora was working in the fields, her room had been repainted, everything from floor to ceiling was covered in gelatinous white. Nora was outraged, she wandered the camp screaming, insulting the people who had done it. It was because of the spiders, she was crying because they'd been chased away.

Esther and Nora had a hiding place, at the far end of the building, under the water tank. It was Nora who'd found the place and they took refuge there in the afternoons, when it was so terribly hot. Nora found the key that opened the door under the reservoir. It was a large empty room, lit by two loopholes. There was nothing there but cases, old gunnysacks, some cable, empty drums. It was as dark and cold as a cave in there. It was very still, only the sound of water running in the pipes, drops falling regularly somewhere. It was strange, disquieting. Under the rocks, Nora found white, almost transparent scorpions. And others, very black. She showed Esther the rings in the tail that indicated how strong their poison was. She said this was where she lived now because they'd painted her room white. She wanted to be in the theater. She walked up and down under the reservoir reciting poems out loud. They were poems that resembled her, vehement and tragic poems that she translated for Esther, exclamations, entreaties. She recited poems by García Lorca, by Mayakovsky. And she recited verses in Italian, passages from Dante and Petrarch, parts of Pavese, *Death will come and she will have eyes.* Esther listened to her, she was her only audience. Nora said, "You know what would be nice? To bring the children here and listen to them sing and play."

There was a heavy silence, as if waiting for something to happen. It was over. Esther wanted everything to remain full, so there would be no room for the emptiness of memories. She had copied the poems of Hayyim Nahman Bialik in her black notebook, the same kind in which Nejma had written her name, on the road to exile. She read,

"Brother, brother,

have pity on the black eyes beneath us,

for we are weary, for we share in your pain.

I did not gain my light in the courtyards of liberty.

I did not receive it from my father,

I tore it from my own flesh,

I carved it in my own heart."

The children's house was in the center of the kibbutz. The rooms of the dining hall also served as a school. There were appropriately sized tables and chairs for the children, but the walls were bare. Painted in that same gelatinous white.

She just couldn't help it. Nora couldn't bear being alone out there in the water tank anymore, with the dripping sound, and that blinding light outside. She walked out into the open through the tall grasses that grew around the tank. She was looking for snakes. Her pale face glowed like a mask over her black dress. She passed Esther without recognizing her. She was in Livorno, the militiamen had taken her sister Vera away. She roamed around like a madwoman, shouting the name out. "Vera, Vera, I want to see Vera right now!" She went up to the children's house, went into the classroom, and the schoolteacher just stood there, the Hebrew phrase suspended on the blackboard. Nora knelt down in front of a little girl, she hugged her close, smothered her in kisses, spoke to her in Italian until the frightened child burst out crying. Then Nora suddenly realized where she was, she was embarrassed, excused herself in French and in Italian, she didn't know any other languages. Esther took her by the arm, led her over to her room, laid her down on the bed very gently, like a sister. Esther sat down on the bed beside her without saying anything. Nora stared blankly at the all too-white wall in front of her, then she fell suddenly asleep.

It was time for The Festival of Light. Everyone had been waiting for it. This was the very first time, it was as if everything would be new, as if everything would start all over again. Esther remembered her father used to say that, that everything must be started over again, from the beginning. The devastated land, the ruins, the prisons, the accursed fields where men had died, everything was washed clean in the winter light, the cool mornings when the Hanukkah candles were lit, and the new flame, like a birth. Esther also remembered the words of the Book of the Beginning when, on the third day, the stars lit up, she recalled the flames of the candles in the church in Festiona.

Jacques was still with her then. He had to leave right after the holidays. But Esther didn't want to hear about that. The grapefruit harvest had begun. Jacques and Esther worked side by side, the grove rustled with all the hands picking fruit. It was a magnificent morning. The sun was scorching despite the cool air. In the afternoon they went back to Nora's room. They just lay there, one against the other, their breath intermingling. Jacques simply said, "I'm going soon." She felt tears fill her eyes. It was the first day, the day they'd lit the first Hanukkah candle.

That was a night she wouldn't forget. The dining hall was full of people, there was music, everyone was drinking wine. Girls came up to Esther, saying to her in English, "When are you getting married?" Esther was with Nora, it was the first time she'd ever been drunk. They were both drinking from the same bottle of white wine. Esther danced but didn't even know with whom. She felt an incredible emptiness. She didn't know why. It wasn't the first time that Jacques had gone away to the border. Maybe it was because of all the sun that had burned their faces in the grapefruit groves. Jacques' hair and beard had shone like gold.

Nora laughed, then suddenly started crying for no reason. She was feeling nauseous, all the wine and cigarette smoke. With Elizabeth, Esther took her out into the night. Together, they held her up while she vomited, then they helped her walk to her room. She didn't want to be left alone. She was frightened. She talked of Italy, of Livorno, of the men that took her sister Vera away. Elizabeth wet a cloth and laid it on her forehead to soothe her. She fell asleep, but Esther didn't want to go back to the party. Elizabeth left to go to bed. Sitting on the bed next to Nora, in the glow of the nightlight, Esther began to write a letter. She didn't really know to whom she was writing, Jacques maybe, or else her father. Or maybe she was writing for Nejma, in the same type of black notebook she'd taken out on the dusty road, and upon which they'd written their names.

It was morning, Esther realized for the first time that she was with child. Even before having physical proof, she knew it, she felt that restlessness, that weight deep inside, something had happened that she didn't understand. A feeling of joy—that was it—a joy like nothing she had ever felt before. It was early dawn, she'd slept with the door open to let in the cool of night, or maybe it was because of the smell of wine and tobacco that permeated the room, the bed sheets. Elizabeth was still sleeping soundlessly, it was so early that nothing moved in the camp, barely a few sparrows flitting between the trees. From time to time, coming from the other end of the kibbutz, the hoarse call of a rooster. Everything was gray, still.

Esther walked over to the water tank, then she followed the path leading to the avocado groves. She was wearing a light dress with the Bedouin sandals she'd bought in the Haifa marketplace with Jacques. She listened to the earth crunching under her steps. As she walked along, day broke gradually. Now there were shadows, the shapes of trees stood out on the hilltops. Birds flew up as she passed, thieving starlings that hovered over the fields, swooped away toward the pond.

Little by little, sounds began. Esther recognized them one after the other. It struck her that they belonged to her, each of them, they were inside of her like the words of a sentence coming out backward, sinking its roots into her remotest memories. She was familiar with them, she had

277

always heard them. They were already there when she was in Nice, or in the mountains, in Roquebillière, in Saint-Martin. The cheeping of birds, the calls of sheep and goats in the stable, the voices of women, of children, the whirring of the water pump, the vibrations of the strainers in the pipes, the wind pumps.

At one point, without catching sight of them, she heard Yohanan's flock moving away in the direction of the pastures, over by the Druze village. Then the cowherd who opened the gate of the corral and took the cows down to drink at the pond. Esther struck out again across the fields. The sun appeared over the rocky hill, lit up the tops of the trees, shooting red reflections off the pond. And that sun was inside of her, that red-hot point, whose name she did not know.

She thought of Jacques. She wouldn't tell him, not right away. She didn't want the slightest thing to change. She didn't want there to be anyone else. Before leaving for the border, Jacques said that they would get married over there, once they were in Canada, he would study at the university. And so Esther didn't want to talk about anything else, not to Jacques or to anyone. She didn't really want to think about the future.

She walked through the fields, still deserted at that hour. She went out into the very distant hills. So far away that she no longer heard the sounds of people anymore, or the cries of animals. She climbed up into the middle of the avocado grove. The sun was high now, it lit up the pond, the irrigation ditches. Very far away in the south, the domed shape of Mount Carmel showed above the sea haze. Never before had Esther stood facing a landscape like that. It was so vast, so pure, and at the same time, so worn, so old. Esther didn't see it with her eyes, but with the eyes of all those who had dreamt of it, all those whose eyes had closed with that hope in them, the eyes of the children lost in the Stura Valley, taken away in the boxcars with no windows. Haifa Bay, Akko, Mount Carmel, the dark line of the hills just as Esther and Elizabeth had seen it appear on the horizon before the prow of the *Sette Fratelli*, such a long time ago already.

Something was growing inside of her, swelling at the core of Esther's being, living within her, she didn't know it, she couldn't know it. It was so powerful it made her tremble. She couldn't walk. She sat down on a rock, in the shade of a tree, breathing in slowly. It was coming from very far away, permeating her. She remembered Joel's words in the prison in Toulon, the words in the language of mystery that welled up in her throat, that filled her body. She would have liked to find each of them now, here in this land, in the sunlight. She recalled the moment that she and Elizabeth had stepped onto this land for the first time, the sand on the beach when they had gotten off the boat, their clothes dirty and damp from the sea brine and their bundles of old garments.

She started walking again. She'd left the groves, was walking through the brush. She was far from the kibbutz, in the realm of scorpions and snakes. And all at once she felt afraid. It was like long ago on the road to Roquebillière, when she'd felt death lying upon her father and a void had opened out before her, and she'd run until she lost her breath.

Esther turned and started running. The pounding sound of her feet, of her blood, of her heart echoed in the hills, in her ears. Everything was strangely empty. The fields seemed abandoned, the even furrows shone harshly in the sunlight, like so many traces of a vanished world. There wasn't a bird in the sky.

A little farther on, Esther came upon the flock of goats and sheep. The animals were stopped in the bottom of a ravine, scattered alongside the field, some goats had even climbed up the embankment and were starting to eat the young beet sprouts. They called out in their sharp bleating voices.

When she reached the kibbutz, Esther saw the men and women gathered in front of the houses. The children had come out of the school. In the shade of the central building, on the bare cement terrace, they'd laid Yohanan's body. Esther saw his very white face thrown backward. His arms lay close along his body, hands open. The light bouncing off the wall made his eyes and his black hair shine. It was terrifying, it seemed as if he were only sleeping in the noon heat. There was a large dark stain on his shirt in the place the murderer had struck.

That same day, Esther learned of Jacques' death—killed at the border near lake Tiberias. When the soldiers came with the news, Esther didn't say anything. Her eyes were dry. She just thought, so he won't come back, he'll never see his son.

Montreal, Rue Notre Dame, 1966

Through the window of the glassed-in balcony, I watch the immutable street. The sky is so distant, so white, it's as if we were in the highest regions of the atmosphere. The street is mottled with snow. I can see footprints, sinuous tire marks. In front of my building, there is a garden with bare trees bristling against the pale sky. It was in that bit of garden that Michel took his first steps. The embankments are still very white. Only crows have left their tracks. On either side of the street stand tall curved lampposts. At night they make pools of yellow light. Along the snow-covered sidewalks, cars are stopped. Some haven't moved for days, their roofs and windows are covered with frozen snow. I can see Lola's VW whose battery went dead in the beginning of winter. It looks like a shipwreck stuck in the ice.

At the end of the street, the rear lights of cars flash on when they brake at the intersection. The orange and white buses drive around the square, go down the street toward the intersection. That's where I take the bus for McGill. That's where I met Lola for the first time. She was taking drama classes. She was expecting a baby too, and that's why we started talking to one another. On Sundays we used to take the VW and go to Longueil, or to Mont-Royal cemetery to watch the squirrels that live in the graves. All of that was so long ago that it seems a little unreal. Now the apartment is empty, there are only a couple of boxes left, some books, bottles.

It's hard to leave. I didn't think I'd accumulated so many things over the years. I had to package, give away, sell things. Yesterday there was the sale in the courtyard in front of Lola's house. Philip carried everything over there, with Michel and Zoé, Lola's daughter. The dishes, appliances, old toys, records, the stack of *National Geographics*. After the sale, there was a kind of party, we drank beer and danced, Philip was talking a little loudly. Michel and Zoé left quickly, they looked as if they were a bit embarrassed. They went bowling with some friends.

It was Sunday, it was snowing. Lola wanted us to go back to the cemetery together, just like when the children were small. It was terribly cold; though we looked very hard, we didn't see any squirrels living in the graves.

It's hard to go back. I watch the street with pained scrutiny, to fix each detail in my mind. My face is so close to the window, I can feel the cold against my forehead and my breath traces two steamy circles on the glass. The street is limitless. It runs out toward the infinity of bare trees and brick buildings, toward the pale sky. As if it were enough to take any one of the buses to go back there, across the ocean, back to my mother Elizabeth's side.

Now just when I'm going away, Tristan's face appears, such a gentle face, still a child, just as I'd seen it in the half-light of the chestnut trees in Saint-Martin, the day we began our wandering through the mountains. A little over a year ago, I found out that Tristan was in this country. It seems he works in Toronto, in some industry, or in the hotel business, I didn't quite understand. Someone spoke to Philip about him, a telephone number jotted down on a matchbook. I thought about it for a minute, but then I lost the number, I forgot about it.

Now, just when I'm going to leave, I see his face again, but it's on the other side of my life, it's the teenager who irritated me because I ran into him everywhere I went, and whom I accused of spying on me. It's not the potbellied, graying, forty-year-old man with his business in Toronto that I want to see. It's the child in Saint-Martin, when nothing had yet been changed in the course of the world, and we still thought everything was possible, even if war was all around us. My father was there then, standing in the doorway and Tristan shook his hand gravely. Or else deep in the gorge with the babbling waters of the torrent, Tristan puts his ear against my bare breast, he listens to the beating of my heart as if it were the most important thing in the world. How can all of that have come undone? Something aches deep down inside of me, I can't forget.

It's hard to go back, a lot harder than leaving in the first place. It's for Michel that I'm going back, so that he'll finally get to know his land and his sky, so that he'll finally be home. Suddenly I realize he's exactly the same age as I was when I boarded the *Sette Fratelli*. The difference is that today it will only take a few hours on a plane to cross the abyss that separates us from our land.

I look at this street, I feel dizzy. I thought everything was so far away, almost inaccessible, at the other end of time, at the end of a long and painful journey like death. I thought it would take my whole life to get there. And here it is, tomorrow. Just at the end of this street. On the other side of the traffic lights, where the orange and white buses turn and disappear between the red cliffs of the buildings.

I think of her now, Nejma, my sister with an Indian profile and pale eyes, she whom I only met once, by pure chance, on the road to Siloam, near Jerusalem. She who emerged suddenly from a cloud of dust and vanished into another cloud of dust as the trucks were taking us to the Holy City. Sometimes it seems I can feel the light touch of her hand resting on my arm, I sense the questioning look in her eyes, I watch her as she writes her name slowly in Roman letters on the first page of her black notebook. It is the only thing about her that I am still certain of, after all these years, that black notebook in which I too wrote my name, as if in a mysterious pact.

I dreamt of that notebook. I saw it in the dark, covered with fine writing, noted down with the same pencil we'd each held in turn. I dreamt that I knew how to decipher the writing and that I read what she'd written, just for me, a story of love and wandering that could have been my own. I dreamt that the notebook had reached me through the post, or else a mysterious messenger—like the children that were abandoned in Dickens's time—had put it in front of the door to my apartment in Montreal.

So I too bought a black notebook in which, on the first page, I wrote her name, Nejma. But It was my life that I put down, a little each day, my studies at the university, Michel, the friendship with Lola, the meeting with Berenice Einberg, Philip's love. And Elizabeth's letters too, the long awaited return, the hills that were so beautiful, the smell of the earth, the Mediterranean light. Was it about her, about me? I wasn't really sure. One day I would go back to the road to Siloam, and the cloud of dust would open up, and Nejma would come walking toward me. We would exchange our notebooks to abolish time, to stop the suffering and the burning pain of the dead.

Philip made fun of me, "Are you writing your memoirs?" Maybe he thought it was just one of those silly girls' diaries, in which they write down their love life and their secrets.

I even looked for Nejma here. From the window, I watched for her to appear in this snowy street. I looked for her in the corridors of the hospital, among the poor women who came for treatment. In my dreams she appeared standing in front of me as if she'd just opened the door and I felt the same attraction and the same hatred. She stared at me, I felt the light touch of her hand. There was the same questioning look in her pale eyes. Nothing had changed in her since the day I'd met her. She was wearing the same dress, the same jacket, gray with dust, the same scarf that half hid her face. Her hands above all, wide, suntanned hands like those of a peasant. She was always alone, the other women and children who walked beside her had disappeared. She came from exile, from forgotten drought-ridden lands, alone, to observe me.

When Jacques died, I was broken, I stopped dreaming. Elizabeth took me to her house. She'd moved to Haifa, lived in an apartment with a view of the sea. I didn't know where I was anymore. I wandered through the streets till I came to the beach we'd landed on, such a long time ago. In the crowd I always encountered the same woman—an ageless shape clothed in rags, her face veiled with a dust-stained cloth—who strode along the streams with a crazed look about her, pursued by children throwing stones. Sometimes I saw her sitting up against a wall in the shade, oblivious to the movement of cars and trucks. One day I went up to her, I wanted to look into her eyes, recognize Nejma's light. As I drew near, she extended her hand, the bony hand of an old woman with protruding rope-like veins. I stepped back, my head reeling, and the beggar woman with crazed eyes spit on me and fled into the shadowy streets.

I was just like Nora, I saw blood and death everywhere. It was winter, the sun scorched the hills of Galilee, seared the roads. And that weight in my womb, that ball of fire. Nights, I couldn't sleep, my eyelids opened, I had salt in my eyes. I just couldn't understand, I felt I was tied to Jacques beyond death, by the life that he had sown in me. I talked to him as if he were there and could hear me. Elizabeth heard me, she caressed my hair. She thought it was grief. "Cry, Estrellita, you'll feel better afterward." I didn't want to talk to her about the child.

In the daytime, I wandered aimlessly through the streets. I had the same stride as the madwoman who begged by the marketplace. Then I did that crazy thing; I hopped on one of the military trucks that transported material and provisions. I succeeded in convincing the two soldiers—so young, still children—that I was going to visit my fiancé on the front. I went to Tiberias, and once there, started walking in the hills, not knowing where I was going, just wanting to walk on the land where Jacques had died.

The sun beat down, I could feel the light weighing on my back and shoulders. I climbed up through the terraced olive groves, passed abandoned farms, walls riddled with bullets. There wasn't a sound. It was just like on the road to Festiona, when I used to watch for my father to appear in the mountains. The silence and the wind made my heart quicken, the sunlight was blinding, but I kept on walking, running through those silent hills.

At one point, I saw a tank stopped by the path. It was nothing but a half burned-out carcass, treads blocked by mounds of earth, but I was terribly frightened, didn't dare move. A little farther on, I reached the zigzags. There was a series of trenches reinforced with logs that weaved sharply back and forth on the hillside like fragments of stars invaded by bramble bushes. I walked along the trenches, then sat down on the edge and looked out in the direction of Lake Tiberias for a long time.

That's where the soldiers found me. They took me to headquarters to question me because they thought I was a Syrian spy. Then a truck brought me back to Haifa.

Elizabeth took care of everything, decided everything. I was to leave for Canada, I'd go to Montreal, to McGill University to study medicine. That's what Jacques Berger would have wanted. I accepted because of the child. It was my secret, I wanted him to be born far away, without Elizabeth knowing anything about it. At the end of March, I boarded the *Providence*, a small liner that brought food and medicine for the United Nations to the Arab refugees and took passengers back as far as Marseille. In Marseille, I boarded the *Nea Hellas* that transported emigrants to the New World.

It was at the end of September when my little sun was born. I had dreamt that he would be born back there, across the ocean, in my land, on the beach where Elizabeth and I first arrived, when the *Sette Fratelli* landed. The last months of the pregnancy were rough, I stopped going to classes, the semester was a total loss. The professors were indifferent, except for Salvadori, the pathology professor, an old man with a mustache and little round glasses like Gandhi. He said, "You'll come back afterward, when it's over." He extended my grant without my having to take the exams over.

It was Lola who took care of me, like a sister. She too was pregnant, but her child wasn't due till just before Christmas. We stuck together, the two of us, we told each other stories, she kidded me about looking like the Michelin Man. She was alone too. Her fiancé had disappeared, leaving no forwarding address. We lived together most of the time. She was teaching me yoga. She said it was good for our condition. Breathe in, push down with your stomach, sit in a half-lotus position, close your eyes and meditate. Lola was funny, so tall and high-strung, with her childish face, her blue eyes, her frizzy hair, and her complexion like that of a Dutch doll. Her name was Van Walsum, I never understood why her parents gave her a Mexican first name.

We discussed names. She wanted a girl, she enumerated first names, changed the order every day, Leonora, Sylvia, Birgit, Romaine, Albertine, Christina, Carlotta, Sonya, Maryse, Marik or Marit, Zoé, she always added Hélène, because of me. I thought that Zoé would fit her well, especially if she looked like her mother. "And your son?" I'd decided it would be my son, my little sun. But I pretended not to have thought about it. Destiny frightened me. I didn't dare tell her he would be the sun. I told her that if it were a boy I'd name him after my father. Michel.

"And if it's a girl?"

"Then you can name her."

Lola had never asked any questions about the father of my child. Maybe she thought it had been the same as with her, a man who had abandoned me. We were so much alike, we'd landed in Montreal like driftwood, one day a wave would carry us off again, we knew we'd never see each other again.

He would be the child of the sun. He would be part of me forever, made up of my flesh and blood, my land, and my sky. He would be carried by the waves of the ocean all the way to the sandy beach where we landed, where we were born. His bones would be the white stones of Mount Carmel and the boulders of Gelas and his flesh the red earth of the hills of Galilee, his blood would be the spring-water, the water in the torrent in Saint-Martin, the muddy water of the Stura and the water in Jesus' well. In his body would be the force and agility of the shepherds, in his eyes would shine the light of Jerusalem.

When I had wandered in the hills in Ramat Yohanan, over the dusty earth of the avocado groves, I had felt it already, the presence, the power. Like a bit of sun, so hot and heavy to carry. How could the others understand? They had a family, a place of birth, a cemetery in which they could see the names of their grandparents, they had memories. I had nothing but that ball in my womb that would appear. That's why I'd been dizzy, I'd felt imminently nauseous, a deep dizziness digging a hole inside of me, a hole that opened onto another world, onto a dream. I remembered Reb Joel's words in the prison in Toulon, when he told of the creation of Ayisha in his mysterious language. The words had made me shudder, and I'd pressed Jacques' hand so that he would translate for me more quickly. Now I felt the same force within me, it coursed through my body as if it were the words that had come to life. The sentences ran on, they were tides moving forward like the ripple of the wind on the water.

I didn't know where I was anymore. The labor room in the hospital, the walls painted bright yellow, the wheeled stretchers upon which the women lay, and that horrid brown door that swung in both directions when the midwife brought in a newly delivered mother, and the ceiling with its six buzzing neon bars, the wide grated windows looking out upon the night, a pinkish gray sky like a glimmer of snow and the silence of the steppes, broken only by the moaning of the women and the sound of hurried footsteps on the granite floors of the corridor.

I dreamt that the sun was going to appear on the other side of the earth, on the wide beach where Elizabeth and I arrived such a long time ago. I dreamt I was back there, lying on the beach at night with my mother, Elizabeth, next to me to help me and stroke my hair and I could hear the soft plashing of the waves slipping over the shore, the cries of the seagulls and the pelicans that followed the fishing boats at dawn. I closed my eyes and I was there. I could smell the sea, I felt the salt on my lips. Through my eyelashes I could see the utterly pure light of the first morning, the light that comes first from the sea and then flows slowly outward till it reaches the shore.

Jacques was with me, I felt his hand in mine, I saw his

face, so very bright, the golden light in his hair and beard, that was why his son was the child of the sun, because of the color of his hair. I could hear his voice translating the words of the Book of the Beginning for me, *And he let fall, He, the Almighty, a mysterious sleep on Adam, who slept, and he broke one of his envelopes and he gave it the form of his beauty, and he gave all of his will to the envelope that he had broken from Adam, and he made Ayisha, and he brought her to Adam. And Adam said: This is now substance of my substance, form of my form, and he named her Ayisha, because she had been broken and formed as he had willed.*

It was the longest night I'd ever lived through. I was so tired that I fell asleep in the labor room between contractions. "When will it begin?" I asked the midwife, I was getting discouraged. She gave me a kiss. "But dear, it already has begun." I knew my son would be born with the rising sun, he was its child, he would have its strength, and the strength of my land, the strength and the beauty of the sea that I love. Again, the crossing of Alon Harbor heading for Eretz Israel, and when I closed my eyes I could feel the soft rocking of the waves, I could see the very smooth expanse of sea at dawn, when the stem of the boat was drawing near the shore and that heavy gravelly voice was singing the blues. And then the baby started to come, and the waves carried me all the way to the beach where I'd fallen asleep while Elizabeth watched over the bags. It was extraordinary. It was so beautiful. I was in pain, but I could hear the sound of the waves on the sand, they were carrying me, I was slipping over the sea as it opened out, the beach was shining brightly in the newborn sun. "Breathe in, push push push push." The voice of the midwife echoed strangely on that lonely beach. I breathed in, I did not scream. There were tears in my eyes, the waves passed through my belly.

And Michel was born. I was blinded with all the light. I don't know who took me away, I don't know what happened. I slept for a long time, lying on the smooth wide beach where I had finally landed.

Elizabeth

Nice, summer of 1982, Hôtel de la Solitude

Elizabeth, she who was my mother, died yesterday—such a long time ago already—and as she wished, I will scatter her ashes upon the sea she loves this evening at twilight, when there will be no one on the beaches, just a few fisherman frozen on the seawall, dazed with the torpor of the evening heat. Then I'll walk through the streets, the ones that skirt the sea and whose names end in *i*, like Ribotti, Macarini, Verdi, Alexandre Mari. At the intersections, coming in gusts, I'll smell the sea wind, the smell she always loved.

The sun burned up so many weeks, so many months. The forest fires ravaged the hills and the sky was strange— half blue, half blackened with smoke. Every evening ash rained down on the sea.

Sitting at the terraces of cafés, German, Italian, American, Argentinean, or Arab tourists. The people spoke loudly, so loudly, the women were so heavily perfumed. There were couples of chilly homosexuals, nurses, Greek, Cypriote, Tunisian, Russian sailors. There were bums from Saint-German-des-Prés, from Boulevard Saint-Michel, there were pizza vendors, fortune hunters, panderers. There were stockbrokers, S.N.C.F. retirees, blank-faced girls with bleached hair, adolescents drugged out of their minds. There were bright red Dutch sunbathers; Kabylian workers, veterans of war, ministers, machinists, hairdressers, ambassadors, and who knows what else?

I saw that world, I wasn't familiar with it. I didn't recognize it anymore. All those people coming and going, passing one another, stopping, talking to each other, touching each other, the crowd that flowed like a thick gum along a groove. There was that sound of footsteps, above all, the sound of voices, despite the rumbling motors. Shut up inside their tight hulls, people have a hard look, distant, like a reflection.

Elizabeth left in 1973 during the war in the Sin Desert and that was the year I married Philip and opened my pediatric practice in a noisy street in Tel-Aviv, near the Habima Theater. How could I have let her go? I should have realized she was already ill, that she was suffering in silence. Cancer was eating away at her insides. And I just wanted to live, hard and fast, not trying to know in advance, never hesitating.

Elizabeth left dressed in black, with her small suitcase, the same one she had when she'd come over on the boat. I tried to keep her from going, but I knew it was useless. I talked to her about my profession, about Philip, about Michel who would need her. She smiled faintly, made a brief gesture to indicate that I shouldn't exaggerate. She said, "He won't miss me. It's I who will miss him." Then she added with feigned gaiety, "When he wants to, he'll make the trip to see me. He'll like that." When she boarded at the airport she said, with a calm cruelty that made my heart race, "Of course you understand that I won't be coming back. I'm going away forever." Now I know why she said that.

I walked through the streets of this unfamiliar city. This is where my mother and father spent their youth. I saw the high school where he taught history and geography, that magnificent prison of gray stone with its towers, its loopholes, its spiked gates. I saw the shrunken olive tree that was planted in the park as a symbol of peace. I saw the sundial with its Latin inscription that made me think of expressions used in the Pickwick Club. I looked for the building in which my mother and father lived, with a balcony overlooking the river. But today the river has been filled in with parking lots and pretentious concrete constructions. Nearby, in an old building, is a hotel with a name that I love—Hôtel Soledad, Solitude Hotel. I took a little room on the courtyard side because of the noisy traffic. When I'm stretched out on the narrow bed, I can hear pigeons cooing, and the faint burbling of a radio, and children shouting. It seems to me that I might be anywhere, everywhere, nowhere.

So many days spent in this strange city, in the blazing forest fires. Every day brought the echoes of war in Lebanon and new fires that had broken out in the Maures, the Esterel, in the hills of the Var. Every day in the narrow hospital room faced with my mother's pallid and gaunt body, every day watching her fade a little more, disappear. I listened to her weak, distant voice, felt her hand in mine. She spoke of the old days, of my father. She said Michel, she spoke of Nice, Antibes, she spoke of happy days, walks along the shore, vacations in Italy, in Siena, Florence, Rome. She spoke to me about it all as if I'd been there, somewhere, already grown up, a friend, a sister, a young woman that a couple meets by chance at a hotel, by a lake, and who shares an instant of their happiness, like an intrusion. The restaurant in Amantea, the sea so very blue, the headlands stretching out into the twilight. I'd been there with her, with my father, I had eaten the fresh watermelon, drank the wine, heard the music of the waves and the cries of seagulls. Everything else disappeared then, when she spoke to me of Amantea, of days during the summer after their marriage, as if I'd been there too and I'd seen their faces lit with youth, heard their voices, their knowing laughter. She spoke, and her hand gripped mine very tightly, as she must have held my father's hand back then when they'd gone out on that boat, gliding over the sparkling sea, surrounded by the riotous cries of seagulls.

Elizabeth's voice was growing gradually fainter every day, she told the same story endlessly, repeated the same names, the same cities, Pisa, Rome, Naples, and always the name Amantea, as if it had been the only place in the world that war had never reached. Her voice was so weak in the last days that I had to lean all the way down to her lips, feel the breath that carried the words, the shreds of memories.

Every day leaving the hospital at dusk and walking aimlessly through the streets, my mind swimming, hearing that name repeated infinitely, until it became an obsession, Amantea, Amantea...Reading in the papers about the fires burning on all the mountains, devouring forests of holm oaks and pines in Toulon, in Fayence, in Draguignan, in the Tanneron Mountains. The fires that lit up Beirut as it lay dying.

So I walked through the scorched streets at night, searching for shadows, memories. And Elizabeth's hand gripping mine and her voice murmuring incomprehensible words, words of love that she uttered on the beach in Amantea, lying close against my father's body, the words that he said—like a secret—and the sea seemed even more beautiful, filled with sparks of light, each wave moving eternally toward the beach. In the last days she couldn't even speak anymore but the words were still in her, they came up to the edge of her lips and I leaned over to grasp them on her breath, to hear them once again, the words of life. I talked to her now since she was no longer able to, it was I who spoke to her of it all, of Siena, of Rome, of Naples, of Amantea, as if I'd been there, as if it had been I who had held my father's hand on the beach, watching the fitful flight of seagulls in the evening sky, listening to the music of the waves, watching the light fade beyond the sea rim. I pressed her hand and I spoke to her, watching her face, her chest barely lifting the sheet, holding her hand tightly to give her some of my strength. In the embattled city, there was no more water, no more bread, just the flickering light of the fires, the rumble of battle, and the silhouettes of children wandering through the ruins. It was the end of August, whole mountains were burning above Saint-Maxime.

At night as I walked through the hills after leaving the hospital, the sky was aglow as if with the setting sun. In the Var, seventeen thousand acres were in flames, there was a taste of ash in the air, in the water, even in the sea. Freighters sailed away from the ruined city carrying cargos of men. Their names had etched themselves in my memory, they were *Sol Georgios*, *Alkion*, *Sol Phryne*, *Nereus*. They were sailing for Cyprus, Aden, Tunis, Port-Sudan. They moved over the smooth sea and the waves in their wakes would widen till they broke upon the shore, upon the beaches. The seagulls kept them company for a long time in the pale twilit sky until the buildings on shore faded to tiny white spots. In the maze of streets, faces questioned me, eyes watched me. I saw women, children slipping like shadows down the crumbling streets, the ruts of the refugee camps in Sabra, in Chatila. The boats sailed away, they were headed for the other side of the world, for the far side of the sea. The *Atlantis* slipped slowly along the wharf, it was moving out toward the glassy sea in the hot evening wind, it was as tall and white as a building. It was going north, toward Greece, toward Italy perhaps. I searched the sea, the ash-gray sea, as if I would see it appear in the dark dusk, its lights shining, gliding along in its wake, surrounded by the whirl of seagulls.

Elizabeth was so weak she couldn't see anymore. I spoke to her for a long time, very close to her ear, feeling the strands of gray hair against my lips. I tried to say the words she loved, the names, Naples, Florence, Amantea, because those were the words that could still penetrate her and mix with her blood, with her breath. The nurses had tried to keep me away but I remained, clinging to the bars of the bed, my head resting on the same pillow, I waited, I breathed, I lived. Water ran into her veins from the tube, drop after drop and the words were like those drops, they came one after the other, imperceptible, very low, very slow—the sun, the sea, the black rocks, the flight of birds, Amantea, Amantea...Medicines, injections, brutal and frightful treatments, and Elizabeth's hand suddenly clenching mine, strengthened by suffering. The words again, to gain time, to stay a little longer, to keep from parting. The sun, the fruit, the sparkling wine in the glasses, the streamlined shapes of tartanas, the town of Amantea growing drowsy in the afternoon heat, the cool sheets under naked skin, the blue shade of closed shutters. I had known that too, I was there, with my father, with my mother, I was in the shadows, in the coolness, in the flesh of the fruit. War had never come there, nothing had ever troubled the immensity of the smooth sea.

Elizabeth died during the night. When I went into the room, I saw her body laying on the stretcher, wrapped in a sheet, her face very white, very thin, with the peaceful smile that didn't seem real. Both suffering and life had ended in her at the same time. I looked at her for a moment, then I left. I no longer felt anything. I filled out the necessary papers and a taxi took me to the crematorium for the sinister ritual. The oven heated to fifteen hundred degrees turned the person who had been my mother into a pile of ashes. Then, in exchange for money, I was given an iron cylinder with a screw-on lid that I put in my shoulder bag. I'd been in this city for years, it seemed to me I would never be able to leave.

Each day that followed I roamed the streets with my bag in the metallic heat of the fires around the city. I didn't know what I was looking for. Maybe the shadows the officers of the Gestapo tracked through this city, all of those they had condemned to death and who had hidden in cellars, in attics. Those who the German army had captured in the Stura valley and locked up at the camp in Borgo San Dalmazzo near the train station, who left in armored boxcars, who came through the station in Nice during the night, who continued their journey northward, to Drancy, and farther still, to Dachau, to Auschwitz? I walked through the streets of this city, faces floated in front of me, lit by the glow of the streetlamps. Men leaned toward me, murmured words into my ear. Young people laughed, walking along with their arms around each other's waists. The people that Prefect Ribières had condemned to death, issuing an order of expulsion against them. On a beach across the sea, while the city seems to stand transfixed in its destruction, the women and children of the refugee camps watch the boats drifting away on the smooth sea. And here in this city people come and go in the streets past the brightly-lit shop windows, they are indifferent, remote. They walk by corners where martyred children were hung by the neck from the moldings of streetlamps like from butcher hooks.

The day after Elizabeth ended in the crematorium, I walked around on top of the hill in Cimiez, through streets gleaming with sunlight, filled with the smell of cypress, of pittospores. There were cats running between the cars, insolent blackbirds. On the roofs of the villas, turtle doves danced. The smell of the fires had disappeared now and there were no more clouds in the sky. I didn't know what I was looking for, what I wanted to see. It was like a wound in my heart, I wanted to see the evil, understand what had escaped me, what had cast me into another world. It seemed as if I could find a trace of that evil, I would at last be able to leave, forget, start my life over, with Michel, with Philip, the two men I love. At last I would again be able to travel, talk, discover places and faces, live in the present. I haven't much time. If I don't find where the evil is, I will have lost my life and my truth. I will continue to wander.

I walked around for so many days through the squares, my bag on my shoulder, past the luxury apartment buildings that look out over the sea. Then I came up in front of a large white building, so beautiful, so peaceful, lit with the last rays of the sun. That was what I'd wanted to see. Beautiful and sinister, like a royal palace, surrounded by its formal garden, its basin of calm water where the pigeons and blackbirds came to drink. How could I not have seen it before? That house was visible from every point in the city. At the end of the streets, above the tumult of cars and humans, stood that white house, majestic, eternal, infinitely contemplating the sun and following its course from one end of the sea to the other.

I walked slowly, cautiously closer, as if time had stopped, as if death and suffering were still in the sumptuous apartments, in the symmetrical park, under the bowers, behind every plaster statue. Walking slowly through the park, I heard the gravel crunching under the soles of my sandals and in that silent domain the noise seemed to make a sharp, compact, almost threatening sound. I thought of the Excelsior Hotel that I saw yesterday near the train station, its gardens, its white baroque façade, its wide entrance adorned with plaster cherubs through which the Jews had to pass before being interrogated. But in the quiet and luxury of the large park, beneath the windows of the white house, despite the cooing of turtledoves and the cries of blackbirds, a deathly silence reigned. I walked on and I could still hear my father's voice in the kitchen of our house in Saint-Martin as he talked about the cellars in which people were killed and tortured every day, cellars hidden under the sumptuous edifice and at night, the screams of women being beaten, the screams of the tormented, muffled by the shrubs and the pools, the shrill screams that one couldn't mistake for the cries of blackbirds, and so perhaps in order not to understand in those days, one had to plug up his ears. I walked along under the high windows of the palace, the windows from which the Nazi officers leaned to observe the streets of the city through binoculars. I used to hear my father uttering the name of the house, The Hermitage, almost every evening I heard him say that name in the dark kitchen when the windows were stopped up with newspaper because of the curfew. And the name remained within me all this time, like a hated secret, The Hermitage, the name that doesn't mean anything to others, signifies nothing other than the big luxury apartments overlooking the sea, the peaceful park crowded with pigeons. I walked around in front of the house looking at the façade, window after window, and the dark mouths of basement windows from where the voices of the tortured rose. There was no one around that day, and despite the sunlight and the sea shining in the distance between the palm trees, a cold shudder arose from deep inside of me.

The Sunday after Elizabeth's death I took the bus to the village of Saint-Martin. In the street with the stream, I looked for the door to our house, a little below street level, with its three or four stone steps leading down. But everything was foreign now, or maybe I'm a foreigner. The stream that bounded down the middle of the narrow street, that was once powerful and dangerous as a river, is but a thin trickle washing a few papers along. The cellars, the old stables are restaurants, pizzerias, ice-cream stands and souvenir shops. In the square there is a new, anonymous building. I even looked for the mysterious, disquieting hotel in front of which my mother and father and I stood in line every morning to have our names checked in the carabinieri's register. The place where Rachel had danced with the Italian officer, where the carabinieri moved poor Mr. Ferne's piano. I ended up realizing that it was the modest two-star hotel with advertisements on the parasols and strange old-fashioned curtains in the windows. Even Mr. Ferne's house—the villa with the mulberry tree—so old and abandoned, where he played Hungarian waltzes just for himself on his black piano, has now become a vacation home. But I did recognize the old mulberry tree. Standing on my tiptoes, I picked a lovely dark green, finely serrated leaf.

I went down below the village till I reached the curve from where you can see the torrent and the dark gorge where we used to go swimming as if in the depths of a secret valley, and once again, I felt all the hairs on my skin bristling with

Wandering Star

the icy water and the hot sun, and I heard the buzzing of the wasps, and on my chest Tristan's smooth cheek lay as he listened to the beating of my heart. Maybe I heard the laughter of the children, the shrill cries of the girls that the boys were splashing, the voices calling, just like before, "Maryse! Sonia!" It made my heart sink and I walked quickly back up to the village.

I wasn't bold enough to speak with anyone. At any rate the old people were dead, the young had all gone. It has all undoubtedly been forgotten. In the narrow streets tourists strolled with their children, their dogs. In the old house where the women lit the lights for Shabbat, there was now a garage. In the square, where the Jews gathered before they struck out walking through the mountains while the troops of the Fourth Italian Army went back up the valley and abandoned the village to the Germans, I saw people playing boules, a Belgian ice-cream parlor. Only the fountain continues to flow, like in the old days, spitting water out of its four mouths for the children who come to drink standing on the edge of the basin.

Since I had no choice, I hitchhiked on the road to Notre-Dame-des-Fenestres. A car driven by a young blond girl stopped. Inside there was a dark young man who looked Italian, and another girl, very dark, with pretty green eyes. In a few minutes the car climbed the road through the forest of larches to the sanctuary. Calmly, I watched the road along which we'd walked, Elizabeth and I, I tried in vain to catch a glimpse of the clearing where we'd slept near the torrent. The young people in the car attempted to talk to me. The young man said something like, "Is this the first time you've come here?" I said no, it wasn't the first time, I'd come once a very long time ago. At the end of the road, above the ring of mountains, the peaks were already hidden in the clouds.

306

The buildings in which we'd slept, the Italian soldiers' barracks, the chapel, everything was there, but it was as if something had been removed, as if they no longer had the same meaning. In the building we'd slept in, facing the solders' barracks, there was now an Alpine Club Refuge. As a matter of fact, that is where the young people put their bags for the night. For a second I felt like staying with them, sleeping there, but it wasn't possible. "Even in this season you have to reserve a bed at least a week in advance." Said the guardian of the refuge to me, looking indifferent. They didn't used to be so picky!

Since it was already late, I didn't feel up to walking on the stone path the tourists took back. So I sat down on the embankment, not far from the barracks, sheltered from the wind by a low stone wall and I looked out at the mountain, at the very place I used to watch until my eyes burned and I shook with dizziness when I was waiting for my father who was supposed to join us. But now I know that he can't come.

The same day my mother and I started out on the road to Italy, my father was escorting a group of fugitives on the path to the border, up above Berthemont. Around noon the Germans took them by surprise. "Duck! Run!" the man from the Gestapo shouted. But as they tried to flee through the tall grass, a spray of machine gun fire cut them down and they fell, one on top of the other, men, women, old people, young children. It was a young woman who hid in the bushes and later in an abandoned sheepfold who told us that, and that's why Elizabeth came back to France, to be in the land where her husband died. She wrote it all down in a single, long letter, on the pages of a school notebook in her fine and elegant hand. She wrote the name of my father, Michel Grève, and the names of all the men and all the women who died with him in the grass, above Berthemont. Now, she too is dead in this same land and her body is closed up in a steel cylinder that I carry around with me.

I walked a ways on the road, in the direction of Saint-Martin. I could hear the peaceful sound of the torrent and the rumblings of the storm behind me in the ring of clouds. Some English tourists picked me up in their car and took me to the village. Despite the tourist season I managed to find a small room in a hotel at the bottom of Rue Central in an old house I wasn't familiar with.

I wanted to see the place my father had died in Berthemont after all. Early the next morning I took the bus to the fork in the road and I walked down to the bottom of the valley till I reached the old abandoned hotel where the thermal baths used to be. I followed the stairway up over the sulfurous torrent, then the path that winds up the mountain. The sky was magnificent. I thought Philip and Michel would have liked to see that, the morning light shining on the grassy slopes, on the rocks. On the other side of the Vesubie valley, the tall blue mountains seemed as light as clouds.

It had been so long since I'd listened to that silence, felt that serenity. I thought of the sea, the way I had seen it one morning when I stuck my head out of the hold of the *Sette Fratelli*, so long ago now that it seems like a legend. I imagined my father being on that boat, just when the sun brushes against the edge of the world and lights up the crests of the waves. That was how he used to talk of Jerusalem, the city of light, as if it were a cloud, or a mirage over a new land. Where is that city? Does it really exist?

I stopped on the side of the mountain, in the place where the huge fields of grass begin and where Mario looked for vipers, the place where I used to dream I'd see my father walking. The sun was beating down, gleaming up in the center of the sky, gathering the shadows into small piles.

The valley was still in the misty half-lit morning, there was not a human shape, not a house, not a sound. The grassy slope rose skyward, as if into infinity. The sole trace, the path.

Now I realized: it was here they had walked, my father leading, the fugitives behind him, in single file, women wrapped in their shawls, children whining or indifferent, and the men in the rear, carrying the suitcases, the sacks of provisions, the woolen blankets. My heart racing, I climbed on through the tall grass. It was the end of summer, just like forty years ago, I remembered it perfectly: the vast sky, so blue, as if you could see the depths of space. The smell of burning grasses, the shrill chirping of crickets. Up above the dark valleys, kites circling, puling. My heart beat faster because I was nearing the truth. It was all there, I hadn't forgotten, it was only yesterday when we walked, my mother and I, on the path of sharp stones, through the storm clouds, toward Italy. The women were sitting on the edge of the path, their bundles on the ground next to them, their eyes staring fixedly into space. The smell of the grass up on the slopes makes your head spin, like a strong perfume does, maybe the farmers in the village had cut it and it was beginning to ferment. Sweat streamed down my face as I followed the path toward the top of the grassy slope. Then I was in an immense prairie that stretched all the way out to the rocky peaks. I was so high up that I could no longer see the valley bottom. The sun had gone back down toward the blue mountains on the opposite slope. The clouds were puffy, magnificent, I could hear thunder rumbling somewhere.

The shepherd's shelters were just ahead. Ageless drystone huts. Maybe they were already there before men built their cities, their temples, their citadels. As I drew near the shelters, a trembling sort of feeling rose inside of me, despite the hot sun and the heady smell of the tall fermenting grasses. Suddenly I knew, I was sure of it. This was the place. They were hiding there in the stone huts. When the fugitives came up onto the prairie, the killers came out, their machine guns on their hips, someone shouted in French, "Run! Quick, quick, run! Get away, we won't hurt you!" It was a man from the Gestapo who had shouted that, he was wearing an elegant gray suit, with a felt hat on his head. Through the tall grasses the women and children started to run, the old women, the men, like so many panic-stricken animals. Then the S.S. pulled the trigger, and the machine guns raked over the grassy field, bringing the bodies down one on top of the other, and the shrill frightened screams were drowned in blood. Others were still alive, men trying to flee to the bottom of the slope along the path they'd come up on, but the bullets hit them in the back. The bundles, suitcases, sacks of flour fell into the grass, clothes, shoes were strewn about, as if in a game. The soldiers left the bundles. They dragged the bodies by the legs up to the shepherds' huts, and they left them there in the sunlight.

In the evening, rain began to fall on the grassy slope, the stone huts. The path led down through the tall grasses toward the valley deep in shadow, just like another time when the sharp blades came up to my lips and I didn't know where I was anymore. No one goes up there now. Maybe at the end of summer the flocks of sheep led by an old deaf man who talks to his dog, whistling, and sits on a rock to watch the clouds scud over the sky.

I came down the mountain at a near run, through the tall grasses on the slippery path. Do vipers still become entangled in amorous combat? Does anyone still know how to call to them, like Mario, whistling gently between his teeth? Everything was wheeling around me, as if I were the only living creature, the last woman to have escaped war. Then it struck me that Jerusalem—the city of light that my father dreamt of seeing—was up there, on that grassy slope, with all of its celestial domes and the minarets that link the earthly world to the clouds.

In the valley, the night was warm. The rain ran over the road with a soft whisper. A truck driven by an Italian brought me back to Nice. I found what I'd come looking for. In two days Philip and Michel will be here. I love them. I'll go back with them across the sea to my country where the light is so beautiful. It shines most of all in the eyes of the children, the eyes from which I hope to drive all suffering. I know that everything will begin now. And I still think of Nejma, the sister I lost so long ago in the cloud of dust on the path, and whom I must find again.

The sea is beautiful in the twilight. The water, the land, the sky melt into one another. A haze is hovering, shrouding the horizon imperceptibly. And the silence, despite the moving cars, despite the city-dwellers' footsteps. Everything is calm on the breakwater where Esther sits. She stares out to sea, almost without blinking. She's been coming to this place for several days, when the sun descends, to look at the sea. Tonight is the last time. Tomorrow, Philip and Michel will be here and they'll all take the train for Paris, for London together. They must go away, to forget.

Each evening at the same time the fishermen come out to set up their lines. On the slabs of cement making up the breakwater they carefully prepare the bait, the poles, the reels, they work with precise and sure gestures. Esther enjoys watching them. They are so busy, so meticulous, it's as if all other things were only dreams, delusions, the imagination of a madman rambling in the halls of his asylum. So Esther thinks that is what reality is, these fishermen in the twilight, the lines that they now cast into the sea, the weights that whistle as they lash the slack waves, and the mirroring of the light as the swollen sun vanishes in the haze. Esther's gaze wanders in the blue-gray vastness before her, then it focuses on a small lone boat, a thin, lone triangular sail slowly traversing the haze.

Once again it is the end of summer. Days are shorter, night falls abruptly. Esther shivers, in spite of the warm air. Out on the breakwater the fishermen have turned on a radio. The music drifts over in snatches on the wind, a woman's voice singing loudly—it sounds off-key—and the crackling static due to thunderstorms in the mountains.

The fishermen turn around from time to time, seeming to jeer, they say things in the dialect spoken around Nice and she suspects they're talking about her because they laugh a little. Some are young men, the same age as her son, very dark, Italian-looking, with pink short-sleeved shirts. What could they be saying about her? She has a hard time imagining what it might be, dressed as she is, like a vagabond, her short-cropped graying hair, her still-childish face, tanned from days in the sun, in the mountains. But in a way, she's glad to hear their voices, their raucous music, and their laughter. It proves that they are real, that all of this exists, the slow sea, the blocks of cement, the sail moving through the haze. They aren't going to disappear. She feels overwhelmed by the lightness of the air, the luminous haze. The sea with its ebb and flow, its bursts of refracted light, has entered her body. It's the time of day when everything vacillates, is transformed. It's been such a long time since she's known such serenity, such detachment. She remembers the deck of the boat in the night when both the earth and time had ceased to exist. It was after Livorno, or maybe farther south, nearing the Strait of Messina. Disregarding the Captain's order, Esther climbed the ladder and went out the half-open hatch, then she'd crawled over the deck in the cold wind as cautiously as a thief till she reached the front lookout post. Sylvio was on watch and he'd let her by without saying anything, as if he hadn't seen her. Esther remembers now how the boat slipped over the smooth sea, invisible in the night, she remembers the gentle sound of the stem, the tremor of the motors under the deck. In the forecastle, the radio was on and the sailors were listening to a tinny and sputtering tune, the same kind that the fishermen are listening to now. It was the radio for Americans in Sicily, in Tangier, the jazz music broke through the night in wafts, as it does now, we didn't know where we were going, lost in space. It drifted away, came back, the powerful, husky voice of Billy Holiday singing *Solitude* and *Sophisticated Lady*, Ada Brown, Jack Dupree, Little Johnnie Jones's fingers on the piano. It was Jacques Berger who had taught her the names, later, when they listened to the records on an old phonograph, in Nora's room in Ramat Yohanan. Esther remembers the song—she sang it in a low voice whenever she went walking around in the streets—and everything she'd discovered in Canada, the music in the apartment on Avenue Notre-Dame that helped her live through the cold and the loneliness of her exile. Now, out on the breakwater, facing the darkening sea, she still floats along on the music coming from the fishermen's radio. She remembers what it was like back then, heading for the unknown across the sea. But she feels a pang in her heart because it occurs to her that for Elizabeth none of that exists anymore, there will be no more journeys. The ship stopped slipping over the sea, borne along on Billy Holiday's music when Elizabeth stopped breathing. She died during the night, alone in her cot, with no one to hold her hand. Esther went into the room and saw her face—so very white, tilted backward on the pillow, the dark stains on her eyelids. She bent over the cold, hard body and she said, "Please, not now. Stay a little longer! I want to talk to you about Italy, about Amantea." She said that in a loud voice, squeezing the cold hand, to let a little warmth into the dead fingers. The nurse came in, she just stood by the door saying nothing.

Now all of that is fading away. It's as if it were in another world, a world where the light was different, where everything had a different color, a different taste, where voices said other things; where eyes held a different look. Her father's voice saying her name, like this: Estrellita, little star; Mr. Ferne's voice, the children's voices shouting in the square in Saint-Martin, Tristan's voice, Rachel's voice, Jacques Berger's voice when he translated the words of Reb Joel in the Toulon prison. Nora's voice, Lola's voice. It's dreadful, the voices that fade away. Now that it is dark, for the first time in years, ever since she'd ceased being a child, Esther feels tears that can come. They spill from her eyes and roll down her cheeks. She doesn't know why she's crying. When Jacques died in the hills of Tiberias, three soldiers came to the kibbutz bearing the news, two men and a woman. They said, as if they were excusing themselves, Jacques Berger died on January 10, he was buried. They left right away. They had very gentle faces.

Esther hadn't cried then. Maybe there had been no tears in her at the time, because of the war. Maybe it was because of the sunlight on the fields, in the groves, the light that clung to Yohanan's black hair, because of the silence and the bright sky. Now she feels the tears come as if the sea were rising into her eyes.

From the bag she's carried around for days through the streets of the city and up in the mountains on the grassy slope where her father died, Esther takes the metal cylinder with the ashes inside. With all of her might she twists off the cover. The wind blowing over the blocks of cement is warm, it comes in gusts, bringing with it the sound of the tinny music, it quite resembles Billie Holiday's voice singing *Solitude* over near the Messina Strait. But it must surely be something else. The wind and the night sieze the ashes spilling from the metallic canister, scatter them seaward. At times an eddy brings the ashes back to Esther, blinding her, dusting her hair with them. When the canister is empty,

Esther throws it far away, and the splash in the sea makes the fishermen turn their heads. Then she closes the bag and jumps from block to block along the jetty. She walks along the wharves. She feels immensely weary, immensely serene. There are bats dancing around the lampposts.

J. M. G. LE CLÉZIO is a distinguished, best-selling French author with 20 novels to his credit. He was born in Nice in 1940, and after completing his undergraduate degree in literature at the University of Nice continued his studies in England. His first novel, *The Verbal Process*, was published in 1963. During the past two decades, Le Clèzio has divided his time between his home in Nice, Paris, Mexico, and Albuquerque, where he began teaching one semester a year in 1977 at the University of New Mexico.

CURBSTONE PRESS, INC.

is a nonprofit publishing house dedicated to literature that reflects a
commitment to social change, with an emphasis on contemporary writing
from Latino, Latin American and Vietnamese cultures. Curbstone presents
writers who give voice to the unheard in a language that goes beyond
denunciation to celebrate, honor and teach. Curbstone builds bridges
between its writers and the public – from inner-city to rural areas, colleges
to community centers, children to adults. Curbstone seeks out the highest
aesthetic expression of the dedication to human rights and intercultural
understanding: poetry, testimonies, novels, stories,
and children's books.

This mission requires more than just producing books. It requires ensuring
that as many people as possible learn about these books and read them. To
achieve this, a large portion of Curbstone's schedule is dedicated to
arranging tours and programs for its authors, working with public school
and university teachers to enrich curricula, reaching out to underserved
audiences by donating books and conducting readings and community
programs, and promoting discussion in the media. It is only through these
combined efforts that literature can truly make a difference.

Curbstone Press, like all nonprofit presses, depends on the support of
individuals, foundations, and government agencies to bring you, the reader,
works of literary merit and social significance which might not find a place
in profit-driven publishing channels, and to bring the authors and their
books into communities across the country. Our sincere thanks to the many
individuals, foundations, and government agencies who have supported this
endeavor: Connecticut Commission on the Arts, Connecticut Humanities
Council, Eastern CT Community Foundation, Fisher Foundation, Greater
Hartford Arts Council, Hartford Courant Foundation, J. M. Kaplan Fund,
Lamb Family Foundation, Lannan Foundation, John D. and Catherine T.
MacArthur Foundation, National Endowment for the Arts, Open
Society Institute, Puffin Foundation, United Way, and the
Woodrow Wilson National Fellowship Foundation.

Please help to support Curbstone's efforts to present the diverse voices and
views that make our culture richer. Tax-deductible donations can be made by
check or credit card to:
Curbstone Press, 321 Jackson Street, Willimantic, CT 06226
phone: (860) 423-5110 fax: (860) 423-9242
www.curbstone.org

IF YOU WOULD LIKE TO BE A MAJOR SPONSOR OF A
CURBSTONE BOOK, PLEASE CONTACT US.